Fate's Monolith
The MacLomain Series-
Book 1
By Sky Purington

~Fate's Monolith~

Dear Reader,

As always, I'm thrilled you decided to read one of my tales. *Fate's Monolith* was originally written four years ago and is now being re-launched. I loved meeting all of the characters once more and helping them tell their tale from a more in-depth perspective. If you love fantasy romance, medieval Scottish history and eighteenth century American history, this story is bound to hook you.

Outside of the magical love story, all the information about Clan MacLomain (Originally known in some circles as Clan MacErachar) is based on historical truth to the best of my research. They were one of the most powerful clans in the Scottish Highlands during the twelfth century. All clans introduced in this story were their allies at the time.

All information about the Broun (Brown) clan is historical truth. They were a lowland clan who were allied and intermarried with the MacLomain clan for over three hundred years, twelfth through fifteenth centuries. To this day, each clan claims the other as their sept.

And so the series goes... The unending tie between two clans meant to forever connect through time.

Did I mention that I descend from the Broun clan and my husband, the MacLomain? Fodder for a good love story or two I'd say.

Thank you for reading.

Best Always,

Sky

~Fate's Monolith~

New to *The MacLomain Series*? Start the journey with *The King's Druidess-Prelude*. It all began in Ireland (Eire'). The true beginning of the MacLomain Clan. Found on Kindle, Nook and Smashwords for .99 cents.

SNEAK PEEK: Be sure to read on after this story to learn which scrumptious character from *Fate's Monolith* will lead the pack and become an unforgettable hero in *Destiny's Denial- The MacLomain Series- Book 2*. (Hint- He's only a teenage visionary with a gorgeous set of icy blue eyes in this book. No worries. He grows up into one delicious Scottish laird.)

Pick up your copy of all four stories (one short tale, three full length novels) in the MacLomain Series at .99 cents per title for a limited time. *Sylvan Mist* (The MacLomain Series-Book 3) is available now.

~Fate's Monolith~

This is a work of fiction. Names, characters, places, and incidents are either the product of the author's imagination or are used fictitiously, and any resemblance to actual persons living or dead, business establishments, events, or locales, is entirely coincidental.

Fate's Monolith [The MacLomain Series 1]

COPYRIGHT © 2011 by Sky Purington

All rights reserved. No part of this book may be used or reproduced in any manner whatsoever without written permission of the author except in the case of brief quotations embodied in critical articles or reviews.

Contact Information: Sky@SkyPurington.com

Cover Art by *Tamra Westberry*

Published in the United States of America

~Fate's Monolith~

Dedication

This book is dedicated to my mom, for never allowing me to give up.

This is also dedicated to my husband, my warrior, for the use of his clan's name and his endless patience. I know it wasn't easy but *wow...* we had fun along the way, aye?

~Fate's Monolith~

Prologue

"Have you the courage to kill me?" Tension fastened together the muscles in her shoulders and neck.

"Aye." The burly, filth-ridden man aimed his weapon at her and narrowed his eyes. A calloused finger twitched on the bowstring.

"You have an enemy," she stated.

His muddy glare flickered with alarm. A stranger stood at the edge of the forest. Weaponless hands clenched and stretched his knuckles white. Immune to nature's movement, a blue and green wool tartan lay still against his muscular thigh. She absorbed the moment.

Him.

Thick, woodland trunks lined in strict formation behind him, ready for battle. Noble mountains loomed beyond, majestic and proud. Lethal emerald eyes narrowed on her captor.

Then, those eyes locked with hers.

Hungry lust sizzled between them. *Thud. Thud.* Her heart beat out of control. Breath ceased. Sweat trickled down her forehead. She couldn't tear her gaze from the man across the way, those parts of him she could see for he was never whole.

Horrible with power, wind seized the land. Her hair whipped and lashed her cheeks.

"Evil." The nearby warrior muttered a prayer under his breath. He released the arrow.

Arianna! Noooooo!

Time slowed. Silence enveloped. Flung back, she landed hard on her back. She gasped for air and wrapped cold hands around the shaft protruding from her chest. Compelled, she peered down at the warm fluid trickling over her hands. Blood. Her blood.

Turning her head, she once more locked eyes with the man across the way. Enraged eyes that wouldn't let her go as he ran toward her.

A wind born of mountain rain blew against her wound. Fresh pained seized her body. The world tilted, then started to fade. Panic robbed coherent thought. Everything began to drift away.

She'd finally met her end.

Chapter One

Salem, New Hampshire 1799

Am I blind? Why can't I see? Gasping for air, Arianna struggled to tear away the arrow only to realize she held the fabric of her nightgown. She blinked rapidly and tried to control the panic. Slowly, bit by bit, the dim room surfaced.

Releasing the cloth, she fisted her hands to stop the tremors. Her body shook as she untwisted from the sweat soaked blankets. The cold hardwood floor underfoot was sweet relief. She swallowed a small sob and worked to regain composure.

A plague of the mind, the same dream/nightmare had been a constant shadow now for ten years. It followed her year after year, forever intense and evasive.

As a child, the dream of death had terrified her. Now, she only wanted to piece the man together. Flashes of broad shoulders, dark hair and verdant eyes teased her to near insanity.

"Who are you?" The wooden walls of her bedroom gave no reply.

She shouldered into a robe and walked to the window. A bare expanse of dirt road lay empty below. Pale, gray clouds hung thin on the horizon of autumn wood line. Wind blew and a mighty oak tree yawned and stretched. With a long armed knock, it rapped on the side of the house.

Arianna leaned her forehead against the windowpane and ran a fingertip down the cold glass. If she closed her eyes his face rose up as though he beckoned her. Needed her. But was only a figment of her imagination. Wasn't he? He had to be.

Staring down the lane she wondered...would he someday walk up it and find her? Would she recognize him when he did? Enough! She had to stop doing this to herself. After all, it was All Hallows' Eve today.

Rolling the remaining tension from her shoulders, she turned and smiled. *The dress.* Many pricks to the fingers and inward curses flowed along the seams of the medieval gown.

Guilty of a competitive nature, she had made the twelfth century Scottish gown with this evening's festivities in mind.

"Take whatever you need and win." Her uncle had urged back in July with a wink and a toss of a brown leather satchel full of coins.

The garment came to life over the months and now hung from the back of the closet door in silky, deep blue waves. The annual costume contest held at the Huntington's party would have one more masterpiece to contend with this year.

The water basin beckoned. She swept back her thick hair into a long braid and washed her face, then slipped into a white day dress.

Ahh. The sweet smell of apples drew her downstairs where Aunt Marie bustled around the kitchen. Bright red hair and wild curls struggled to defy her white cap. An apple juice stained apron clung to a comely figure. Slightly swollen, her stomach pressed against the smock where her pregnancy began to show.

"There you are." Cheer charmed Marie's words as she rushed over and gave Arianna a quick kiss on the cheek.

"I told Liam ye would be up the very minute my baking tickled yer wee bonnie nose." A chuckle bubbled forth and pretty blue eyes flashed. Everyone knew Marie was giddy with pleasure when a Scottish brogue thickened her tongue.

Arianna smiled. "Mmm. It smells so good down here."

"We've got our work cut out for us, lass." Happy with the challenge, Marie eyeballed the slew of food to be prepared for the evening feast. Every woman would bring a favorite dish to the event. Her aunt would arrive with at least half a wagon full of baked goods.

"The girls will awaken soon," Marie declared. "Which means we should take advantage of an empty space while we have it."

Arianna grabbed an apron and pursued Marie across the kitchen.

"There's a cup of tea on the table." Marie leaned over and carefully extracted a hearty loaf of pumpkin bread from the cast iron Dutch oven over the hearth.

"Thank you," Arianna murmured between sips, accustomed to her aunt's uncanny ability to always have the hot brew ready.

"Get to it." Marie handed her a clean griddle for muffin batter.

"I can't believe All Hallows' Eve is here already." Arianna stirred the batter full of cut apples and brown specks of cinnamon.

"Aye, the kelpies will be about tonight. I stayed up after you went to sleep last night and finished sewing the costumes for the girls..." Back turned, Marie continued to chatter.

Arianna set the pan of freshly scooped batter on the table, her thoughts adrift. Her death dream stranger haunted her. What would it feel like to touch him? The glimpse of a muscled arm and a small black braid skimming a square jaw filled her vision. She licked her lips. How would it feel to kiss him? What would he taste like? Agreeable warmth burned her cheeks. Face aflame, Arianna struggled to catch her breath.

"Lass, why are you blushing like that?" Her aunt's voice cut through her reverie.

"What?" Arianna fanned her face.

"Aye, you were thinking about him, you were." Marie said, pleased.

"How could you know?" Arianna replied without thinking. Not again. The minute a thought came into her head it rolled right out of her mouth. Marie couldn't know what consumed her thoughts.

"Well, it's obvious to everyone Edward has his eye on you, perhaps you've an eye for him as well," Marie provided.

"Who?" Arianna's mind went blank.

"Who, my arse." With a wink and a snicker, her aunt planted her hands on her hips. Arianna adjusted her expression one second too late and Marie's eyes narrowed.

"We are talking about Edward, aren't we?"

Arianna avoided Marie's gaze and placed scoops of batter onto the griddle. "Of course we are."

Edward was the son of Richard Huntington. He worked hard at the gristmill for his father. In due time, he would inherit the family business. Edward was everything Arianna's family could hope for her—ambitious, well educated, and smitten with their niece.

Thump. Thump. Grateful for the reprieve, she turned away when her aunt became distracted by the endless thumps from upstairs. Multiple feet pattered across the floor, then resounded in another thump. Muffled words were thrown back and forth as doors slammed.

"Get out of my way," one young voice yelled.

"I was here first, you spindly legged little mothball." Another voice retaliated, and then screeched.

Before Marie made it half way across the kitchen, havoc let loose. It sounded as if two big bags of potatoes were thrown down the staircase as her daughters tried to outrun one another. As Marie reached the bottom of the staircase, Annie slammed face first into her thigh with Coira right behind her.

"How many times have I told you two not to run on the stairs?"

The children quieted under their mother's stern look. Annie, the youngest, sidled past her mother and skirted across the kitchen. She grabbed Arianna's hand and wrapped her free arm around the waistline of her nightgown.

Coira apologized to her mother. Proper, she walked as though a book balanced on her head. Back ramrod straight, she angled away from her mother. She stuck out her tongue, facial features going smooth and serene the moment Marie passed. Arianna glanced down at Annie in time to catch the same sentiment retreat back into her mouth.

"Grab yer aprons you little scoundrels." Marie issued two small aprons to her daughters and removed a kettle of porridge from the hearth for their breakfast.

As the hours ticked by on the grandfather clock, the family labored together. Arianna prepared the recipes with her aunt, Annie mixed the batter and Coira washed any kettles, bowls or spoons they finished with.

Marie believed that the chefs should always sample their creations to ensure quality taste. Good parental cooking beliefs belied the promise of full bellies. Hence, when the hour arrived, heavy eyelids graced the children and they went peaceably for their noontime naps.

After everything was set aside and ready for travel, Arianna decided to make the best of her free time. The barn beckoned. Liam had purchased horses for both Arianna and Marie five years earlier.

She named her horse after the Scottish loch that bordered the village of her childhood. Buckskin colored, Fyne had a black tail and a mark much like a Celtic cross on her forehead.

A whinny welcomed Arianna from the nearest stall. Fyne poked her head out and nuzzled the side of Arianna's hair. She opened the door and stepped beside the great beauty.

"Hullo, my luv." She kissed Fyne's forehead. Arianna only allowed her long abandoned Scottish brogue to erupt when she was with Fyne.

She mounted the horse and scowled at the expensive saddle on the wall. She much preferred to ride bareback. Comfortable, Arianna grabbed the thick, leather lead line attached to the halter.

The two became one as Fyne led her out the backside of the barn into the New England woodland. She let the horse take the lead. Uncle Liam would've had a fit.

"You lead the horse, the horse never leads you."

What he didn't know wouldn't hurt him! Trees rushed by as Fyne ran through the forest. Alive in flight, the horse skirted in and out of tree trunks. Arianna blinked against wind-spawned tears. The fresh scent of potential snow mixed with pine. A light pull on Fyne's rein slowed her gate as they drew up to her favorite spot. She swung off the horse, rewarded Fyne with a quick pat and tied her to a tree.

Arianna stood at the threshold of ancient stone formations. The town called the Stonehenge Pattee's Caves. She ducked into the largest chamber with two dark passages in the shape of a "T". Mysticism and melancholy housed here. She ran a hand along the cool, jagged wall.

Arianna stopped short. Had the ring on her finger just glowed? No. It must've been her imagination. The ring consisted of two hands coming from separate directions holding a crowned heart at the center. Twirling it on her finger, she continued to stroll and recalled the eve she'd received the trinket. It was about a year after she and Aunt Marie had fled the Highland Clearances in Scotland. The event had left her traumatized and without parents. Luckily, her young mind had repressed whatever happened.

Regardless, she'd become a withdrawn little girl until Liam had come into their lives. His warm disposition had healed her immensely. The night before they'd set sail for America he gave her the delicate ring saying simply, "I want you to have this, lassie. It's a family heirloom from Ireland, one of only three. It is to let you know that I will treat you as one of my own. Mayhap one day, there will be more of its kind."

Since then, Arianna had cherished the piece. To her, it symbolized love and new beginnings.

Further along the woodland path, she stopped in front of a wide, spear-like monolith positioned in the ground. This was one of three placed at astrological edges of an unseen border that surrounded the original chambers. On occasion, Arianna would watch the Northeast horizon welcome the sunrise in alignment with this particular stone.

She ran her hands over the abrasive surface and stared at the slice of land beyond. Late October yearned for winter. Very little time was left. Soon, heavy drifts of snow would cake the landscape.

Lost in contemplation, her vision blurred. Unable to move, frosty air steamed and compressed around her. Total silence engulfed the area. Vibration emanated from the stone. *Oh my Lord!* It ran from her fingers, crawled up unsteady arms and massaged her center.

Trancelike, Arianna watched everything change.

The ground deep with copper leaves and drowsy trees awoke as though it were spring. Long grass sprouted and twisted a path of dark green. Arched, feathery ferns swayed, cocooned beneath a heavy canopy of lush leaves.

With a backdrop of sapphire sky, white clouds swelled, flattened on the bottom, and then spindled upward. A combination of new earth and clean spice filled the air.

"I'll find you." A masculine voice rode the warm, salty wind.

Suction fused her to the monolith.

Now loose, Arianna's braid unraveled and her long hair whipped forward. She struggled to see past the tornado of locks. A horrible roar passed over. Unable to use hands to cover her ears, she endured what sounded to be the thunderous heartthrob of an immortal god.

Then it stopped.

Dead silence.

Her hair dropped and gravity gave loose legs ground. Instinct and reflex made Arianna grab the top of the stone. *Air! I need to breathe air!* Trying to calm herself, she took slow, deep breaths.

As quickly as it had happened, it was gone. The new grass, springtime trees and warmth...all gone. Was she mad? She pushed away from the stone abruptly. Her knees buckled and she fell backward landing with a heavy thump on a log.

This was all becoming too much to handle. It was one thing to dream about a man over and over again but to actually hear him? Pure insanity. She sat for several minutes until she felt calm enough to leave.

The last thing she needed to do was worry her aunt and uncle.

Twenty minutes later she was heading back into the house. As she passed the swing hanging from the old oak, she gave it a push.

"That was me first order of business," Liam said. He stood in the doorway, smiling.

"Aye, you were a good uncle and still are." She leaned back to eye the two knots, which supported either rope high above. "You chose a good, sturdy branch."

He laughed. "If I recall correctly, you picked that branch, I wanted the other one."

"Thank God for good, Scottish sense," Arianna said. Back in 1791, the branch Liam had thought preferable cracked and fell one blustery morning.

"Where would I be without it?" He shook his head. "Come in lass and join us for a bit."

She followed him inside.

"My lady." Liam pulled a chair away from the kitchen table.

Thank you." Arianna plunked into her usual chair.

Marie slid a cup of tea her way. "Edward Huntington stopped by while you were gone. I think he's wanting to court you, lass."

She should've known he'd be by. After all, she allowed him a kiss but a day ago. "Aye, he's a nice man."

"Good catch, that lad," Liam said. "You'd do well to consider his offer."

"He's made no offer *yet*." Marie winked.

Arianna rolled her eyes. The two were determined to see her wedded. Even though she'd kissed Edward, could she really marry him? Love him? Strangely enough, she felt almost obligated to this mystery stranger who didn't even exist. The thought of committing to another man felt almost…dishonest.

"So where have you been off to love?" Marie asked Arianna. Absently, she intertwined the fingers of one hand with Liam's upon the table.

"I took a ride through the woods."

"Quite the ride Arianna, you've been gone nearly four hours."

Four hours? Impossible! A strange sensation rolled through her when she glanced out the window. She frowned. Marie was right. It was late in the day. No doubt, the lost time occurred at the monolith.

"I must have lost track of time. I was at Pattee's caves again."

A brief flicker of tension passed between Liam and Marie. Or Arianna thought that's what she sensed. Before she had a chance to further analyze the odd exchange, Liam spoke.

"Is your costume ready to claim this year's grand prize?" Eager anticipation lit his face.

"Bloody hell right it is." She clamped a hand over her mouth at the vulgar admission.

"That's the O'Donnell spirit." Marie tore her hand from Liam's and slammed her palm on the table. Eyes round as saucers, her cheeks turned rosy with excitement.

She fought the urge to correct her aunt's choice of words. Marie may be an O'Donnell at heart, but Arianna would always be a Broun. Immediately after her aunt and uncle married, her family surname became a middle name.

"We leave in a few short hours and the sun will soon set." Liam pushed away from the table.

"You ladies best have yourselves prepared. The children are outside playing Graces. I believe I might join them for a bit." Liam kissed his wife on the mouth and his niece on the cheek.

An hour later, a wealth of baked goods were tucked into the back of the wagon and Arianna stood at the window combing out her hair. The sun hid below the tree line. Deep orange flooded the western sky. Liam and Marie stood close together by the wagon below. Did they realize it was time to get ready?

A red and black tartan was neatly folded and placed on the large trunk at the end of the bed. She scooped it up and held it against her chest. This meager wool blanket was all that was left of her parents. Somehow, Marie had managed to salvage the family plaid when they fled the Clearances.

She sat on the bed. What a strange day. The monolith and the odd loss of time all fought for precedence in her thoughts. Absently, she twisted a long strand of moist hair around her finger.

The room shimmered. Entranced, she marveled when nearly black hair blended with golden-red. For a brief moment, she wondered at the whiteness of her hand against such a color.

Arianna's eyelids turned heavy as she followed the dark strands inch by inch. *Oh!* Her breath caught when she met powerful green eyes.

Though unable to focus, she knew it was he.

The Scotsman from the edge of the forest sat close beside her on the bed, huge and possessive. The same blue and green tartan spread across his strong thighs and wrapped over a well-muscled shoulder. Her throat tightened. Her mouth went dry.

Arianna squinted but couldn't make him complete. How she longed to see his face. She inhaled deeply. He smelled wonderful and masculine, like spice and wood. An intoxicating combination of fresh cut cedar, pine and new grass.

Unable to move, she felt the back of a large, tender hand touch and roam her sensitive jaw line.

Painful and urgent, an anxious heart pounded against her ribs. His bold hand fell and fingered the plaid strewn across her legs. Torment magnified the verdant intensity of those sensual eyes. His eyes, the kind designed to seduce.

A deep, beautiful Scottish brogue rumbled within his chest. "I am sorry, but you are destined to marry a MacLomain."

Though fascinated, irritation preceded all else. "Who are you to tell me whom I will marry?"

Heat stifled her. His eyes narrowed and turned such a deep shade of green one might think them black. She could see his lips, wide, not too full, but not too thin, perfect. They wore a crooked grin.

There were no more words. His arm moved fast and wrapped around her waist. Hot, hard flesh pressed against her. So close, but where was he? Why could she only see bits of him?

The physical affect he had on her was immediate. She wanted to run her fingers over his skin, feel the shape of his face, the texture of his hair. Fire, liquefied and fast, spread throughout the lower half of her body and she groaned. Clenching her thighs, the bold urge to taste his lips overwhelmed and she leaned forward.

Chapter Two

"Arianna, are you in there?" The small sound spliced the core of her eardrums. Images snapped shut as a loud knock resounded.

"Arianna, come on, let me in." Annie's half whine, half yell broke through. Her eyes flew open. *Oh no.* Not another dream, during the day no less. But why should that surprise her when she'd heard him at the monolith. Arianna groaned and rolled onto her side. She closed her eyes, pulled her legs up to her chest and willed the moment back.

"Arianna. Let me in now, please." Annie pleaded. Her small fists pounded persistently.

Body shaking, she slowly sat up. He'd been here, in her room, she was sure of it. Arianna stood up and her legs crumbled like slender matchsticks beneath a thirty- ton boulder. She grabbed the edge of the bed and managed to sit.

Lord, what had she come to? Nervous laughter dribbled from a wry mouth. A handsome, flesh and blood man giving her a kiss could not nearly incite from her what an imaginary Scotsman in medieval attire could. Aye, it was coming to pass, she was losing her mind.

"Arianna?" The child's plea turned to a whimper.

"Yes, Arianna, I'm here too. We are extremely worried about you cousin," Coira said. She sounded so stern for a young girl.

Arianna concentrated, focused on the sound of her cousin's voices. Resolute, she walked on now sturdy legs and opened the door. Two bodies nearly fell to the floor, they were pressed so tightly against it.

"Hello, my luvs," Marie said from behind. "Is everything well?"

"Hello mama," Coira and Annie greeted in unison.

"Are you two bothering your poor cousin again?" A mock glare challenged them.

Arianna schooled her expression. She didn't want Marie to worry about her. "Aunt Marie, you know these two angels are not capable of bothering me."

Though Marie's gaze lingered on her a second too long, as though she knew Arianna wasn't quite herself, she declared the hour had arrived to prepare for All Hollows' Eve.

Excited, she joined in with the children's pleasure. Cries of delight trailed out her door while everyone made their way to their own costume. She shut the door behind them and did a little jig across the room.

Time to adorn her new dress.

With great care, Arianna removed the garment from the wooden hanger. After the kirtle was in place, she pulled the dress over her head. How she admired the way the hem swept the floor. The slim waistline fit to perfection, adding to the elegance of the long, sweeping sleeves. To top the look off, she intentionally cut holes in the outer garment, which allowed it to gather at the waist. This look revealed the fancy kirtle beneath.

Arianna sat down at her vanity and began the next stage. She opened the instructional book and strived to execute the chore of maidens past, the headgear.

She styled her hair to accommodate and wrapped the Barbette around her chin, then pinned it at the top of her head. Over this she placed a round veil with a face hole cut out of the center. To complete the look, the Filet was placed on top. She turned her head.

Arianna smiled at the cloth that straddled her head. Not bad.

Finally, she slipped on her shoes. Made of leather, Arianna implemented the, "turn shoe," method of the time. Though not the most eye appealing in that they were turned inside out, when she curled her toes the sheer comfort made the style irrelevant.

Her family plaid came last. Arianna wrapped and tucked the material into the folds until it appeared part of the dress. Not easy. At last, she gazed into the cherry wood full-length mirror. She was pleased with her ability as a seamstress. The dress fit perfectly.

She walked down the stairs with great care so as to not step on the delicate material. The family chattered away in the living room. As usual, everyone talked over one another. She stopped at the entrance to the room. One by one, each family member spied her and sighed away their next word.

"Hello all," Arianna said, uncomfortable under their immediate scrutiny.

"Cousin, you look beautiful." Ever the most prominent, Annie flew across the room.

Liam nodded in agreement while Marie embraced her. When she pulled away, Arianna was shocked to see a tear glistening in her aunt's eye.

"You know I love you my family, but I do believe our Arianna will walk away with this year's prize." Liam eyed his niece with unrestrained pride.

"I have to agree, you're so lovely. It's clear that twelfth century attire becomes you," Marie said, her expression melancholic and distant while she continued to hold Arianna at arm's length.

"You flatter me." Heat scorched Arianna's face. "You aren't too shabby yourselves."

Handsome, Liam was a domineering pirate clothed in black. Her aunt was his claimed treasure. Gorgeous in a gown of white with a ring of flowers made to encompass her head, she was his bride to be. Marie's sense of humor gave the costume character when she covered one eye with a black patch.

Annie was adorable dressed as a fairy. She swung her magic wand in an arch over Coira's head. Liam had made the unique piece for his daughter from a stick in their back yard. Two fingers thick, the foot long branch was full of tiny carved leaves and rose petals. Marie had attached a small star made of corn stalks to the tip.

Coira sat in a wing-backed, burgundy chair in a very regal position. She was dressed as an English noblewoman. A tall, white wig swallowed her head and a horrid cascade of fake jewels weighed down her neck. Her pastel dress was so loaded with lace, ruffles and underskirts it seemed a decorated church bell set to ring at Easter mass.

"Do you like my costume Arianna?" One part Irish, one part Scottish and Coira chose to speak with a rough English accent.

"Give it a swirl, child."

"You like it then?" Coira held her head high and looked down her pert nose as she twirled once.

Puppet-like, Arianna smiled. "Aye, it's beautiful."

Why would the girl choose such a costume? Then again, she was only eight and knew naught of prejudice. The English were kind here. This was America, not England or Scotland. Though she loved the Huntington's, some small part of her would always be wary of the English.

"I borrowed the dress and wig from Sarah, her pa brought it overseas from London just last year. The jewels I made myself." Coira twirled around twice.

"Well," Liam said, "are we ready to disembark?"

"I believe we must be," Marie confirmed. She still pinned Arianna with a forlorn expression.

"Is everything alright?" Arianna asked softly while the children were bundled into overcoats and ushered out the front door.

With a brief nod, Marie smiled and rubbed Arianna's shoulder as she passed.

"Of course, sweet child, everything is fine."

As they strolled to the wagon, Arianna touched her aunt's elbow to signal that they pause for a moment.

"I was wondering if you could answer a question?" She toyed with the plaid at her waist. Marie nodded with interest.

"Do you know of a clan by the name of MacLomain?"

A startled look crossed her face. "MacLomain," Marie said. Her Scottish burr rolled the syllables. "MacLomain is the Gaelic word for Lamont."

"Do you know of Clan Lamont, then?"

"Well, the Lamont, Broun and MacMillan clans were intermarried for generations hundreds of years ago in Scotland. All three clans claim the others as their sept. But it's rather unclear when they all began."

"How interesting," Arianna replied.

"Why do you ask?" Marie's eyes narrowed and her brows furrowed.

"Oh, no reason." Arianna continued toward the wagon.

Arianna, you haven't asked me a question about Scotland in...well, it's been a very long time," Marie said.

"No, I haven't." Arianna hopped into the wagon next to Annie. "Well, if you ever want to learn more—"

"Thank you so much but no. That's all I needed to know," Arianna replied. The last thing she wanted to do was prolong this conversation.

Thick pools of twilight's purple colored their surroundings. A chilly autumn wind blew piles of leaves across the drive. The children's laughter mixed with the patter of acorns.

Pulled by two horses, the family wagon made its way down the dirt road. Arianna gazed at the faint twinkle of stars erupting against the darkened sky.

So the saga deepened. Her mystery man gave her a clan name, one interwoven with her own. How could this be?

"Now, there's a sight to see," Liam said. As the wagon topped the hill, they stared in wonder.

Rising like the mighty sails on a monstrous ship was a swollen moon of orange. Miles wide, it loomed over the Spicket River.

"'Tis a full Harvest moon we witness tonight, a moon of true telling it be," Liam murmured.

The way he said it sent chills up her spine. This day had been an endless stream of bizarre happenings. Could it be that even stranger things were yet to come? Would the moon's telling reveal even more before this day was over?

One part of her hoped not.

Another part felt almost eager.

****

The Huntington's house was full of life and light. Various sized pumpkins lined the walkway to the laughter-filled home. A slew of disagreeable expressions were carved into the sides.

Thrilled by the extent of candlelit spheres, Arianna walked behind everyone as they streamed into the house. Warmth and laughter saturated the front foyer as Richard Huntington and his wife, Edna, greeted her. Both were dressed in Roman attire. Richard was such a rail of a man she was amazed his shoulders didn't slide through the neck hole of his chest armor.

"My dear, you look wonderful," Edna said.

"Thank you, you look beautiful as well." Arianna embraced the woman with care. Edna's narrow frame and twig-like bones made her husband appear muscular.

Richard smiled and praised Arianna. "My wife is most observant. Excellent attire my lady. You have a talent with the needle, gifted I'm sure."

"Thank you as well, please don't think for a moment that my uncle didn't stand over my shoulder every minute." Arianna shot Liam an exasperated grin.

Everyone laughed and continued their banter.

Arianna drifted through the crowd until she leaned against the wall of the parlor. The interior of the home was adorned with deep, glossy furnishings. Thick gold candelabras supported beeswax candles that burned bright on each end of the mantelpiece across the room. Plush mauve chairs were coupled in front of a roaring fire. A combination of rich aromas suffused the air. Squash pies, cinnamon muffins, corn bread, pumpkin pudding and sweet candied apples.

"You certainly try to look the part in that costume, huh?"

Arianna turned and came face to face with a she-devil.

She stepped back and glared at the attractive, willowy woman. Arianna wrinkled her nose at the five foot eight blond and narrowed her eyes in challenge. Pale green eyes shot daggers at her beneath a healthy set of red, pointy horns.

"It seems to me you're not far off the mark either," Arianna said.

Beth Luken lowered her voice an octave. "Scottish hussy. Aren't you pushing it just a bit, dressing like some sort of barbarian royalty?"

"Now who is the real barbarian with such words?" Arianna was always eager to goad her opponent.

"German royalty, of course."

"Good evening, ladies." Edward smiled. "Are you two at it again?"

Beth sighed with exaggeration and spoke with a sloppy English accent. "Why Edward, this is what best friends do for entertainment when they're both official wallflowers."

Arianna laughed and took Beth's hand. "You look fantastic, maybe a little too fantastic."

Beth grabbed her tail and wagged it around. Beth Luken, her fast friend since they had met nine years before. The two shared a common bond, difficult childhoods prior to coming to America. Nowadays, they rarely saw one another. Though one would never guess it by her jokester attitude, Beth was a talented writer and spent the majority of time working on her first novel.

"I agree with Arianna's assessment my dear. No doubt you'll bedevil every man here this night," Edward remarked.

He eyed Beth up and down with mock provocation.

"And may I add you're much better at your native German accent."

"My, say it isn't so. Does president John Adams have an eye on the devil?" Beth gave him such a look of disappointment that they all burst into laughter.

Edward and Beth had always been close friends. Their personalities were kindred. In Arianna's opinion, the two would have made a great match. She thought it curious that they never developed romantic feelings for each other.

"You do look quite presidential." Arianna's cheeks burned when she addressed Edward. She regretted the earlier kiss. It changed everything.

Tall and blond, Edward struck her as classically handsome. He stood straighter at Arianna's compliment of his costume. "Well, it seemed more appropriate than dressing as King George the Third of England."

Edward touched the corner of her tartan. "You, my dear girl, look breathtaking."

Arianna squirmed beneath his appreciative gaze. Did he expect her to flirt? Banter back and forth like lovers? This was nonsense. Then again, by allowing him that small kiss she'd clearly sent a certain sort of message.

"Enough of this silliness, Edward, take the devil by the horns and come dance with me," Beth said while yanking on the two points attached to her head.

Before she led Edward to his doom, Beth whispered in Arianna's ear. "We'll talk later princess. I'm eager to discover why talking to our friend Edward makes your skin sizzle so."

Arianna grimaced as the two joined in with the fiddle and pianoforte. Beth was too sharp for her own good. With a sigh, she turned to the crowd. Time to join the fun. So, for the next few hours she mingled with friends and acquaintances. Edna played the piano alongside the fiddler, her brittle frame jerked side to side with the music.

Eventually, the judge for the annual contest rapped his gavel on the pine podium. Arianna sidled her way into a room not nearly large enough to accommodate the amount of people trying to infiltrate it. At last, she could see Richard Huntington as he pounded the gavel again to gather everyone's attention.

"Arianna, can I show you something really quick?"

She smiled. "Of course, Coira."

Aye, she was eager to find out who won the contest but her niece never asked anything of her. How could she refuse?

"Come with us Arianna, you just *have* to." Coira led Arianna down a hallway. Near the end of the candlelit hall they joined two of Coira's friends.

"Cousin, it would mean very much to me if you will join us in a game. We have taken it upon ourselves to disprove an old wives tale," Coira declared.

"That's *disprove* an old *wives* tale, darling," Arianna said.

Coira pouted. "Oh."

Arianna introduced herself to Coira's friends, Elizabeth and Florence.

"This is how it goes," Coira continued. She waited until everyone looked at her. "There's an old superstition that says we can all determine who our one true loves are on this very night." She removed an oval shaped mirror from a table beside her.

"Legend has it if you walk backwards down stairs on All Hollows' Eve and look into a mirror, your one true love will appear."

Her friend's eyes rounded with amazement.

"It cannot be true," Elizabeth said. The girl rubbed her arms together.

"Oh, but it is. I was told so by a very reliable source."

"I would love to go first, that is unless someone else would?" Arianna volunteered. Though she knew it to be a silly game, she enjoyed playing along.

All three girls nodded with vigor. As they watched with interest, Arianna took the mirror and walked to the top of the cellar stairs. Florence skirted around her with a candle and walked down the stairs ahead of Arianna to provide light.

Close by, the other two girls watched Arianna hold her skirts up with one hand and the mirror with the other. She stepped backwards down the staircase. When she arrived at the bottom stair, Arianna held the mirror in front of her face. "Please expose my one true love."

Arianna peered into the glass and waited.

Nothing happened.

She was about to lower the mirror when a small flash of light caught her attention. Narrowing her eyes, she looked closer and froze. It couldn't be. Blinking rapidly, she tried to clear her vision. But the pinprick of light turned to foggy mist. Through that swirling mist, a Scottish loch materialized. An impressive figure on a black warhorse rode along the shore. He traveled with vigor toward her while dodging flashes of white hot lightning. She caught a glimpse of determined emerald eyes.

Oh no! This is impossible! She dropped the glass and ignored the sound of shattering glass as she rushed up the stairs.

"Arianna, what happened?" Coira yelled after her.

Arianna ran out the back door, desperate to suck icy air into her shrunken lungs. She braced her body against the side of the house while trying to regain control.

The moon rested heavy and obtuse. The orange had deepened and now cast shiny puddles over the varied depths of land.

He was coming for her.

Arianna squeezed her arms tight and balled her fists. She had to get out of here. With no thought to her destination, she ran into the night. Trees spilled moonlight as she raced through the forest, catching her sleeves on sticky pine needles and stumbling over random sticks and stones.

Eventually, she stopped at the only place that could possibly soothe her, Pattee's caves. She headed for a jagged rock related to the monolith she visited earlier in the day. This one resembled half a bumpy oval. It marked the sun during both fall and spring equinox. With a stagger forward she fell against it and slid down the rock.

I'm going insane! This simply can't be happening. Her labored breath hit the cold air in small clouds of wispy vapor and she buried her face in her hands, eager to erase the image in the mirror from her mind. Eyes closed, she pressed her cheek against the cool granite.

He was hunting her... haunting her. Arianna clutched the rigid rock. She ripped off the face veil, curled into a ball and sobbed.

Time curled away on a fine mist. It wrapped her in a heavy cloak of despair. Even the curious moon vanished. She was confused when dawn teased her swollen eyelids. It'd only been a few hours at best.

Panicked, she sat up. Her family would be worried.

Arianna leaned against the rock and tried to acclimate to her surroundings.

Thick, white fog made it difficult to see beyond her hands. She struggled to remember if she'd ever seen such a wall of moisture overcome Salem. Cold and tired, Arianna stood and shook the dirt from the bottom of her skirts.

She froze as a strange sound whistled toward her. An arrow?

Recognition came too late.

Oww! Pain seared her shoulder and her body twisted as she fell backwards. She slammed into the ground. Her vision dimmed. The last thing Arianna saw before she plummeted into darkness was her own blood.

Chapter Three

Scotland 1199

Iain was amazed to discover he still possessed feet as warmth started to penetrate his chilled bones. The fire blazed high on the hearth and invited rest for the weary.

"Brother?" Though spoken softly, the word broke through the haze of impending slumber and he smiled.

"Iain, are you still awake?"

"What is it Muriel?" His head snapped back from its perch on his chest and he eyed his sister. Could she not see he was resting after a long journey?

"Would you prefer ale or wine?" She was quick to look concerned.

"You woke me to ask if I would have something I obviously dinnae need?" He sighed as she plunked down next to him.

"Nay, brother, you do need fluid, for surely you're dehydrated," Muriel assured. "But now you are awake, tell me everything."

Iain laughed, leaned over and gave his sister a kiss on the cheek. Only fourteen winters and she already had the look of their Ma.

"What of it will you have, child? The endless hours astride my horse or the cold nights watching a barren landscape with anticipation?"

"Aye, Iain, all of it you sarcastic ox." She winked. "It's obvious your betrothed is still amongst the missing." With practiced efficiency, Muriel handed Iain his preferred ale and waited.

"No luck, lassie." He took a long frustrated swallow.

Muriel eyed her brother with worry. She'd been but a child when his marriage had been pre-arranged. The ceremony should've taken place years ago but the father of the bride was closely affiliated with Scotland's king, William the First. Caught in abiding his ruler's whims the marital event was delayed. When the time was finally opportune, he became ill. Still determined to fulfill his agreement to Iain's now deceased father, he ordered his finest warriors to escort his daughter to her future husband.

"There was no sign o' her this trip to the borders, then?"

"Nay." He gave his empty cup to his sister. His future betrothed came from the far distant eastern shores of Lothian.

He couldn't meet her along the way for he could not leave his lands unattended. The times were perilous, structure was thin, and clans allied themselves to each other through marriage and war. Frankly, he was impressed this foreign laird honored a pledge made so long ago. Theirs were old clans and the tie would be a good one.

"Seems it may be true after all." Muriel handed her brother another cup of ale.

"What's that?"

"Naught brother," she returned. "But there *are* the rumors."

"Aye, I know of the talk. It matters little." Iain stretched and crossed his legs out in front of him. He reflected on his future bride. The tale had traveled far, the love she was said to have for one of her father's warriors. He believed none of it. A woman of her clan would be disowned if she did not honor her father's wishes. It was gossip, formed by rival clans to travel the land and spit in his face.

"You are right." Muriel eyed him. "You are nearly too old to take a bride. If Da was still alive, he'd surely have broken the agreement by now. If for nothing else than to ensure a male heir! And your bride, she's already near past her childbearing years."

Iain rolled his eyes. Old his arse. He would honor this agreement if it was the last thing he did. Nothing mattered more to him than loyalty and duty. If his Da had made a pact, he would see it fulfilled. Their clan had descended from the great Irish kingdom of Dalriada, marrying into the finest Viking families, and producing a strong Celtic-Norse bloodline. Their Da and older brother died years before in one of the many battles between rival clans.

Shortly thereafter, their Ma died while giving birth to his youngest sister, Catherine. Iain, the surviving son, became chieftain of the clan. He'd done well so far. He'd allied their clan with many others and used the years well, both in battle and in fortifying the castle. The fortress was renovated from log to stone. He added a second surrounding wall and moat around that which already existed, making it the most impregnable fortress in Scotland.

Gods above, he was tired.

"We will find her soon," Muriel assured softly and gently removed the tilting cup from his drowsy hand.

"Laird Iain!"

Startled, he shot up. Had he dosed off? Disoriented, he noted his sister still sat next to him.

"What is it, Ferchar?" He turned towards the entrance.

"There's action, 'tis the enemy. We believe they have your bride," Ferchar provided.

"Talk, lad," Iain said to his nephew.

"Movement, twenty men, an hours ride north." Ferchar followed him out of the keep.

Fifty warriors stood ready in the courtyard awaiting his orders.

"We ride. Now." Iain swung onto his black warhorse and departed.

The wait had been long enough. Was she really finally here?

The sound of hooves echoed behind him as Iain rode hard along the western shores of the Holy loch into the hills and mountains of the north.

Eventually, he slowed enough to enable his first in command, Hugh, to ride alongside.

"Tell me cousin, how bad is it?" Iain said.

"Bad," Hugh responded. "She traveled alone."

"Alone? What o' her men?" Iain reigned in his aggravation.

"We know naught."

"What of their scouts?"

"None, the fools found her on our land, they fled quickly."

"We'll speak later about how they made it as far as they did." He cast his man a look of reprove.

"Ride hard!" Iain bellowed.

They caught up with the enemy quickly. The journey was not far and their horses were still fairly fresh. With a signal, he deployed the strategy for attack.

"I want her capturer." Bloodlust rippled through him. Years of comradeship in battle had sharpened the clansmen into a formidable weapon. Through signals and soft sounds they worked together in stealth and surrounded the intruders with deadly efficiency.

Making ready his blade, he watched his men filter through the woods. Some were on horseback and others afoot. He slid off his mount and snuck through the brush until the rear guard appeared. With a graceful leap, he swung up and ran a sharpened dagger smoothly across the pliant neck of the rear warrior.

This was the signal to break their silence. His men unleashed battle cries as the enemy clan was attacked.

On his horse again, Iain charged ahead through the tall pines. He pulled free his axe in full gallop and his weapon met its mark as it lopped off the head of another. He rode until he had his man in sight.

A gray mare trailed behind the enemy clansman. A body lay slumped over the sweaty horse. Long hair hung nearly to the ground from the limp figure.

Pure rage bubbled up. Anger flared anew as he rode up alongside the man. *I'll kill you over and over you bloody bastard!* Iain had him to the ground before the stranger's axe made full swing. The two rolled. Iain's dagger fell against the man's throat before the stranger had a chance to reach for his knife.

"So you thought to claim what was mine." Iain dug the blade into the man's flesh until a thin trail of blood curled around the blade.

"Aye." The intruder sneered and laughed roughly. He knew his time was done. "I did claim what was yours."

Why kill you when I can make your fate so much worse? Iain smiled and retracted the dagger from the man's neck. Before the clansman understood what was happening he was fully castrated. A cry unlike any other emitted from the broken warrior.

"Aye, and so did I," Iain said grimly. The enemy clansman passed out.

"Leave him for the scavengers." Iain spit on the body. "If they'll have him."

He was pleased with his men. Broken bodies lay astride their horses, wide eyed with quick death, none were left alive.

Astride his horse again, Iain pulled the lifeless sack of woman onto his lap. It was then that he discovered a broken shaft of arrow wedged within her shoulder. The arrow had not come out the other side; therefore, the horse had hidden the damage. Blood coagulated around the plugged wound. He grabbed her wrist and felt a faint pulse. She was still alive.

Barely.

Fools. There was no doubt in his mind that these men had been ordered to keep this woman whole for their Chieftain. This was not the way to do it.

She needed medicinal aide immediately.

Iain confronted his men. "The enemy fell before us."

He nodded to his kinsmen and shouted his next words. "Clan Cochran will think before bride stealing again."

He held his bloodied axe in the air and cheering erupted.

"'Tis a small ride back, but you may rest here if you desire. I will reward you upon return. You have done well."

Iain spurred his horse and rode like the wind back to his castle.

As he galloped up to the front door he urged the servants to rouse Muriel. It wasn't until his future bride was taken from him that he realized his men had followed.

"The men prefer to take you up on your offer when the lass is well," Hugh said as they entered the hall.

"Very good." His was an accomplished group of warriors. They were generations of men devoted to one thing, their clan. Hugh chose to remain and the two let the fire warm their bones.

"None of the enemy's horses were injured. All of them are being corralled in. Not a bad lot. Twenty-five total."

"Aye. Good." Iain sighed in spite of Hugh's positive report. There were many questions on his mind.

"They've sent a man ahead. It won't be long before our enemy's laird knows your intended has arrived." Hugh looked his cousin in the eye. "Arthur is talking to our men along not only the northern border but the others as well."

"Ten years as Chieftain and no one has ever made it by my men. I know it's no fault of yours Hugh, 'twas just frustration that laced my earlier words." Iain stared at the fire. Theirs was a good location. Surrounded on three sides by water, only the north was land. There was something else at work here.

Hugh said nothing but Iain knew his friend dwelled upon the same puzzle. How had the enemy made it past their border and why did the girl lack an escort? He crossed his hands behind his head, eyed the fire and mentally utilized the comfortable silence of an old friendship.

****

As the first dim light of the new day filtered through the hall, Muriel appeared on the stairs. The men slumbered before the hearth.

"She will live." Muriel stood in front of them. Neither man woke at her words.

"Iain." She gave him a hard kick in the shin.

"Ouch!" Iain sat up. "Bloody hell."

"Watch your tongue brother." Muriel stood with her hands on her hips. "Aren't you the least curious how this woman o' yours fares?"

Iain and her second cousin sputtered to life. *Men.*

"Is she alive, then?" Hugh asked.

"Aye, Muriel, is she?" Iain arched his brows.

"Aye." She smiled at Hugh. "May I have a moment with my brother."

Hugh nodded. "I'm glad to hear she's well."

Muriel waited until he left the hall before she spoke.

"The arrow was removed, the wound washed, and then treated with Apothecary's rose petals. When she is more able I will have her drink some wine spiced with the last of my cloves, this will help restore health and strength depleted from such loss of blood. As you will see, the wound is wrapped with fresh cloth. There will be a period of fever, but she will live."

"'Tis good news. No doubt she has been through much. Thank you." Iain leaned forward and rested his elbows on his knees. "Will she be well enough to marry by the coming festivities?"

Muriel rubbed her hands together in front of the fire. "I would think so. I implore you to keep in mind, however, that she is without anyone familiar to her in a land much different from her own. Is it prudent you marry so soon?"

"I have waited long for this pact to be made. The marriage will take place upon the Samhain."

Muriel frowned.

He softened at the worry in her eyes. "She will be unfamiliar for a time whether she is married or not."

"Mayhap you misunderstand me," Muriel said carefully. A slight blush touched her cheekbones.

"I understand your concern clearly, but I do believe 'tis time to produce an heir. Dinnae you agree?"

Muriel shrugged and sat. This was about the last thing she wanted to talk to her brother about so she said no more about it. "Have you heard anything about how this all happened?"

"No." Iain consumed the entire glass of watered wine a servant set beside him. "I have some theories."

"I suppose you're not going to tell me what those are."

Muriel and her brother were close, yet he had always protected her from talk of war.

Iain shrugged and gave her his famous crooked grin.

A scream tore from above.

Iain jumped from his chair and flew up the stone staircase. He entered the room to find the girl wailing in her sleep. Muriel came in behind him.

Without a second thought he sat on the edge of the bed and gathered her into his arms. She was delirious with fever. As he held her head against his shoulder, he whispered reassurances into her ear. Her burning, sweat slicked arms grasped him weakly.

"The fever rakes her." Muriel's voice remained calm as she wet a cloth in the cool water from the pot beside the bed. "I will stay with her."

The woman moaned against him. Gently, he attempted to lean her back but she would not release her hold.

"Where am I?" She murmured the slurred question against his shoulder.

"You are home," he said. She shuddered and he pulled her tighter against him.

"I had such a dream." She snuggled closer.

"What of?"

"Violence," she said. "Then he saved me."

"Who saved you?"

"The man. My man, the one with the beautiful eyes.

"He was there and angry. He saved me..." Her words were drowsy.

Iain scowled. The rumor must be true. This warrior of her fathers. Well, no more. He would not stand for it. She was his now. They would be married at once. Irritated, he tried to pull away.

"No," she gasped with the last of her breath and clutched his neck in desperation. Her body jerked.

How could he leave her like this? Iain took the damp cloth from Muriel and held it against the girl's steamy forehead. "I will stay with her. Get some rest sister."

"As you wish," Muriel said. "Come for me later."

Iain nodded. "Blow out the candle."

As darkness fell, he laid down beside her and held her close. She was so soft. Her hair smelled so sweet. She was a slim, fine-boned lass as far as he could tell. Who was this slip of a girl that despised a marriage arranged by her father, her clan?

Though weary, Iain didn't sleep but continued to administer the cool cloth until her breathing fell to a slow, even rhythm. How was it that he already enjoyed the feel of her in his arms so much?

Many hours later, Iain felt satisfied that she was at peace and somewhat reluctantly left.

The new sun sat low on the morning horizon when he stepped outside. Stretching, he eyeballed the stretch of loch beyond the wall of trees. A group of his men practiced mock combat with each other as a light mist slid over the green field between his fortress and the trees. His castle was built strategically in that it allowed a panoramic view of miles of surrounding countryside.

"Good morn to you, my laird," said Ferchar.

"Good is yet to be seen lad." Iain smiled and slapped his nephew on the shoulder. Tall for fifteen, he had the look of his father with blue black hair and pale blue eyes.

It'd been ten winters ago that Iain's elder brother was killed. He kept his sister-in-law and her son in the main keep and watched over Ferchar as though he was his own son.

"'Tis good we found the woman before the Samhain fire celebrations, is it not?" Ferchar walked with him to the field.

"Aye, it does please me. Perhaps we will make it a duel celebration this year."

"'Twould seem a practical thing to do." Ferchar nodded. "'Twill be a grand celebration."

Iain was relieved that the search for his betrothed had finally come to an end. The previous year had been a long one spent scouting the land for this lass. With many cold, unprotected nights spent out in the forest and mountains. Most of the surrounding clans were allies, yet many of their clan trekked further into the wild, tempting onslaught from those whom were enemies.

"My laird," Hugh acknowledged. He crossed his long sword in front of his face as Arthur's blade came down with brute strength. He jumped back, and then slowly circled the other man.

Both men were aware Iain watched them with scrutiny. Plunging forward, Arthur invoked Hugh into a rapid dueling succession. The other men watched in appreciation. Besides Iain, these two men superseded all others with their swordsmanship.

Metal blades hissed and clanged while sweat poured from the two warriors. Iain knew before the fight began who would be victorious. Where Arthur would always be a towering wall of force, Hugh was a man of endurance and wit. He wore his opponent down with small movements intended to extract unnecessary effort from Arthur, who now panted from the excursion.

In a final attempt, he swung his 40-inch steel blade toward Hugh's throat. That was his mistake. Hugh crouched as the metal whistled over his head and jutted his own blade forward. He halted as the sharp point pricked bare skin.

"You would have taken my head clear off my shoulder man," Hugh cried and tossed the blade aside. He stood up and dealt a solid punch to Arthur's face.

With a backward stumble, the boom of Arthur's laughter would probably awaken all of Scotland. The two men proceeded to clap each other on the shoulder as they jested back and forth.

"Well done." Iain praised them both then turned his attention to the men present.

"The skill of this clan in retrieving my betrothed will be rewarded. There will be a celebration in the great hall this eve."

Cheers erupted and he unsheathed his own sword. "Now, who would like to fight me?"

Ferchar accepted the challenge and the two battled as Iain taught his nephew new tricks.

That evening, hundreds of his clansmen gathered in the great hall. Barrels were rolled out and great amounts of ale were consumed. Music played and women joined the festivities.

After he announced his appreciation for the safe arrival of his bride, Iain set no limits on his men this night. A great fire roared on the hearth and created a thin veil of smoke that hid the stone ceiling high above.

Platters heavy with beef and mutton filled ten long tables. Big bowls of stewed kale were plunked next to those full of fruit. It was an easy feast. In a weeks time the occasion would be far grander, with added breads, fish, whiskey and wine.

The servants were instructed to bring food to those men who drew watch. Iain would allow them ale the next evening when those that now attended sobered up. He was not a man to take chances. Although it was unlikely his enemies would dare retaliate. He had not taken his clan this far by being a trusting laird.

He would take no lass to his bed this night.

He'd waited long for this girl and he would not disrespect her. Iain only hoped that she would be worth the wait.

Chapter Four

Surrounded by hazy, mammoth shadows, Arianna blinked. *Where am I? Am I dead?* Not yet based on the searing pain in her shoulder. She moaned and clutched at the arrow that protruded from her left shoulder. She was so weak. What was happening? Was she dreaming?

"Good clean shot." A deep sandpaper voice boasted with a heavy Scottish brogue.

She squinted and watched in horror as she was encompassed by a slew of men on horseback. They towered over her and carried massive weapons. Some had long swords; while others were adorned with battle-axes, maces, war hammers, daggers and long bows.

Filthy tunics and wool plaids covered large, muscled bodies. Their hair hung unkempt and long with small braids that hung by thick necks. Hardened faces portrayed eyes full of hatred.

"Bonnie thing, make a good whore," one burly giant grunted as he grabbed his manhood.

"Aye, but our laird wants her first," another reminded while he slid from his horse.

He sauntered over and ripped off the headpiece. Her hair fell free and the men roared with approval. The man yanked her to her feet. Eye level with his chest, she cringed. His red hair hung limp and greasy.

Terror seized her. A far away memory threatened to return. She would not scream. He would not get that much from her. "Och, I thought it foolish, him looking for you, waiting. I'm impressed. I think I might have done the same for such a wee bonnie lass." His thick Scottish burr stained a wide smile and his sour breath stung her nostrils. "Mayhap now I understand my enemy."

He pulled her close. His sticky tongue licked her cheek as he dragged one large hand over her breast. He smelled like horse manure mixed with month old body odor. Bitter bile rose in her throat.

"Damn you," she seethed and met his lusty gaze.

His fist struck the side of her head so hard she must've passed out because the next thing Arianna remembered was being thrown over a horse. This only pushed what was left of the arrow deeper.

There was no saddle. Sick to her stomach, Arianna's hands and feet were tied together. Blood rushed to her face. Her vision swam with the dirty and faded colors of a plaid wool blanket beneath.

Time blurred.

Every jaunt of the horse tortured her shoulder.

Pain seeped from the wound into every muscle in her body. Her head pounded as minutes turned to hours and her sole view was the ground passing below. Small pine needles and dry leaves crawled over small earth embedded rocks.

She closed her eyes and prayed for death.

Distant voices talked to one another. Laughter echoed in her head. Then the voices quieted. She was losing touch with reality.

At some point the horse stopped and cries of agony screamed through her head. She couldn't open her eyes anymore.

Fresh pain ripped through her when she was pulled from the horse into strong arms. With all the effort left to her, she managed to crack one eye open a mere sliver.

Through a veil of exhaustion she discerned a warrior. Blood dripped from his arms and speckled his face. He smelled like pine and spice. His expression was savage. This man was familiar to her. From where did she know him?

He was a safe place.

She felt warm and protected in these arms. This must be Heaven. She closed her eyes and welcomed peace.

****

"Are you awake?" The feminine voice sounded full of compassion.

"Hmmm?" Arianna slowly opened her eyes and gasped when her vision cleared. A stranger sat on the bed. The young beautiful girl smiled down.

"Who are you? What are you doing here?" Arianna sat up too quick. Her vision darkened as the women gently pushed her back down.

"Have care, you are still too weak." She repositioned the pillow under Arianna's head. "I'm Muriel, your new sister."

Long ebony hair fell in waves over her shoulders. She wore a simple dress made from un-dyed wool cloth over a linen kirtle. Big, luminescent eyes fringed with thick lashes graced a well-sculptured face. High cheekbones accentuated her full, wide lips. She reminded Arianna of someone. But who?

"My sister? Are you mad? Where is Aunt Marie?" Arianna tried to sit up again. Blood drained from her face as she looked around.

This wasn't her room. Where was she? The walls were made of stone. A light wind whistled through one thin wall slit and ushered in a subliminal hint of sea salt. The meager sliver allowed dull daylight to enhance the golden blobs of fire dancing within torches set in heavy, pewter wall brackets. A wooden chair stood in the corner of the room by a large chest. A brown animal skin rug was laid in the middle of the small chamber.

"You suffered from a great fever but it has broken," Muriel said gently. "It appears there is confusion left in its wake."

"What fever? Whose room is this and who did you say you were again?" Arianna attempted to stifle panic.

"You ask too many questions." Muriel laughed. "You have been fighting a fever from the arrow in your shoulder. You are in a servant's chamber. I'm Muriel, the sister of your future husband. I have a question for you as well, why do you sound so funny?"

Arianna stared at the girl in amazement. For indeed her own Scottish burr sounded faint compared to Muriel's.

Future husband? The most recent dream bombarded her. She looked down and realized there was a cloth wrapped around her shoulder beneath the thin chemise she wore.

Tentative, she touched the bandage. What had once been a horrible throb was now just a dull ache. The pain from the brute's paw hitting her was completely gone. A shiver ran through her.

If there was ever a time to keep a level head, it was now.

"Muriel, where am I?" This had to be some sort of prank.

"You are in the castle of Clan MacLomain, Arianna. We didnae think you would come, but you have. Now my brother can fulfill his promise." Muriel sounded pleased.

"MacLomain," Arianna whispered and shrank down further into the bed. This was beyond comprehension. The only person who had knowledge of that name was Aunt Marie and she was one person Arianna knew would never play a practical joke such as this. There's no way this could be happening. She dug her nails into her arms to ensure reality and winced at the very real self- inflicted pain.

Breathe. Just keep breathing.

Arianna ran her hand over the scratchy wool blanket covering her, suddenly grateful for the chemise that protected her skin from the abrasive material.

"Yes, ours descend from the great kingdom of Dalriada. We are amongst the oldest clans in Scotland," Muriel said with pride.

"Scotland you say?" Arianna looked around the room again. Insane. Dead. What difference did it make? At least Heaven was Scotland.

"Arianna, I understand that 'tis been a trying journey for you but has the fever stolen your mind completely?"

Fevers in Heaven, what next?

Fear flared her temper. "Well Muriel, you could not comprehend how dimwitted I feel at this moment. You know my name, inform me I'm in a Scottish castle and you are the sister of a man intended to be my husband whom I do not know. All of this in a room I don't recognize. Now you question me about my feverishly stolen sanity induced by an arrow, a weapon in which I have only seen pictures of in books."

Arianna sighed and tried her best to keep aggravation at bay. "You have spun quite the tale, but I'm curious Muriel. I see the dress you wear, which is obviously very ancient attire. I can only assume there is a great gag being imparted. Tell me. Who are you in league with? So help me God, this has gone too far."

Arianna had leaned forward as her distress increased, as her set of circumstances became clearer. She had to admit it would have been an impossible feat for any of this to be a joke yet the idea of this all being real numbed the mind.

"I've spent the entire week nursing you to health, hoping we would become friends when you were finally coherent Arianna Broun." Muriel walked over to the slit of a window. "I am in league with no one. You have suffered from fever. I can only hope this is a temporary affliction with your personality."

Arianna frowned at the girl. She had nursed her back to health? How sick was she? It was quite obvious if this was a trick this girl had no knowledge of it.

"I'm sorry." She looked over at Muriel. "I...I'm confused, please don't be upset."

"Of course." The red drained from Muriel's face. She sat back down on the bed and took Arianna's hand.

"I ask these questions because I've forgotten so much," Arianna lied and squeezed Muriel's hand in assurance. In her experience, you got more with sugar than with vinegar. Muriel's expression softened.

"Did your brother shoot me with an arrow?" She needed to understand what was happening.

"No, Arianna, 'twas our enemy clan that injured you." Muriel sniffed with derision. "They are monsters."

"Why did your enemy shoot me?"

"To claim you as their own," she responded. "'Tis a great feat to steal the promised bride o' such a man as my brother."

"What is your brother's name?"

"Iain," she said with a smile. "I think you will be quite content with him."

Arianna stiffened though her muscles felt nonexistent. The dream. Her bedroom. The man who had sat on her bed and said, "I am sorry, but you are destined to marry a MacLomain."

"Why is he such a great man?" Arianna's words came out in a squeak.

"Arianna, he is the laird o' the mighty MacLomain clan, Chieftain o' all Cowal," she said, incredulous.

Forget about Heaven, I should be waking up anytime now. Arianna chewed her lip. How did one wake oneself up?

"Come," Muriel responded to a light tap at the door. A young girl entered the room with two pewter mugs. She handed one to Arianna and the other to Muriel before she departed.

"Cowal in Argyll?" She turned the heavy mug and admired the engraving. A single raised hand palm forward perched over intricately carved words. Arianna ran her fingers over the motto. *"Ne parkas nec spemas."* "Neither spare nor dispose," she said.

"Argyll shire, aye, that's good." Muriel smiled and nodded.

"The Cowal Peninsula?" Arianna sniffed the liquid in her cup.

"Aye. Many peninsulas really. The whole of Cowal is surrounded on three sides. On the West by Loch Fyne, the Strath of Clyde to the south, and Loch Holy to the East."

After she was assured the content was merely ale, Arianna took a tentative sip from the given mug. The warm, bitter fluid slid down her throat.

Muriel smiled when Arianna grimaced at the taste of the ale. "It will warm your belly and calm your spirit."

A warm spirit. Good. "No doubt it will."

Arianna relaxed as warmth filled her. "Tell me again, why am I here?" Arianna drank more.

"Your father and mine made an agreement a long time ago," Muriel said, patient. "I'm amazed my brother upheld such a promise. My father has been deceased ten years now and Iain is no longer a young man."

"How old is he?" Arianna envisioned an old man. The dream has gone astray.

"Twenty and six winters." Muriel shook her head, a look of true remorse on her face.

"What was this agreement?" Arianna said, relieved. He was only seven years older than her. Thank the good Lord. She giggled at Muriel. The ale was doing more than warming her belly.

"That you and Iain would be married, uniting our clans." Muriel sighed as Arianna stared wide-eyed at her.

"Where is my father, then, Muriel? Should he not be at my wedding?" Arianna was convinced she would either receive the truth now or wake up.

"He is dying and you know that...at least you did." Muriel's eyebrows drew together.

"Where am I traveling from?"

"Lothian, near the shores of the North Sea."

Muriel simultaneously cupped her chin between the flat of her forefinger and thumb, bit her lower lip and shook her head. It was clear the girl thought Arianna's mind had snapped.

Arianna sat back. This stranger did weave a great tale. As if on cue, the servant child appeared again and took her empty mug. She replaced it with a full one.

"So, let me make sure I have my facts straight. I am Arianna Broun, to which I readily concur. I'm in the great Laird Iain MacLomain's castle in Cowal. As you say, I'm to be his wife based on an agreement made years ago between my dying and his deceased father. I was shot by the arrow of an enemy clan trying desperately to intercept me as I traveled from Lothian near the distant Eastern shores of Scotland."

Arianna held up her hand before Muriel could talk. "I can only hope my dying father sent men to protect me. Assuming something happened to these men, I stumbled forward alone. At some point, I was attacked. Horrible men from your rival clan intended to keep me but your brother's men intercepted them, hence saving their beloved laird's bride-to-be."

"You understand well now my sister." Muriel took a sip from her own cup. "You are wrong about one thing, however."

"That is?" She really was better at vinegar than sugar.

"My brother led the men who intercepted the beasts attempting to steal you. 'Twas he who saved you, Arianna. The man rode madly through the black of the night to ensure you lived," Muriel provided.

Arianna couldn't help but like this girl. She had an honest countenance. Muriel defended family and Arianna appreciated that.

She pulled the blanket more tightly around her and gave the room a third appraisal. The wind had stopped which enabled the torch's flames to stabilize. Straight edged shadows skimmed along the outer rims of firelight hiding the corners in pockets of new nightfall.

"Why is he not here to talk to me if he is to be my husband?" Arianna's voice cracked as she imagined the man in her dreams. As absurd as this fairytale was, who wouldn't be curious to meet the man they were supposed to marry? In a dream, of course.

"'Tis not proper sister." Muriel cast her eyes down. "I'm glad we had a chance to become familiar with each other."

Something in Muriel's tone implied she didn't really believe it so improper. The girl stood and gazed down at her with an unreadable expression. Muriel grabbed another blanket from inside the trunk and spread it over her.

"Me too." Arianna was genuine. Perhaps they would meet again in another dream. She yawned and fought the heaviness of her eyelids. "Thank you for taking care of me, your skills in healing must be superb."

"You are welcome and thank you." Muriel preened and blushed. She fiddled with her skirts in contemplation and then confided, "He has checked in on you every day."

"Your brother?" Arianna blanched. The idea of a strange man present while she struggled through a forgotten fever was beyond embarrassment.

"Aye, who else?" Muriel chuckled and winked. "Fear naught my friend, I made sure you were covered."

Arianna groaned.

"You're feeling better at a good time. On the morrow we begin the Samhain celebration," Muriel said.

"Samhain, you say?" She was beginning to drift away. Almost time to wake up.

"Aye, 'twill be a grand occasion this year," she said. From a drowsy state Arianna was aware of Muriel tucking the blanket beneath her chin like her aunt had done when she was a child.

"Muriel?" Arianna murmured her name before she slipped out the door. "What year is it?"

Muriel turned and stared at her. "It is one thousand, one hundred and ninety nine years after the death of Jesus Christ."

Then she was gone.

Arianna snickered as she gave in to an alcohol-induced slumber. The last thought she had was a promise to herself that she would never, ever again dream of a Scottish warrior.

Chapter Five

"My lady? Are you awake?"

The timid words teased Arianna's ear like a distant wind. Opening her eyes a crack, she saw the same brown-eyed servant girl who had brought her the ale before. She prodded Arianna's arm gently.

Wary, she hoisted herself upon an elbow and sighed. This was one long dream.

"'Tis little time before the Samhain celebrations begin and your presence is required," the girl said while she busied herself in the corner of the room.

"What is your name?" Arianna said. The girl turned.

A look of amazement stretched her youthful features. "I am Emma, my lady," she said and bowed.

"Please don't bow to me Emma, you are my equal," Arianna said. Being opposed to one human being owned by another, her family kept no slaves.

"Yes, my lady." Emma eyed Arianna with open curiosity. "Lady Muriel sent this heated tub of river water up for you to bathe."

"I see." Arianna sat up with care. She was nude! Who removed the chemise? Better not think too hard on that one. Modest, she pulled the blanket back over her.

"Come, my lady, we will make you ready." Emma took Arianna's hand, led her across the room and motioned to the water.

With a sigh of surrender, Arianna dropped the blanket and entered the water quickly. When Emma made to start washing her she declined. It felt odd enough having the girl present, never mind bathing her.

Though Emma graced her with a peculiar look she said nothing more. With expert hands, she dressed Arianna's nearly healed wound. After she wrapped it with a light cloth she implored that Arianna wait a moment.

Arianna was delighted when Emma returned with her kirtle and blue, silk gown. *It's free of blood! And the tears have been sewn!* After Emma helped her dress, she combed her long, wet hair until it dried into shiny, soft curls. There would be no headpiece.

Emma bowed her head, blushed and then disappeared.

Regrettably, there existed no mirror so Arianna distracted herself and tried to peer out one of the slits in the wall. It was difficult to see anything but gray.

"Oh! Just look at you."

Arianna turned.

"You are breathtaking, my sister," Muriel said from the doorway.

The girl held a noble stance and wore a dress Arianna would not have dreamed existed in this time. Created with a light wool material, it was dyed a beautiful light green that complimented her eyes.

A deep blue kirtle peeked from beneath the bottom of the skirt. The colors at the neckline plunged from the spectacular hue of green to darker shades of green, which melded with turquoise until it finished at the bottom with a shade of blue that matched the undergarment.

The front of her long hair was braided and interwoven with silver material and then tied back.

The remainder of her hair curled in long tendrils down her back.

"I pale in comparison to you," Arianna said.

"You know naught then," Muriel scolded. "'Tis time for you to join the festivities."

Eager to finally leave the room, Arianna followed Muriel. Her mouth dropped open in amazement. This couldn't even exist in a dream.

Arianna's chamber was among many others that lined a pathway behind a waist high stone wall. Beyond the barrier and far below lay the largest room she ever saw. The ceiling towered far above her head. This is medieval Scotland? She felt as though she stood in a great fortress portrayed in tales pertaining to ancient Greek mythology. How she wished she had asked Aunt Marie more about this clan.

Twenty long trestle tables lined the floor below and overflowed with people. Hazy smoke drifted from a fire she couldn't see. Hundreds of torches lined the staircases and walls below, burning brightly against the rock. A group of three men created the foreign music that filled the chamber.

She worked hard not to appear timid as she trailed behind Muriel to the right. They stopped at the top of a staircase, which was identical to the staircase they would have reached had they turned left outside her room.

Enormous tapestries hung from the walls and depicted various battles, the Scottish land and woman entwined with men. Arianna gasped when she locked on a forty foot intricately woven tapestry that depicted a heavily armored, horn helmeted Viking running his sword though a man on bent knees begging for mercy. The picture was so well created she thought she saw the look of triumph through the thin slices of metal that adorned the victors' head.

"Are you feeling well enough for this, Arianna?" Muriel's brows knit together in concern.

"I'm fine." She straightened her back. Wherever and whenever she was, now was not the time for weakness. Arianna pulled back her shoulders and nodded to Muriel.

"Now is the hard part. You do not follow me until I reach the last stair," Muriel warned. "Just sort of a tradition."

Tradition? She didn't like the sound of this. Arianna watched Muriel walk down the stairs, well paced in her descent. Arianna doubted she could look so regal. Which made sense, in that she was not nobility but simply an American from New Hampshire. Well, at least she was last week.

Many men turned to stare. When Muriel reached the bottom stair she turned her head briefly and gave Arianna the cue to follow her.

Ugh! This is bad. Very bad.

In an attempt to mimic her predecessor, Arianna began her walk down the stairs. Sweet Lord, don't let me trip. Elegance was not something in which she had been trained yet she wasn't doing too badly. Arianna held her head high as though there was a book on it, just like her cousin Coira had. Though a bit of a challenge on stairs, she managed.

Then the situation got worse.

About three quarters of the way down the stairs, the music thinned to the single trill of a lone bagpipe. The sound enchanted the soul and was as solitary in its melody as she was in this moment. Every person in the room stopped their chatter and watched her with intensity.

Her mouth turned dessert dry. She pressed slick palms into the folds of the skirts she had held up to descend. There's nowhere to go but forward. *I can do this.*

Then Arianna met the eyes of the tall man standing at the bottom of the stairs. Muscular and tan, he was clad in a black tunic partially covered by a dark blue and green plaid. Wavy black hair accentuated his intense emerald gaze.

Arianna's legs turned numb and her torso shook.

She would've been wise to stop at that moment but the thought didn't connect with the body. Thank the angels above there were but two steps left because she missed them both and fell right into his arms.

He dragged her against him as he brought her to her feet.

"A bit clumsy, are you not?" He whispered; his brogue thick and his breath warm against her ear. Her body felt aflame. Her heart stopped. She dimly recollected being cradled in the arms of a familiar man high astride a horse. She struggled for breath. While she regained both her footing and dignity, the rowdy crowd applauded.

"I know you," Arianna said low enough for only him to hear. "But I regret to inform you, sir, I am intended for the laird of this establishment."

"The laird, you say?" He put a single finger to her lips.

Arianna froze in his arms. That deep voice and those eyes. The man she had dreamed of for so long. It had to be him. Nobody had eyes that color. Their intense brilliant green desecrated her. Heat rose and she felt weak. *Am I swooning?* She felt one arm lock behind her back and he held her closer yet. Her breath caught.

He was so tall, his face a work of art. With a strong jaw, well sculptured lips, high cheekbones, a strong brow and straight nose she had never seen a more handsome man. His finger felt hot on her lips as his gaze sparkled with mischief.

"Come forward my laird. I meant naught by holding your woman so close, she but fell into my arms," he declared.

He motioned to another attractive man who stood nearby. Slightly shorter than he, the warrior stepped forward, grabbed Arianna gently from her captor and pulled her next to him.

The man who now held her spoke to the crowd. "My future wife, sent to ally us with another great clan on the far distant shores of the North Sea, Arianna Broun!"

The room boomed with rambunctious cheers. She looked around and marveled at the medieval attire of the crowd. People were people, however, and this crowd was in a jovial, celebratory mood. Every eye in the room accosted her with open curiosity.

"What if I challenge you for her?" A man bellowed from across the room. Arianna moved closer to her betrothed as a man larger than any she had ever seen drew a great battle-axe. As he barreled across the room, the bear of a man raised the axe over his head. This beast clearly had the devil in his eyes.

The man who held her pushed her behind him. "Are you that brave, you big galoot?"

"I am." The giant let his axe swing with promise by his side.

Arianna stepped back a pace in fear and shook her head.

"That's enough, you monsters," Muriel broke in with a look of reprove. "She doesnae ken."

Arianna watched in amazement as Muriel stepped forward and positioned herself bravely between the savages.

"Arthur, Hugh and you." She tossed a glare at the man in black. "Shame on you all. My whole life I've had to put you in your place and you choose this moment to act like a bunch of barbarians. You put your clan to shame."

"Apologize, now." Muriel pointed a finger at the lot of them.

The crowd chuckled with appreciation.

Arianna was baffled. If she was correct in her historical recollection, the medieval period was an age when a woman had no say. Yet, no one stepped forward to silence Muriel. What a foreign place.

The man from her dreams spoke. His voice carried the distinct edge of authority. "Aye, lassie. You said your piece."

He gave a single nod to the other two men.

Arianna watched in disbelief as the towering man with long, flaming red hair and ready axe bent onto one knee. The top of his head reached her chest. He kissed the back of her hand and welcomed her to the clan then stated his name as Arthur. The man who had pushed her behind him followed suit and bowed his head. He was Hugh.

She thanked the men and faced the remainder.

"That only leaves you, Iain." Arianna was amazed her voice held steady as she met his humored gaze.

"It does, lass." He granted her a smile that nearly made her knees buckle once more.

"Have you had your fun now?" Arianna tried to reign in her temper. Beautiful dream warrior or not, she didn't like to be mocked. She was in no mood for jokes. Arianna would just return to her room and regain some semblance of dignity. She excused herself and began to walk back up the stairs.

"Thank you, lads. As you can see, she was well worth the effort." Iain laughed and pulled her back into his arms.

Before Arianna could fire off a healthy stream of insults his mouth came down on hers. Stunned, her hands clenched over his strong forearms. Iain's lips were warm and sweet. His tongue flicked lightly over her lips and every nerve ending in her body ignited. She should fight, push him away. Instead, her eyes drifted shut. The world faded.

The crowd roared.

Startled, she snapped back to reality. Just as Arianna found the will power to push him away, he released her. Dumbstruck, she could only stare up at him. With a cocky grin he helped her regain her footing.

Apparently finished with her, Iain turned to the wall of admiring clans-folk, declared that the celebration should resume, then sauntered off.

"Welcome aunt." A young man embraced her. "I'm Ferchar, Iain's nephew. I look forward to talking to you later."

Arianna started at being called aunt by a complete stranger. Never mind the fact he was not all that much younger than her. She smiled at the handsome lad whose facial features could have been a younger version of his laird's.

Ferchar must have realized the way Arianna's evening would proceed for everyone wanted to congratulate and welcome her to his or her family. Many women eyed her with envy. Most made her feel welcome.

She didn't see Iain for a good part of the evening but spent ample time with his fellow clansmen who spoke a mixture of English and Gaelic.

Hugh was a very personable man who looked to be about the same age as Arianna. Turned out he was first in command of the soldiers when his laird was not present. With light brown hair, deep set black eyes and rugged, carved features, he caught the attention of woman all night. Arianna wondered at his lack of response until Muriel joined them. He was smitten.

She could only hope a man looked at her like that someday.

Arianna felt a kindred spirit in Arthur, Iain's second in command. Though not handsome like Hugh, he held his own appeal. A big, tough man with a soft heart. Every conversation he held shaped his face into a new expression. With merry eyes and a laugh no man could compete with, he had his own string of admirers.

After some time, she strayed from the crowd a bit and looked at the tables full of food with curiosity. They held crude platters that overflowed with thick slices of pink salmon accompanied by big bowls swimming with black-shelled mussels, swollen scallops and moist shrimp.

Hard cheeses sat in random piles. Interlaced were platters full of goose meat, capons, pheasant, partridge and wood pigeon. Wooden platters stacked with small, round, flat loaves of bread were placed at the ends. Peas and beans were mixed into tempting concoctions.

Six large pewter bowls were the centerpieces, which lined the center of each table. The bowls overflowed with cherries, apples, blackberries, blueberries, elderberries, rowanberries and hazelnuts. What century was she in?

Big barrels of whiskey and ale lined the entryway. Gallons of wine sat like snobs beside them. Instead of rushes on the floor there were hundreds of animal skins and furs. Servants scurried around as they cleaned behind the guests. Was there no end to this man's wealth?

"He's not as bad as he looks," a petite, comely woman said while grabbing a cherry. "Or should I say he's not as bad as he acts."

What to say? *Aye, your laird is rude for not even talking to me. Are you sure this is the man I'm meant to marry? No? Excellent, I'm leaving and returning to my home. Wherever that is.*

"I'm Helen, Iain's sister by marriage and Ferchar's mother." She handed Arianna a pewter wine goblet. "This is for you."

"Thank you." Arianna smiled at the woman with pixie features and long pale blond hair.

"Och, he's just not used to being devoted to one woman," Helen provided.

Arianna held her tongue and eyed Iain across the room. He stood chest deep in a throng of adoring women. Ridiculous to be jealous but she had little doubt that the irritation she felt was just that. He *had* haunted her for the past ten years after all.

She chomped down a juicy blueberry with too much vigor and sipped her drink. Arianna choked on the taste and gaped at Helen. Light gray eyes sparkled with humor.

"'Tis just a wee dram, though 'tis a bit strong." The woman gave a wicked grin.

"I do not doubt you that." Arianna took another sip of the whiskey disguised as wine. She was pretty sure her future sister-in-law was a bit of a hellion. She caught the laird in her peripheral vision and proposed a toast to Helen.

"To women," she said, pleased when the woman raised her glass in agreement. Things hadn't really changed so much in six hundred years.

The rest of the night was enjoyable. Arianna met Catherine, a happy child with curly brown hair and hazel eyes. The youngest sister, she looked nothing like Iain and Muriel. The child's features were rounded and jovial with freckles that covered her cheeks and nose.

Arianna executed dances foreign to her as the willing crowd forgave her lack of knowledge to having come from the lowlands. Many handsome men talked and danced with her, which made her more aware that Iain did not. When the midnight hour arrived an old man with long, pure white hair made his way to the stand before the fire burning on the great hearth.

"I welcome you, Arianna of another place." His wizened eyes shot sparkling shards of blue ice across the room. For a moment, she had the impression he understood who she really was.

"Who is he?" She asked a girl beside her.

"He is our Shaman."

It was so quiet one could drop a piece of cloth and it would be heard landing on the floor. The Shaman appeared small as he stood in front of the gigantic fireplace. A strong wind howled outside as though in acknowledgment of the man's speech.

"On the morrow the veil between this world and the otherworld, Sidh, will be very thin and the divine beings, the spirits o' the dead and mortals can move freely between one world and the next. This clan follows the old ways. I will oversee you as you run the boundaries of your farms at sunset with blazing torches to protect your families from the faeries and malevolent forces free to walk the land this night, full o' mischief."

He appeared so solemn as he gazed at the faces before him. Everyone in the great hall wore grave expressions while they awaited his next words. When he spoke, his voice rang loud and joyous.

"The spirits will protect your clan." He stomped his cane thrice.

Arianna cheered along with the buoyant crowd and swigged the last of her whiskey. She felt a bit off kilter and chastised herself. At home, she had an occasional glass of wine. With a slight sway, Arianna went to stand before the flames. The crowd returned to their merry banter. She hoped to see the old Shaman again.

"Perhaps, you've had enough to drink."

Arianna turned and found herself nose to chest with the man who'd avoided her all night. No small thing considering she stood five-foot-nine inches tall.

Startled, her hands came to his well-muscled chest. He was as hard and immovable as a rock. She had the sudden urge to run her hands over his wide shoulders and feel the strong slopes of his cheekbones and jaw. Perhaps feel the soft heat of those stern lips beneath her fingertips. Yet touching him, feeling a living, breathing man was almost too much to bear after so many years.

I can't do this. He's too much for me to handle. Shaking her head, she pushed away.

****

"Arianna." Iain held tight and looked down into her eyes. Their gazes locked. He grabbed her around the waist and pulled her close. Desire ignited. Her small struggle dissipated.

She arrested him. All night long he made a point of avoiding this. Her. Now she was in his arms. He remembered how magnificent she looked when she came down the stairs earlier. The blue of her dress had made her gold mane come alive.

Iain hadn't realized she was such a great beauty. With flawless features and a long, curvaceous figure, she'd had an immediate effect on him, as well as every other hot-blooded man in the room.

He was grateful for his position within the clan in this matter. He could stay clear of her and not worry about his territory being breached. Now that she stood within his arms again he was grateful for their previous distance. He wasn't good at not taking what he wanted when he wanted it.

"My children." The words cut like a double-bladed sword through his intentions.

Arianna ripped away from Iain and he turned to the old Shaman with a scowl.

"My boy, have I not taught you everything I know?" He questioned Iain, though he looked at Arianna.

Iain could almost feel what she felt when she looked upon Adlin. Awe. Trust. The need to believe. Adlin did that to all.

"I am Adlin." He took Arianna's hands and cocked his head. His oddly youthful eyes were nestled in a craggy, old face. Their intensity stole her. The man's stare sucked her into a whirlwind of confusion. Iain knew that to Arianna, it felt as though her life flashed before her eyes.

He remained quiet beside her.

"That is what I thought." The Shaman said softly. He raised one ancient, vein filled hand to her cheek and touched her but a moment before a slight smile folded the corners of his eyes.

Adlin turned to Iain. For a time immeasurable, the two looked upon each other until the Shaman turned and walked away. The old man had this all figured out. Iain didn't doubt it for a second.

Wary, Arianna thought to do the same.

Iain grabbed her arm. *Please don't go. I want to keep staring at you. Memorizing your features. I've waited so long.* But he didn't say what he felt. Instead, he said what a chieftain should. "You will stay by my side the remainder of the night, lass."

"What makes you so sure?" It was obvious that Arianna was fed up with his indifference.

"I am the laird, you will be my wife. 'Tis time to play the part." He didn't spare her a glance but gazed around at his clan.

"As you played the part all night, my laird?"

She wasn't afraid of him. Did he really want her to be? Of course not. Yet her lack of respect was irksome. Was this how the lowland lassies treated their

Chieftains? Well, she'd soon learn it wasn't as accepted with the Highlanders.

He tightened his grip on her arm. "Dinnae test me."

"How dare you?" Arianna tried to tug her arm away.

"You are not under your Da's roof anymore lass." His tone turned curter, needed to. Her days in the lowlands were over. Best that she understood that now.

"Seems to me, I would be better off if I still was." She tore her arm free and ran up the stairs.

Iain glared at her retreating form. Damn sharp-tongued lass. Who did she think she was? She should be grateful, marrying into one of the most predominant clans in Scotland. Most women would murder for what she'd been given.

"You never fail to amaze me." Muriel came up beside him.

"Sister, that woman is the devil's own," he murmured and turned to the fire.

"If she is the devil's own, you must be the devil reincarnate."

Iain looked at his sister in amazement. "You grow bold."

"Michael, could you move the party outside? 'Tis very late," Muriel said to the head servant as he passed.

Michael looked at his laird and waited. Iain nodded his approval and the man shuffled off to do his bidding.

"I have always been under the impression that I was free to say what I feel to you," Muriel said.

Iain huffed and shook his head. "You're my sister and I love you but you must ken that there are some things that are mine alone to dictate."

"First war, now love?" Muriel raised her brows. "She will be my sister and you've not been kind to her this eve."

He was too aggravated for this. "You will learn in time that matters o' the heart aren't always up for discussion."

Muriel waved goodbye to a friend. "Perhaps, but matters o' the family always are. A fine line, no?"

Iain sat and watched the hall clear. Muriel was still so young. Iain patted the seat next to him. "Child, come sit."

She did and he took her hand.

"You remind me of Ma. She was always very good at saying what was on her mind. That is a good trait when tempered with the ability to know when the time is right to use it. I know that you are trying to understand what is in my heart. If I could give you a straight answer then I would." Iain squeezed her hand. "I didnae intend to mistreat your new sister."

Muriel met his eyes. "She is a kind person. As are you. Why did you avoid her all night? She's so alone."

Iain signaled a servant who was quick to bring a mug of whiskey. Once the servant departed he continued.

"Perhaps I didnae give that much thought." Iain took a long drink. Yes he had. "I'm new at this."

Muriel looked hopeful. "So you'll be more kind to her in the future?"

"Aye, 'Twould be easier for us all," Iain replied. After he told her exactly how he felt about her sharp tongue.

"You might just find that you like her." Muriel gave him a sly glance.

"I'm sure I will," Iain agreed. Or maybe I won't. Time will tell.

The hall had cleared and only the two of them remained. Drunken laughter could be heard outside the keep as men found their way to sleep. Servants moved quietly behind them as they cleared the tables.

"Go get some rest," Iain urged.

Muriel yawned and nodded. She leaned over and gave him a kiss on the cheek, then departed.

Iain sat back and stared into the fire.

At the top of the stairs, Muriel glanced down at her brother. She had never known him to love a woman. Was he capable of loving this one? On impulse, she snuck inside Arianna's chamber.

Chapter Six

Arianna awoke immediately when Muriel shook her shoulders.

"Are you awake?" Muriel was nose to nose with her.

"How could I not be?" Arianna muttered. Alerted, she nearly banged heads with the girl.

"Good, I just cannot handle the servants anymore. They won't listen to me, things need to be attended to and the evening is over. I think they must have snuck some whiskey, they are so defiant." Light from the hall shone in and Arianna saw that Muriel rung her hands. "Would you please talk to them?"

"Me?" Arianna sat up, confused. "If they won't listen to you, why would they listen to me?"

"You're marrying their laird. They would be thrown from the clan if they chose not to heed your command." Muriel's eyes were round with fret.

"Of course, I'll talk to them right away." Arianna tried to reassure Muriel and wondered at the state of things before she had arrived. Why wouldn't Iain support his sister? Impart the delegation surely privy to the laird of a castle. Most likely he didn't care.

"Thank you so much, sister," Muriel said, relief apparent on her face. Without another word she raced from the room.

Bleary eyed, Arianna stumbled into her dress and made her way down the stairs. What on Earth did one say to a servant? Upon reaching the bottom stair, it occurred to her nobody was left in the hall. What was Muriel talking about?

With a heavy sigh, she decided to take advantage of a good situation. Arianna walked to the ongoing fire and rubbed her hands together, grateful for the warmth. *Ooooh. Felt good.* She studied the carvings that peaked out from heavy stones above the impressive hearth.

More than three times her height and three horses in length the fireplace alone was intimidating. Detailed portrayals of strong, god-like faces were chiseled where a mantelpiece would normally be. They glowered down at her. The fire beneath them carved deep shadows in the concaves of high cheekbones and strong brows. Crimson light shifted across demanding eyes as though they were alive. They looked to judge her in a purgatory they alone controlled.

"Are you that cold?"

Arianna whipped around and spied Iain. He appeared a king sitting in a high-backed chair positioned before the flames. His dark, brooding gaze locked with hers.

She turned back to the fire abruptly as though that would make him disappear. She would not run from him again. Arianna crossed her arms in front of her chest.

"Do I appall you that much?" He came to stand directly behind her.

Appall me? No. Intimidate me? Aye. She took a deep breath and measured her response. "Your attitude could be better but that's beside the point." She shifted, uncomfortable. "You do not understand. I don't belong here. Whatever woman you waited for, I'm not her."

It was hard to be reasonable with the man when he stood so close. Arianna felt his heat against her back and glanced up. Was it her imagination or were the hearth's faces laughing down at her?

"Look at me." He turned her. One strong hand cupped her face and tilted back her head. "Look at me."

She did. Golden flames swam within bright emerald.

"I have heard the rumors." Brief distress passed over his features. "But you *are* the woman I have waited for.

"Are you not Arianna of the Broun clan?"

Shivers ran through her. God, he was handsome, and so intense. "I am her, but not the same woman you waited so long for." She challenged his eyes, those lethal eyes as green as newborn grass. How bizarre it was to be this close and having a conversation with a man who had never been whole. He was whole now. Incredibly, beautifully whole.

Exasperated, he peered down. "You are the woman 'twas described to me." He fingered her hair. "Your hair matches the wildness of the fire, your eyes are the color o' blue ice and you've a defiant temper."

"This all fits the description you were told?" His eyes ensorcelled her. They turned near black as they sought to rip her apart.

"You are not entirely as the tales tell you, Arianna," he whispered and pulled her against him. "They did the color of your eyes no justice, nor the magic that is yours."

"Magic?" Perplexed, she stiffened when he tightened his hold on her.

"Aye, magic," he said, voice hoarse. It suddenly seemed as though she could read his mind. He thought her all soft molded curves against him. The smell of smoke from the fire was smothered by her sweet scent. He held a delicate, seductive rose in the palm of his hand. Blinking, she shook her head. There's no way he could so soon think such thoughts.

But more came as her heart pounded against his chest and his lips hovered close. He'd not forgotten the taste between them. Of their lips when they'd met before. To his eyes, she was no average lass. The realization burst from his eyes, even if it would never from his mouth. *No.* She shook her head. How could she even contemplate that he would think such a thing? They'd only just met.

"You dinnae believe in magic?" He kept a low tone.

"Of course not, are you serious?" She muttered under her breath. Frankly, such talk was the last thing on her mind. Magic?

"You are a strange woman, Arianna. Scottish blood runs in your veins like fine wine, yet you are convinced of the truth behind your own words."

He needed to understand. Enough of this! "Aye, I am as you say but not from this era. In my time magic is something out of an old novel loaded with fairy tales and folklore."

Arianna couldn't control the low tremble that began to fill her body.

"You are still suffering from the effects of your fever I believe." He sighed. "Muriel said as much."

What? "I am suffering from no such thing. Do you hear yourself? Magic? You cannot be serious." At the moment, even the contemplation of magic was the furthest thing from Arianna's mind. He smelled wonderful, like spice and woods. His skin burned her. His wide shoulders encaged her.

You do not think I know magic?" He whispered the taunt and leaned his forehead against hers.

A strange feeling overcame, as though her body propelled forward yet didn't move. A feeling of *power*. "Let go!" She tried to pull free from his grasp. He mesmerized, even more so than in her dreams. Were his eyes the green she remembered or this fathomless, seductive black? Was his skin bronzed gold before? Were there tints of auburn in his locks or were they as ebony as his eyes at this very moment? She was no longer sure.

It was obvious he wanted to show her his magic but Arianna had a good idea what that meant. Perhaps just a little kiss wouldn't hurt. Then he would surely release her. Anything to escape from this unpredictable feeling of energy and... something else.

"Show me your magic if you must." The words were out before she gave them much thought.

What happened next was not what she expected.

His hands fell from her yet she was unable to move away. She didn't want to. His raven hair shimmered as his eyes sparked to life. All she could see was the man before her. He controlled her.

His muscles rippled with provocation as he brought her to him. An inch from him, he seized her and pulled her so close she felt part of him. For long moments, he made her look at him.

Want him.

Let go. Don't let go. Confused, she attempted to speak, fight, but he laid claim to her, his mouth covering hers in a swift movement. Wild and untamed, Iain's lips coaxed and caressed. He drank deeply from her lips, prompting an equal response. When his tongue swung into her mouth, Arianna didn't feel appalled as she surely should have. Instead it felt wonderful, natural, beyond perfect. Was she evil? Was she wrong?

She felt them swirl together before the fire. Smoke twisted into delicate tendrils forming a tornado above that curved up to the ceiling. Flames spun around them and rose like a rattlesnake. The fiery serpent slithered through them. Heated lust flooded through her arms and legs, filling her chest. She was thirsty for him. Moaning, she gave into the passion.

"No!" He mumbled into her mouth and whatever held them left in a rush of wind that blew the fire down to a pile of glowing logs.

Iain pushed her away. "Leave me."

Cleaved from oblivion, Arianna stared at him in confusion. *What?* He'd just introduced her to *bliss*. His eyes were cool. Distant. What had happened? Why did he now look at her as though she had the plague?

If he thought her kiss was that foul, so be it. She pulled her shoulders back, held her head high and narrowed her eyes.

"I would be a fool to marry the likes of you," she declared, voice unwavering. With a last look of disgust, Arianna walked up the stairs.

Her time with him was finished.

Iain ignored her departure and crouched in front of the fire. The embers jumped to life and he dared the flames to defy him. How sweet her lips had tasted. How well she fit into his arms. Who was this temptress?

He regretted his outburst of anger but he was uncomfortable with a magic that met his own. He disliked the way his energy succumbed entirely to a woman he'd just met, even if she was to be his wife. 'Twas a dangerous thing, twin magic. *She* was a dangerous thing. He'd known her but a night and already he respected Arianna. The way she'd taken to his clan as though they were her own. The way she stood up to him and spoke her mind. She'd give him a good chase and he could not help but relish the challenge. Another part of him knew to be careful. Arianna had affected him too soon.

Too fast.

Iain tried to let his desire blow free with the flame. He attempted to allow his want to dissipate with the sparks, his need to float lonely in the smoke that sucked at the ceiling. Nothing he'd been taught worked. He closed his eyes and felt fate saturate him. Of all the women he was to marry, why such a feisty lass?

He opened his eyes when he heard the answer in the fresh flames now licking and teasing the hearth...

Because you like a woman full of fire.

****

The next day cast a meager needle of gray into the small chamber. Arianna slipped out of bed and splashed cold water on her face. She grabbed a comb and began to work out the knots in her hair from tossing and turning in bed.

She'd cried herself to sleep the night before and prayed her dreams would lead her home. How could this be happening? The man who had invaded her thoughts for so long scorned her. She despised him for it. The only thing the two shared was a shamefully strong physical attraction.

The idea that magic existed in reality left her in profound awe. She couldn't help notice that she was more hurt by him than afraid of the knowledge of magic.

"Good day," Muriel said from the door and popped her head through. "May I enter?"

"As you wish." Arianna played coy. "It seemed the servants had everything under control last evening."

She didn't realize how hungry she was until Muriel set down a plate loaded with fruit accompanied by a goblet of liquid. Arianna sipped it and enjoyed the taste of the watered wine.

"Really?" Muriel shrugged. "Odd ducks, those servants."

"Aye, those servants." Arianna knew what the girl had been up to but had no desire to go further with it. No doubt the lass only had her best intentions in mind.

She grabbed an apple and crunched into the sweet nectar.

"You slept late, 'tis well past noon," Muriel informed.

That didn't surprise Arianna, between the late night and lack of light in the room.

"I brought you a dress to wear today. 'Twas my mother's." Muriel held a beautiful cream-colored gown up to Arianna. "You are about the same size and height. I think 'twill fit you perfectly."

Arianna gaped at the gown, similar in design to the one she had made. The arms were wider and longer and the bodice cut lower. Threads of gold and bronze were interwoven along the edges of the soft, plush material. Dripping from the middle of the bodice was a hand's length of intricate gold threads that portrayed a delicate cross.

With Muriel's help, Arianna slipped the dress over her kirtle. Its length hung to the floor in the front. The back hosted a small trail of extra material. Unlike her own dress, this one wasn't tucked up.

"Oh my, you do fill this dress splendidly." Muriel marveled and spun Arianna around.

"Do I?" The low cut front showed ample cleavage. She'd never worn anything so revealing. Carefully, she tried to pull the bodice up a bit.

"'Tis a good thing." Muriel giggled. "My brother will be even more jealous than he already is when all the men stare at you."

"That is the least of my concerns." Arianna discarded the apple core and popped a cherry in her mouth.

"Today is the most favored celebration o' the three," Muriel informed. She took the comb from Arianna and brushed the long reddish blond hair.

Arianna lost her appetite.

"How long have I been here Muriel?" It was early morning, the first day of November when this all began. The Samhain celebration had been yesterday.

"This night, Samhain's Eve, will mark your tenth night here." Muriel struggled with a difficult knot.

"Ten nights?" Arianna frowned. "I thought last night was Samhain's Eve?"

"No, we celebrate for three days. Before, during and after the day of observance. Last night was very unusual in that it was inside. The rains were too heavy outside." Muriel's gaze narrowed. "Surely, you know that?"

"Aye, I do." Arianna didn't know this morsel of history. There was a ten-day gap between her time and this?

With a secretive smile, Muriel requested that Arianna wait a moment as she disappeared out the door. She returned with a lush ringlet of white, crème and pale pink flowers. Muriel placed the crown of petals on top of her head.

"Ahh..." Muriel put a hand to her chest and stepped back. "You are a sight."

"The flowers are beautiful, if not a bit elaborate, aye?" Skeptical, Arianna fingered the soft flowers atop her head.

"Nay, 'tis tradition." Muriel wore a dreamy look. "Now, let me show you this great land that is your new home."

About halfway to the door, Muriel paused. A strange look passed over her face.

"Muriel?" Arianna stopped beside Muriel and a shiver ran through her.

Muriel appeared daunted. Her skin turned white, almost as though she saw a ghost. "I just had a strange feeling overcome me."

"Are you feeling sick?" Arianna asked.

"Of course not, why? Do I look ill?" Muriel's skin color returned.

Confused, Arianna replied, "Well, not now."

Muriel's lips thinned and she shook her head. "That silly fever of yours." Brief melancholy blossomed into a smile. "Let's go."

Arianna shrugged her shoulders.

Could things get any stranger?

She followed Muriel down to the great hall. Men ate in sporadic clusters amidst the numerous tables. Heat rose to her face as many turned their heads and gaped.

At least Iain didn't stand at the bottom of the stairs this time, waiting for her to dive into his arms.

The lad from the night before, Ferchar, approached them. "So nice to see you again." He bowed and kissed the back of her hand. Very chivalrous.

"To you as well." Arianna smiled. Ferchar continued to stare at her, his face turning red.

"Put your eyes back in your head Ferchar." Muriel snickered and guided Arianna outside through the huge front doors.

Arianna stepped into the cool air and froze. Such impressive splendor lay before her.

The castle sat atop a massive hill of plush green grass speckled with white sheep. Many stone cottages with thatch roofs littered the immediate vicinity. Even with two tall stone walls layered in protection she could see many more cottages at the apex of a wide field that rolled beyond.

A huge fire burned bright in its center and sent a tall spiral of thin smoke into the sky. A large stretch of forest lapped from the shores of a wide loch tucked within surrounding mountains and glens. A moist, salty wind blew her skirts.

"I have never seen such beauty," Arianna murmured.

Muriel snaked her arm through Arianna's and they walked down the steps. She gawked at the display of community. Sweat gleamed off stocky men laboring with diligence in the smithy while young boys eyed her inquisitively from the stretch of stables. The building housing the kitchen was the size of a ship. Shameless scullery maids flirted with passing warriors as a rotund woman bellowed a steady stream of orders at them.

"That is our head cook, Euphemia," Muriel warned as she followed Arianna's line of sight. "I'm willing to introduce you but we should retrieve defense shields from the armory first."

Arianna shook her head immediately when she witnessed the woman whip a wooden jug at a nearby servant who attempted to sneak a bit of ale from the barrel. The boy dodged the angered Euphemia as she thundered towards him, her jowls swaying back and forth.

"She is tolerated because she descends four generations within our clan. That and there is not a more talented, efficient cook to be found. Her methods of management are sometimes questionable but in the long run she does things well. Believe it or not, she can be quite likeable. It being such a big event right now she has her hands full," Muriel said.

Not convinced, Arianna decided it best to avoid the kitchen. Across from the smithy stood the armory. Mesmerized, she drifted towards the slew of weaponry lined in long neat rows. Thick-chained maces hung with heavy metallic spiked balls dripping off the bottom. Bows of varying shapes were hung in organized bunches over stacks of wooden arrows. War hammers, spears and daggers boasting different lengths and widths graced the far walls.

She walked into the long structure and almost tripped over her own feet at the display of battle-axes on the opposite wall. Some had oblong blades more than double the length of her arm. Others preened with broad, half moon edges that glistened silver in the dim light. A select few differed with half moon, razor sharp axes attached to both sides of the hilt.

"If you think this is something, follow me." Muriel passed Arianna and vanished into another section of the abode.

Arianna entered behind her and was astounded by the vast array of swords.

"This is Iain's preferred choice. 'Tis about the only thing I know about him and war." Muriel removed what appeared to be one of the least elaborate of the expanse. "He claims it to be the most practical for warfare. It is simple steel with double fullers that both lighten and strengthen the blade."

Arianna grinned with sheepish indecision when

Muriel prompted her to take the blade. "'Twill not bite."

She laughed and placed it, hilt first, into Arianna's hands.

Riveted, she wrapped her hands around the wooden handle wrapped with black leather. This was Iain's chosen weapon? For a moment, she relished holding what he might have held in battle, feeling the handle that his hands might have held to protect his life. Strangely enough, it both aroused and empowered her. She licked her lips and for a split second imagined his lips licking hers. *No!* What was she thinking? Testing the weight, she carefully lifted the sword in the air.

"Good choice."

Startled, Arianna turned. A man watched them. With dirty blond hair and piercing silver eyes he was classically attractive, a near feminine sort of handsome. His appreciative gaze roved over her.

Muriel retrieved the blade from Arianna, an undistinguishable mutter on her breath.

"I am Malcolm, second cousin to Iain," he provided, "and Muriel." He shot his cousin a pointed look for her lack of introduction.

He took Arianna's hand and lifted it to his lips. His kiss lingered. A Scotsman that reminded her of an Englishman. Disturbing.

"Malcolm," Muriel said, "we were just leaving."

"Before I've a chance to acquaint myself with my cousin's new woman?"

"Aye." Muriel grabbed Arianna's hand. "There will be time enough when my brother is present."

She let Muriel lead her away. Malcolm shrugged and winked at her as they retreated.

"I take it he is not amongst your most favored relatives?" Arianna said as they exited the armory.

"You could say that."

Arianna returned her survey to the inner compound, pleased to behold a chapel. Although it was autumn, bright purple heather, yellow rue, pink roses, white Madonna lilies and honey-suckle were clustered on either side of the entrance.

"How is this possible at this time of year?" She leaned down and fingered the petals.

"Magic I suppose." Muriel turned and walked in the direction of the open portcullis. In hot pursuit of further details she trailed the girl over the first drawbridge.

She became distracted by the spikes of the portcullis overhead. This was truly amazing. She kept a keen eye on the moat below and walked over the sturdy drawbridge. At the end, they passed beneath a second portcullis. This iron structure was much newer and taller than the last. After transcending a second bridge she finally arrived on solid ground. Arianna followed Muriel's lead quite a ways until she stopped short and turned back.

"Behold your new castle, my sister." Muriel spread her arms wide.

Arianna turned and gasped.

It was glorious. Originally a moat and bailey castle built for its time, the structure was rebuilt into a work of art. The two layers of curtain walls that circled the keep insured added protection. Concentric in design, the castle was square at its heart with immense circular towers that branched from four corners. Multiple smaller towers and buildings also branched from the main structure, which gave it depth and dimension. Sporadic semicircular arches softened the glorious monstrosity. Squinting, Arianna was able to discern men strolling atop the tower battlements. Others stood unmoving upon the wall walks that separated the towers.

"Are you positive your brother is not the king of Scotland?"

"One would hope not." Muriel laughed, took Arianna's hand again and led her through the village.

For many hours the women roamed as Muriel introduced Arianna to an ancient way of life. Hours later they joined Iain and his men on the field.

"So you think you can do better?" Arms crossed, Iain goaded Hugh.

"Aye, my laird, I shall split your arrow with mine." Hugh raised his armed bow. He released the bowstring and the arrow sailed through the air until it spliced Iain's in two.

With a victorious yelp, Hugh turned to mock his laird only to discover he wasn't paying attention. When Iain turned, Arianna knew she'd gained undivided attention. The man had some nerve even looking at her!

"Hello men." Muriel eyed Hugh. He bowed from the waist and kissed her hand.

"You look enchanting, Arianna," Iain said.

She nodded her head in thanks and willed the fire not to flood her face as he stared at her. It was obvious to all that his appreciative gaze was eager to take in every detail of her person, including the low cut bodice.

The daylight only added to his appearance. The green of the grass behind him made vibrant his lustful scrutiny and contrasted with his near black hair. Mahogany highlights showed true in the sun.

"I'm glad I do not disgust you this day, my laird." Arianna couldn't help herself. The ignorant brute had no right to pay her a compliment.

"You've a sharp tongue. It would serve you well not to cut me with it." He burned her with a look that no doubt most men must wither beneath. Not her!

The next look he tossed her was that of a predator on the hunt. Before she realized his intent, he grabbed her.

"What are you doing?" Arianna tried to push him away. Why did he always feel the need to grab her? His warm lips took her mouth. *Oh no. Not this time.* She turned her head and slapped his face. Thoroughly irritated, she balked at Muriel and Hugh's laugher.

"You little vixen." Iain released her. "I will have you yet, lass."

"So you think," Arianna said to his back as he walked away. Who did he think he was? This was the villain she fancied herself in need of when she dreamt? Never. Had he so soon forgotten his treatment of her last night? She surely hadn't! Then again, she was dealing with a medieval male. Best to keep that in mind.

Muriel and Hugh were deep in intimate conversation so she turned to walk back to the castle.

"Not so fast, lass." Hugh caught her arm.

"I thought I would allow you two a moment alone."

Arianna smirked at Muriel. The girl blushed and fidgeted with her skirts.

"Your presence is required," he said.

"My presence? What for?" She stumbled forward as Muriel pulled her toward the line of pine trees nearby. Out of nowhere, tall warriors surrounded her.

"What is happening?" She directed the question at one of the nonchalant giants at her side. No one responded.

"Craobh," Muriel whispered.

"Among the trees?" Arianna repeated the Gaelic word. The forest reminded her of home. Great shafts of sunlight streamed through the canopy overhead. Men stood throughout the tall pine and birch trees, nodding their heads when she passed. They entered a small clearing and she stopped. Muriel released her hand and backed away.

A small river flowed, tinkling over smooth pebbles. Nearby, a waterfall fell in gentle sheets of hazel over a dark gray ledge. Thunder clapped in the distance. The air smelled of pine, earth and salt. She gazed around and noted many more clan's men, women and children.

A clergyman in long brown robes stood with Iain beside the shallow water.

"My dear, Arianna." The old Shaman, Adlin, suddenly stood before her. His cold, thin fingers took hers. The breeze stilled. The air electrified and caused the fine hairs on her arms to rise. A delicious chill ran through her body and left her calm.

She felt serene, at peace. His eyes sparkled and his gaze entranced her once again. Though words never left his lips, Arianna heard him. *This day signifies you chose the correct path, followed your soul's direction. Destiny awaits you child. Dinnae be afraid.* Arianna blinked at the old man. *You will speak the words today, binding you to fate.*

"You have a gift my dear," Adlin murmured. He led her forward and placed her hand in Iain's. With great care, he wrapped a blue and green plaid around their joined hands.

In a daze, Arianna fell to her knees with Iain. The bible was placed between their hands. She drowned in the green pools of Iain's eyes as the robed man spoke foreign words.

She was here, before the flowing water, an emblem of eternity. How did she know that?

"I, Iain MacLomain tak thow Arianna Broun to my spousit wyf as the law of the Haly Kirk schawis and thereto I plycht thow my trewht and syklyk." Iain vowed solemnly and tightened his grip on her.

What did he just say? None of this made sense. Or did it? The man in robes talked further and gazed down at her.

When she looked at Iain, she knew what to say. "I, Arianna Broun, takis you Iain MacLomain to my spousit husband as the law of Haly Kirk schwas and therto I plycht to thow my trewth," she vowed in return. What words came from her mouth? What had she done?

The fog in her mind cleared. Everything became sharp and vivid. The priest still stood in front of them and spoke a few more words.

She was married!

~Fate's Monolith~

Chapter Seven

The forest broke into hearty cheers. A strong wind blew through the woodland. Thick black clouds battled with a crystal blue sky. Thunder boomed and lightning sizzled. Half the clearing became drenched in a heavy wet downpour. The other half remained warm with sunshine.

A rainbow formed and sparkled with colors as it rocketed from the sky into the river they knelt before. Arianna and Iain remained kneeling in the sun, blinded by the beauty of nature.

"There is no omen better than this." The shaman stepped forward and raised his arms wide. With unusual strength, the old man pulled the couple to their feet. When he met Iain's eyes, he nodded.

Arianna gasped when Iain swept her off her feet.

He walked into the river and set her down. Icy cold water flowed over her feet. It carried the trail of her dress upon the surface of luminous water. They stood in the midst of the rainbow. Bedazzled, she surveyed the cave of iridescent colors.

Stunned, Arianna was pulled into Iain's warm embrace.

Time ceased to exist as his head lowered. His kiss felt soft and tender. Laughter and cheering sounded from everywhere. All she could feel were his lips on hers as they caressed and molded hers into submission. God, he felt so good. Her resolve weakened.

Unable to deny him any longer, she snaked her fingers around his neck. Stifling heat filled her body as his kiss deepened. All awareness outside of him fled.

"Arianna." He murmured her name before his tongue collided with hers. Her limbs went weak as he explored. Her body arched and molded against his. Heat pooled in her groin. Clasping her legs together, she tried to keep from moaning.

"There *is* a priest present." Muriel's voice reminded from far away though she stood at the edge of the stream. Her laughter brought Arianna back from wherever she'd been heading.

Pushing away from Iain, she stumbled. He raised his hand and curled his fingers. As if a person stood behind her, she felt her body saved from falling backwards into the water. She glanced over her shoulder and realized nobody stood behind her.

Few people remained to witness the anger that erupted.

"What sorcery is this?" She said, passion forgotten. They both knew what she spoke of and it wasn't the prevented fall into the water.

"Sorcery?" Iain smirked. "What do I know of sorcery or magic?"

"Bastard." She waded from the river and rung out the bottom of her skirts. Surprised, she realized they were now alone. How quick people were to evacuate when they sensed a bicker on the horizon.

"Such words from a lass who just kissed me as if I was the last man alive." Iain came to stand beside her. "And I assure you, I'm no bastard."

"I kissed you because you made me."

"How did I make your lips touch mine, woman?"

His eyes slid down her body and Arianna suddenly realized that he wouldn't mind being the soaked garment that clung to her calves. Where'd that thought come from? It felt as though his mind had entered hers for a moment.

"Bloody magic, that's how." Arianna flushed at his bold appraisal. A warm vibration ran through her body. When she looked down she found that the bottom of her dress was now dry. She glared back in frustration.

"Aye, magic, that which you do not believe in," he reminded. "Know this though. No magic can make a lass kiss me like you just did"

"You flatter yourself." She put her hands on her hips. His hair looked wonderful damp from the rain's mist. Black and sleek. God, how could she hate and admire a man simultaneously?

"No, you flatter me wife."

"I'm not your wife," she spat. Arianna toyed with the skirt of the gown she wore. Of course this was a wedding gown. His mother's wedding gown. How could she not have realized? She had been thoroughly swindled. Ensorcelled.

"That." She pointed back at the river. "Did not count, you did not have my consent."

"Actually, I did." He whistled and a huge black warhorse approached. "And many witnesses as well."

Arianna stepped back as the horse stood before her. She swallowed. The mirror. This horse. She tried to mask her fear as she looked back at Iain.

"He willnae hurt you." Concern lit his eyes. "Are you well?"

She tried to speak but couldn't. He brushed the hair from her face and cupped one cheek with his hand. "Arianna?"

"I want to go home," she whispered. She also wanted to cry again but that wasn't an option.

"Are you afraid to ride the horse?"

Arianna looked at him, confused. "No."

"Then give me your hand," Iain said as he swung onto his mount. She did and found herself up in his arms. A strange way to ride a horse.

"I am not your wife." Arianna felt small in his arms.

"Are we back to that lass?" Iain let the horse take the lead. The sun had fallen below the distant mountains. In its wake a pink twilight colored the Highland woods.

"Aye, we are. You tricked me. There's no way that in God's eyes we're married."

Iain did nothing Arianna could see but the horse stopped anyway. Vulnerable, she met his eyes. Now, he was the great Chieftain of Cowal and she could understand why. His features hardened and the fury twirling in his gaze scared her. *I can't turn and walk away this time.* She would give anything to be able to get off this horse and flee.

"God was there. The holy man was there. We are married."

This would be one of the few times in Arianna's life that she set her temper aside and decided this argument could wait until later.

"Fine, take me home."

Ten minutes later Arianna turned. Not to her home but to his.

"I present my wife, Arianna MacLomain." Iain's deep voice rumbled his deliverance far and wide.

A vast sea of people stood in the field. Women, men and children applauded. The behemoth fire amidst them sparked and roared, eager to join in the applause.

This was easily the most uncomfortable moment in her life. She backed into Iain. "This is so unfair," Arianna whispered. "I am pushed into a position I do not wish to be in. I see these people love and respect you. I do not. Not inhuman, I would ask of you what protocol says I should do this day to aide the people in their celebration. It is Samhain and the day of their great Chieftain's wedding, no? What do they wish to see?"

"Stay by my side." Iain's order bordered hostile. Again, she felt as though she heard his thoughts when he put his arm around her and walked forward. He felt she'd do well to accept her role as his wife or he'd personally throw her over his horse and take her back to her father. Let the Broun clan be his enemy and his own father roll in his grave. Damn woman.

Shaking her head, she disregarded the errant thoughts. After all, she couldn't possibly be hearing his thoughts. Could she?

He sauntered forward with her through the throng of people. The storm clouds retreated beyond the mountain peaks. A full moon stood dull, caught between day and night.

Arianna straightened her stance and walked with a pride she didn't feel. Children touched her skirts and smiled with innocent adoration. Women bowed their heads then met her eyes with kind smiles.

A petite, brown haired girl stood in front of her.

"Congratulations." She nearly glared at Arianna. "I am Florie."

"Very nice to meet you, Florie." This woman didn't like her. She dislodged from Iain for a moment and turned in confrontation. If she couldn't have it out with him she would vent elsewhere.

"Tell me, Florie, why do you look with such disgust at me?" Arianna said.

"My lady, I look naught that way at you," she said as she eyed Iain with her heart in her eyes.

"Ah ha." Arianna glanced at the tyrant beside her.

"Mayhap you have feelings for your laird."

"Mayhap I was here long before you." Though Florie was tiny, she stood tall.

Arianna grabbed Iain's arm and stopped him. "That you were, but what good did that do you?"

She reveled in the flicker of recognition that flashed between the two.

"He married you because 'twas good for our clan. Laird Iain will return to my bed," she promised, her lips drew into a sneer.

It was obvious to Arianna based on last night that Iain liked a variety. Therefore, what better way to irritate him than to be a thorn in his side? Let him think she would cause a ruckus if he sowed his oats beyond their bed.

"Wise as you may think you are Florie, please be quite sure, my arrival will keep him from you from this day forward. I'm a woman that no man abandons seeking to fulfill his lust with another." Arianna smiled at the woman.

"We will see," Florie said.

"Know that if I do catch you embedded with my husband, the last thing you will see is my dagger shredding your throat." That should make him mad. Pleased with her sadistic act of bravado, Arianna walked away.

What she didn't see was the pleased expression on Iain's face when she stalked away. Nor the words exchanged between Florie and her new husband.

"My laird." Florie ran her hand over his chest. "We will meet later, aye?"

As he still gazed after his new wife he turned to meet his former lover's implicative gaze. "I think, mayhap, you underestimate my new wife."

Without a backwards glance, he followed Arianna into the crowd. Later, after endless hours of mingling, Iain pulled Arianna down to sit beside him in the cool grass. She scowled as he placed his plaid of blue and green over her shoulders.

"'Twould please me if you wore my plaid, whether you like me or not," he said.

She pulled the rough wool material around her shoulders and refused to meet his eyes even though he'd been kind to her all evening. So they were married. She could have found a worse fate traveling back to this time period.

No more dreaming, this was real.

"Think what you will, but I mean you no harm." He gazed straight ahead. "I didnae mean to push you away last eve. I am not used to...you. It was wrong."

How flattering. Arianna nearly rolled her eyes. Regardless, he'd caused more harm with today's actions. She may as well be honest and tell him what bothered her. She was hurt and shivered in spite of the plaid and monstrous bonfire. "You married me against my will. You don't even have the truth of things."

"Pray tell then, what is the truth of things?"

Here goes, again. "I'm not of this time, Iain."

"Not of this time?" It was more than apparent that he humored the obvious ill effects of her fever in hopes to pacify her current mood.

"No." Arianna didn't like the look on his face.

"You must think me a fool." He leaned closer.

"You hit the nail on the head." Arianna could not have a civil conversation with this man. She grumbled and attempted to stand.

"What words do you speak?" He pulled her back down and pushed her to the grass where he covered the top half of her body with his.

Arianna didn't move, not sure she remembered how to at the moment. She tried to recall what she'd been about to say as he pinned her arms beside her head. His body held her captive. The smell of grass and wildflower mingled with the spice of his skin and the wood burning in the fire.

~Fate's Monolith~

A bagpipe trilled somewhere in the distance. At long last she'd returned to her homeland and the pure power of the intimate moment with him made the world fall away. "I. Am. Lost." Each word was hard to say.

"You are not lost. You are home," he said.

"You *must* listen to me." Arianna wasn't sure she spoke until he replied.

"I hear your heart." He lowered his head.

"Iain." She relished the taste of his name on her tongue. If his lips met hers there was no hope.

"There's a sight if I ever did see one." Arthur plunked down in the grass beside them.

"Arthur." Arianna struggled to sit up. Thank the Lord for small favors.

"'Twould have done you no harm to have left the sight alone." Iain's thickened words held no mirth.

"Aye, no doubt my friend." Arthur's lopsided grin welcomed Iain's irritation. "But the festivities begin and your presence is required."

"Festivities?" Arianna tossed her hair over her shoulder. "Has this not been a constant stream of it?"

"Aye, my lady, but tonight we dance in the open air." Arthur stood and took Arianna's hands. After he pulled her to her feet, he spun her around.

She followed his lead and whirled in merriment. This was fun. This she could handle. Arianna took the hand of the child beside her and joined the ever-growing ring of happy clans-folk dancing around the fire.

The moon sat pregnant and bright. Its feet tiptoed upon the Eastern peaks of the tallest white-capped mountains. Thin, gauzy pinstripe clouds stretched across the broad sky.

When she tired, Arianna broke from the chain. She stood back and admired such unity. Throngs of happy children played together. Clusters of men stood together as they engaged one another in mock sword battle while women gossiped.

"'Tis impressive, aye?" Ferchar now stood next to her. "Nothing matches it." Arianna was glad for the company.

"I am pleased you enjoy Cowal's clans-folk, 'tis very important." Ferchar clasped his hands behind his back.

"Aye."

"He waited for you a very long time," he said.

"So I've heard."

"Will you be happy here?"

"One could only hope." Arianna sounded uncertain even to her own ears.

"My laird cares for you, 'tis obvious." Ferchar straightened his shoulders. "You should re-evaluate what it is you think will make you happy."

Arianna only looked at him. It was obvious his laird cares for her? Aye, up until he got her into his bed.

"Sister, are you enjoying everything?" Muriel walked up to them.

"Very much so." Just the person she wanted to talk to.

"I'm so glad." Muriel avoided Arianna's eye.

"Why did you not tell me I was to be married this day?" She gave her sister-in-law her undivided attention.

"I assumed you knew, with the head dress of flowers and the dress." Muriel bit her lip.

"You assumed?"

"Helen." Muriel made a show at becoming distracted by another phantom cause. "I must be off, will you stay with Arianna?"

"I would be honored," Helen said.

She watched in dismay as Muriel flitted off. Arianna had only just begun chastising her new sister.

~Fate's Monolith~

The chit was becoming a meddlesome cupid. She took the given pewter mug from Helen and wasn't surprised to taste whiskey.

"Much thanks." Dependable Helen. Here when I need her the most. She took a sip. Arianna would certainly watch what she drank this night remembering the headache she awoke with earlier.

"Welcome to the family." Helen raised her mug.

"What are they doing now?" Arianna lifted her mug in salute. A large group of warriors were coming together.

"They dance to victorious battle."

"Ahhh..." Arianna breathed, entranced.

The tall, muscular Scotsmen formed a huge circle. Iain stepped forward and placed a long, wide sword into the center of the ring of men. His face devoid of emotion, he turned to Hugh, whom handed him a mighty battle- axe.

Turning, Iain swung the axe over his head. Firelight reflected off the dry blood still caked on its blade. Muscles flexed and rippled as he arched the blade. Then he leaned over and swung the blade down, slowing the momentum until he placed the axe across the massive claymore on the ground.

"Victory." The lone word rose into the night and fell on the clan in a harsh wave of emotion. The firelight chiseled his face into that of a reverent, devoted leader. His expression was savage and intent.

"What does this mean?" Arianna looked at Helen. The woman's jaw was clenched and her chin jutted forward with pride.

"'Twas a battle won. Our enemy fell before us."

"What battle?" Arianna was taken with this foreign ceremony. The men now danced around the weapons.

"The battle to retrieve you my lady, hence the cry of the war pipe," Helen allowed and walked away. The lone wail of an angry bagpipe haunted the night as it led the men in their dance. Iain wore his kilt, or plaid as they called it, around his waist only. The dark magnified the fire as it glorified the lines of his upper torso. His muscular form moved with magnificence as he danced the bizarre dance. What a physique.

As soon as it began, it ended. The three men who sat on their tripod of logs swiftly began a lighter, more cheerful melody.

"A grand night, this one." Arianna sidled around a cluster of people deep in conversation until she found the source of the rickety declaration.

An elderly woman sat hunched over with a cluster of attentive children kneeling at her feet. Her hair was slate gray and her skin hung off her skeletal frame in leathery folds. The MacLomain plaid was wrapped tight around her hunkered form. A wizened voice crackled forth as she continued.

"'Tis the day that marks the setting of the sun; the "Light half" of the year. We begin our winter season, "the Dark half." Her voice lowered in warning.

Arianna smiled and sat to listen on a nearby log. It was clear this woman had been telling stories for many years.

Her opaque eyes seemed to suck life from the fire as she continued. "More importantly, on this very night 'tis possible for someone to drop through the crack of time and find himself in the inner world. Whether it be the realm of faeries, the ancestors or the other-worldly folk." The woman's gaze met hers so briefly she thought she imagined it.

"'Tis also a time when beings of the inner world can enter into the realm of the outer world." Solemn, she looked from child to child. "Our world."

The children jostled and squirmed closer together.

"Keeping this in mind there are precautions to be taken. It might be prudent to assume a disguise, mayhap change your appearance in some way. I can see some of you have painted your face. 'Tis good." The old woman pulled the blanket tighter around her.

"'Twould also be very wise to leave a saucer of milk outside your houses this eve for the little people." The children nodded in quick agreement as the woman continued.

"'Twould be an even grander idea to give something to anyone who comes to your door, not knowing for sure who or what it might be. Any fruit on trees which have not been gathered must be left, for there will be a puca on any such fruit. The light half of the year is left to the men and women, but the dark half belongs to the deer, the beasts of the field; to ravens and owls and such. Nothing should be swept out of human habitation, for to do so is to show a lack of respect for the creatures of the out-of-doors, and most especially the wee folk."

The old woman was wracked with a cough before she continued. Arianna stood and stretched as the woman began a tale of a fairy frog.

"Care to dance?" Malcolm stood before her.

"I suppose." Arianna regretted not having asked Muriel more about him earlier. He led them into the crowd of dancing couples that moved around the bonfire.

"I am sorry we did not have a chance to talk earlier," he said.

"Well, I'm really not much of a conversationalist." She felt uneasy under his forward gaze. Malcolm pulled her closer as he danced them through the crowd.

"Your incredible beauty suits me." The corner of his mouth lifted with a calculating implication.

"It matters little to me if anything about me suits you." Who did this man think he was?

"So, you *are* as feisty as they say you are, aye?" He chuckled with appreciation.

"Excuse me?" She attempted to pull away only to have him pull her closer.

"You heard me lass." He moved them faster.

"I will dance with my wife now, cousin." Iain's tone from behind left no room for debate.

"But, of course," Malcolm said. A thin grin appeared then vanished.

Arianna was tossed from one man to the other.

Relieved to be free of Malcolm's grasp she found herself in a far more dangerous one.

"Are you enjoying yourself?"

"Aye."

"Is Malcolm to your liking?"

"He's nice enough."

Iain tightened his hold on her. "Nice enough? What do you mean by that, lass?"

"I mean that he's nice enough but I'm glad that I'm not dancing with him anymore.

Iain's stern expression softened considerably. Arianna's heart paused. "Are you jealous?"

Iain slid his hand down her back. "No."

"No?" Her body reacted when his hand slid even lower.

"No." He pulled her lower half against him.

"No." This time she gasped the word against his chest. Something hard and long pushed against her stomach. She closed her eyes. Her breath became irregular.

Iain's other hand cupped the back of her neck beneath her hair. He moved slower. The man could dance. His head lowered and nuzzled the side of her neck.

Ripples of pleasure washed over her. Was she still saying no?

"I never imagined..." He whispered in her ear. "This." When his lips met her neck Arianna shivered. A new sensation swallowed her.

"Iain."

"Aye."

"I, I'm not, I, this is...I." What was she saying?

He silenced her with his mouth. Nothing felt real anymore as his lips covered hers. When his tongue swung into her mouth her knees almost buckled.

When he slowly pulled away his eyes held hers.

"I will not tolerate another woman in your bed."

Arianna didn't intend to say what she'd been thinking but she meant it. Something had changed.

"Who's jealous now?"

She saw how he struggled. Knew without a shadow of a doubt that he wanted to drop her to the ground and consummate their marriage.

"Me."

"Good." He waited.

"And you?" Arianna said.

"No." Iain smiled.

She frowned up at him. "Stubborn?"

"Mayhap," he said.

"Fair enough." The music ended.

Iain grabbed her hand and led her beyond the swell of celebration to the quietness of the meadow. Distant chips of diamond starlight bubbled across the black sky. The moon cast white light upon the wall of loch and mountains.

He pulled her onto his lap as he sat on the grass. "I want you."

She tensed at his soft admission. They might be married but another woman existed out there for him. "I know."

Strange how all her anger at him had dissipated, as though she'd simply given all the expected responses earlier. Perhaps it was because she'd known pieces of him for so long.

"Arianna, I have waited for you for a very long time. I know you dinnae wish to be here, but you are. I have not taken a lass to my bed since you arrived and have no intention to do so."

This time Arianna put a finger to his lips. If she didn't say no now, she might soon be incapable. "Please allow me but one more night of maidenhood."

Iain pulled back. His brow furrowed. "Why?"

"I've come a long way from what I know and I have just met you. Whatever you may believe, I do not come from this time. Where I come from there is a period of courting, engagement and then marriage. I beg of you just one more night for me to come to grips with what is happening to me?"

Arianna saw the continued disbelief in his eyes. But there now existed some indulgence. Perhaps he was simply grateful that she'd come. The possessive way his eyes roamed her face made her blush.

"I will give you this one night, Arianna. Dinnae ask me this again. You are my wife now and I desire you."

"Thank you." She leaned forward and gave him a feather light kiss on the cheek.

"Let us rejoin the festivities then," Iain said. He took her hand and led her back to the boisterous crowd she knew he'd hoped they wouldn't be joining again.

~Fate's Monolith~

Chapter Eight

Arianna woke early the next morning. She opened her eyes and smiled to find she was still in the small, stone chamber. *Thank God I'm not dreaming.*

The remainder of the previous evening had been wonderful. Iain stayed by her side this time. They ate, drank, and danced. He'd proven to be an amiable companion.

Only once did he steal another kiss before she returned to her chamber. Warmth flooded her as she recalled the passionate embrace at the foot of the stairs.

Then she remembered what she'd promised him. Her chest tightened. Arianna could *not* stay. She could not allow him to consummate their marriage. There was another woman out there to whom he belonged. Where was she?

I should leave.

But not yet, I have to see him again.

He'd become so important in very little time and even though she knew deep down inside it was because he'd haunted her for so long, she couldn't convince herself to flee in such short time. What harm could a few more hours do?

A small bowl of porridge and fruit had been left for her. Delighted, she sat down and ate it all, then dressed and went downstairs.

Muriel caught her at the door. "Will you join me for a ride?" Excitement shone in her large eyes and rose tinted her delicate cheekbones.

Though she knew she had little time, Arianna didn't have the heart to say no. "I would love to."

She followed Muriel outside and was given a chestnut horse to ride. Oh, how she missed Fyne.

They rode their horses beneath the portcullis. The dawn was majestic. Tall mountains were steeped in fog and light purple against a backdrop of sunrise that fanned into the sky. An explosion of dusty peach mated with deep melon giving way to vibrant gold and lavender.

"Come on." Muriel urged her mare into a gallop.

Arianna's horse kept pace through the woodland. When they reached the river, the women traveled at an easy pace upstream. The surefooted animals maneuvered up thin pathways between rocks, dried grass and purple heather. White water foamed as it rushed over tumbled gray pebbles. The air cooled as they climbed higher. Touches of autumn splashed the forest.

"We shall bathe here." Muriel slid off her horse.

"What?" Arianna averted her eyes when she realized that Muriel was taking off her clothes.

"Would you prefer the salty loch?" The water splashed as Muriel dove into the deep, green pool of water.

"I suppose not." These were not modest people. Arianna admired the thirty-foot waterfall yonder as she removed her dress. Tentative, she waded into the freezing water.

"Dive right in, 'tis easier that way," Muriel said, and then sunk beneath the water.

"I'm not convinced." However, this was slow torture. She shivered, closed her eyes and plunged into the frigid liquid.

After a brief period of adjustment, Arianna admitted the water was actually quite nice. She ran her toes over the well-worn rocks at the bottom.

She'd never felt more free and alive then she did at this moment. The mist off the waterfall caressed her face. She'd married the man of her dreams. Amazing how that thought now pleased her immensely. But with that thought came the sure knowledge that she had to let him go.

"Here." Muriel tossed her a crude square of soap.

"Thank you." The soap smelled sweet. Was that ginger she detected?

This wasn't such a bad way to bathe. Arianna leaned back in the water and admired the view.

Massive, kingly pines lined either side of this part of the river and cast sword-like blades of shade across the varied depths of crystalline water. A timid sun lay low on the eastern horizon. Its malignant rays splintered through the tree trunks. Clear mountain water slid down the richly dyed rocks and churned one side of the pool into white frothing bubbles.

"'Twas a wonderful night, was it not, sister?" Muriel smiled and closed her eyes.

"Aye, it was." Arianna was interested by Muriel's far away expression. "Perhaps more so for you?"

"You are perceptive, Arianna. I'm in love." Muriel spread her arms and twirled in the water. She laughed and splashed the water over her.

"This doesn't have anything to do with a tall handsome man, would it?" Arianna grinned.

"That it does. Hugh." Muriel dunked under the water and came up again. Her smile was as wide as the river.

"Well?" Muriel's comfortable friendship made Arianna think of her friend Beth back in Salem. What would Beth make of all of this? Scotland would never be the same again if she were here.

"Well, the two of us wandered down to the loch last night." Muriel scrubbed her face and acted nonchalant.

"And?"

"And we went for a swim," Muriel provided.

"You went for a swim?" Arianna balked. "Did you wear clothes?"

Muriel shook her head. "No."

Arianna was speechless. Muriel was so young. She couldn't be more than fifteen or sixteen.

"And he kissed me," Muriel murmured and hugged herself.

"Muriel, did he—"

Muriel interrupted her. "No, we just kissed. 'Twas magnificent."

Arianna sighed with relief. She was pretty sure Iain would have destroyed his friend had the man taken his sister's virginity out of wedlock.

"He asked me to marry him and I said yes!"

"You're getting married?" Arianna was stunned. "But you're too young."

"Too young?" Muriel laughed at this. "I'm already fourteen winters. That's the perfect age to marry."

Fourteen? Then Arianna remembered Muriel's previous statement about Iain being an old man. This was the twelfth century. If anything, fourteen almost made Muriel a spinster.

"You're right." Arianna smiled. "Congratulations!"

"Thank you," Muriel said. "I'm so happy."

"Does your brother know the good news yet?"

Muriel's face darkened and the sparkle left her eyes.

"No, please don't say anything to him."

"Of course not. You are going to tell him though, right?" Arianna was confused.

"When the time is right." Muriel waded out of the water.

Arianna followed and adorned her clothing. "I would think Iain would approve."

"Me too." Fully clothed, Muriel swung up onto her horse. "I just hate to think of the consequences if he doesn't."

On her own horse, Arianna rung out her hair. Consequences?

"I noticed last night that you and Iain are getting along well," Muriel said and turned her horse back down the path.

That's an understatement. "Aye, he isn't so bad."

Apparently, Muriel did not wish to speak further about her betrothal.

"I'm glad. You're a good woman for him. I've never seen him look at another the way he does you."

Arianna's heart skipped a beat. Despite herself she hoped Muriel told the truth. It would give her something to hold onto when she was gone. "Then I'm glad we're married."

"As am I."

The third day of celebration was underway as they reentered the field. The bonfire blazed bright. Arianna ran her fingers through her hair to dry it. After they returned their steeds, the women mingled with the crowd.

Arthur ran up behind them, lifted Muriel and spun her. "How is my little tree fairy today?"

Playful, Muriel laughed and whacked him. Hugh joined them and gave her a swing of his own. The trio was merry as they turned to Arianna.

"How is my fair lady this day?" Mischievous to the core, Arthur eyed Arianna

"Quite well," she said, intoxicated by the joyous group.

"Excellent." He leapt forward.

Before Arianna could deny him, Arthur flung her over his shoulder. She stared at the ground far below her while she both screamed and laughed at once. The grass passed underfoot as she struggled half-heartedly.

"Let me down you brute." Where was he taking her?

Grass flipped into blue sky as Arianna was dropped into Iain's arms.

"I believe she belongs to you." Arthur gave him a mock salute. "You best watch her, my laird. I believe she has taken a liking to me."

"Silly man," Arianna said. She supported herself with one arm around Iain's neck and attempted a swat at Arthur. The large man dodged out of the way.

"She tried to strike a man," he accused. "If you do not punish her, I will."

"You commit a great crime, lass." Iain hung his head in shame.

"And what is the punishment for such a crime, my laird?" She fluttered her eyelashes. Arianna had never been one to flirt but the man provoked her to act and think in a whole new way.

"Hmmm." Iain looked up at the sky as he contemplated. "Mayhap isolation."

"Isolation?"

"That sounds just to me my laird." Arthur nodded his head with enthusiasm. "Isolation until she is judged suitable to be in my presence again."

"And just who would do the judging?" Her fingers played along the length of Iain's solid shoulder.

"The Chieftain is the only one capable o' such a decision," Arthur declared.

"He has the right of it lass. I believe I am the only man qualified." Iain set her down but didn't let her go.

"Oh?" Arianna stared at his bare chest in the daylight. A light sheen of sweat glistened off the well-defined muscles. Arianna looked up. Intimidated, she took a step back. The twin blades of a huge battle-axe attached to his back caught the sunlight on its sharp metallic edges. Multiple daggers adorned his waistline.

This was a very dangerous man.

"I am a man of war at heart, my wife," he murmured, aware of her trepidation. "Know this though, I would never hurt you."

"I know." She met his eyes.

Then as seemed to happen often lately, Arianna swore she heard his thoughts. He wanted to pull her back to him. She smelled of wildflowers. When he had seen her ride across the field earlier he had been dumbstruck by her beauty. Though beautiful afoot she became an enchantress upon a horse. Her long, golden tresses flowed free and she was but a singular entity of graceful movement with the great beast between her legs.

Thud. Thud. Arianna's heart nearly burst from her chest. Could he possibly be thinking such things?

"I would suggest the shores of Loch Holy an excellent source of isolation," Muriel said and grinned at Arianna.

"A brilliant idea." Iain removed his weapons and flashed Arianna one of his wicked smiles. Straight white teeth shone against his suntanned face as he held out his arm in invitation.

"Subtle," Arianna said over her shoulder to Muriel as they departed.

The forest was quiet. A golden carpet of needles and cones lay before them as he led her through a stretch of pine trees with wide girths of gray and red.

She cast him a sidelong glance and was struck by his regal bearing. His posture and expression seemed comparable to what she imagined the great knights of the past would have projected. Her past. His present.

Iain's strong profile pleased her. He watched his surroundings with a keen eye and made her wonder at the wars he had fought to ascertain such a demeanor.

Why was she so privileged to have such a prominent man by her side? It seemed only fair a woman of this time deserved such a treasure.

Arianna sighed with remorse. There *was* a woman of this time meant for him. She had yet to arrive.

A strange sound brought her eyes to a nearby rock where what looked to be a brown squirrel sat. It cocked its head at her with curiosity.

"And how are you this fine day, little squirrel?" She stepped closer and smiled.

"'Tis naught a squirrel but a degu. A pest."

The degu stood up much like a squirrel would and seemed to chitter a friendly welcome.

"But it's adorable!" Arianna reached her hand toward it. The degu rocked its head and sniffed at her fingers.

"Nay, lass, let it be." He took her hand and led her away. She looked back and gave the little animal a wave goodbye.

"Besides, you wouldn't want the critter to end up without a tail would you?"

Arianna looked at Iain. "What do you mean?"

Iain raised his eyebrows. "Well, one never knows. You may have decided to grab its tail."

She stopped short. "I would never grab its tail and even if I did, the poor creature would not end up without a tail."

Iain graced Arianna with a crooked grin. "Aye, lass. 'Tis well known that if you pull the tail of a degu, 'twill defend itself. The only way a degu knows to do that is to shed its tail from its body. A shed tail will never grow back."

Arianna burst into laughter. "You can't be serious."

"Och, I'm very serious." He laughed as well. "'Tis the silliest thing to behold."

"I can imagine," she agreed.

Theirs was a comfortable silence as they continued to walk. After a time Iain spoke, his deep voice tender.

"Do you like it here?"

"Aye, it's very beautiful." They left the trees behind.

Arianna stopped and took in the splendor of the sea loch that curved like a massive serpent as far as the eye could see. This was the very same shoreline Iain had ridden upon in the mirror.

"I always thought so." He took her hand and led her to the water's edge. The mist had evaporated from the mountains and left them crisp and defined against a deep blue sky speckled by creamy whipped clouds. A flock of black and white barnacle geese flew overhead. Tears welled. Scotland was much the way she remembered it.

Arianna wanted to share her thoughts with him but didn't. For right now, these precious few moments, she would pretend she belonged here with him. That this twelfth century Scotland belonged to her as well.

The Scottish loch was choppy under the wind. Sun spilled on miniscule waves and illuminated the volatile surface. Deep gray, the water lapped at her feet. The cool wind blew against her face as they walked the shore, hand in hand.

"Have you heard the tale of the Sons of the North Wind from your far off Lothian?" Iain said. "Its lore springs from the western isles."

She shook her head.

"It explains the very wind that blows this shore." He steered her closer to him.

Arianna sunk her toes into the sand underfoot. It felt so natural to be next to him. His voice was deep and melodious as he began his tale.

"Well, the North Wind had three sons. These sons were called White Feet, White Wings and White Hands. When the three first came into our world from the invisible palaces, they were so beautiful that many mortals died from beholding them, while others dared not to look, but fled frightened into the woods or obscure places. So when these three sons saw that they were too radiant for the eyes of the Earthbound, they receded beyond the gates of the Sunset and took counsel with the *Ollathair* or All Father." Iain paused as a gorgeous white eagle soared over above them. He looked up and smiled.

"When, through the gates of dawn, they came again. They were no longer visible to men nor, in all the long gray reaches of the years, has any been seen by mortal eyes."

"How are they known now then?"

"They are known of old, lass. They are known by the white feet of one treading the waves of the sea; and by the white rustle and sheen of the myriad tiny plumes as the other unfolds great pinions above hills and valleys, woodlands and garths and by the moving waters, and the windless boughs of trees, upon the silent tarn, upon the bracken by the unfailing hill stream hanging like a scarf among the rock and mountain ash. We know them only by the radiance of their passing and we call them the Polar Wind, Snow and Ice yet fairer are their ancient names, known since the dawning of the day as White Feet, White Wings and White Hands."

Arianna stopped. What a nice tale. What an incredible man. "That's beautiful."

"Aye, my Ma used to tell me that story when I was a wee bairn."

"You must miss her so much."

He nodded, eyes evasive. "I miss all of those who I've lost but they're never far from me."

"I wish I could believe the same," she murmured.

Iain squeezed her hand. "Never doubt it, lass. Not for a moment."

Arianna didn't know what to say. She wished she could tell him more about herself and wished that he would believe her. But she knew better.

Iain released her hand and waded into the water. He turned and urged her to do the same. The wind blew back his hair. His environment complimented him. As tall and strong, the mountains peaked over his shoulder and wondered at her next move.

She waded to him.

"This is real wealth." Iain spanned the Loch and distant mountains with one mighty sweep of his arm.

"Is this all yours?" Arianna's skin tingled at his touch when he held the back of her arm.

"Nay, lass, this is God's," Iain said. "Those mountains beyond are claimed by other clans but like the land of Cowal, no mortal man can truly own them."

Arianna was impressed. "Wise words my laird."

"True words."

Iain faced her as they stood ankle deep in the salty water. For a split second she thought she saw his eyes flare a brighter emerald. Again, her imagination. His gaze remained so intent, so sensual, that she hid behind her lashes.

"The eyes are the windows to your soul Arianna, do not deny me them." He ran his thumb along the fine arch of her eyebrow.

She trembled. Desire rocketed through her body. Soon, very soon, this terrible need would end. All she had to do was put distance between them. All she needed to do was flee. He turned her and pulled her back against him. At this angle the Holy Loch disappeared into the sky. One arm remained locked around her waist as he pulled her hair aside and exposed the delicate ivory of her slender neck.

Distance and fleeing would have to wait. This felt too good.

"There are no words." He ran his warm lips slowly up her neck. She closed her eyes and leaned her head back against him. Arianna was grateful for his supportive embrace for she was sure she would crumple into the water otherwise.

She reveled in the feel of his lips as they explored beneath her ear and down her neck. A shiver ran through her when his tongue flickered over her sensitive skin and his large hand found her breast. Inch by inch, he traced its outline. Heat throbbed and filled her body.

Arianna's heart pounded against her chest, its vibration filled first her stomach and then down lower. Her breath became labored when she felt his arousal against her back. *No. I can't allow this. I'm not the right woman.* She jerked away from his embrace and chewed the corner of her lip. How should she proceed? How was she supposed to tell him that they couldn't do this when every bone in her body wanted it?

The moment stretched.

Iain crouched and splashed cold water on his face before he finally grumbled, "Och, I'm tempted to dunk my whole body, lass." He stood and sighed. "And dinnae stand there looking so bloody innocent. A lad knows when a lass wants him." Shaking his head, he whispered, "You're ready for me, Arianna."

She blinked rapidly and shook her head.

"Lass, I have no intention of taking your maidenhood from you as we stand amidst the loch's shoreline." He edged closer.

"Assuming I have one," she countered.

"As for that I have no doubt." Iain chuckled

She didn't look away when he came to stand before her. Tiny rivers of water ran over his high cheekbones. They gained speed as they plummeted past the slopes of his cheeks and jaw. Polished gold ignited the center of his eyes. He frowned and cupped her face with his strong hands.

"Trust in me, that's all I ask. I willnae hurt you."

Iain's gentle voice mixed with the lapping water and the birds that cried overhead. She closed her eyes as his salty lips skimmed hers. Chilled from the loch, they tilted until claiming the full of her mouth. Skilled, his tongue wound with hers as he removed his hands and wrapped his arms around her. The kiss at the base of the stairs and in the midst of the rainbow paled into comparison to the one he introduced now. The chill of the water around her ankles vanished, as did the persistent pull of the wind. Dead silence and pure feeling became Arianna's world. She wrapped her arms around Iain's neck and leaned into him.

He tightened his embrace. There was only this. Mutual desire. How long they stood that way with the dirt beneath the water eager to bury their feet, she couldn't be sure.

When he eventually pulled away, Iain murmured, "You test my self-control, lass."

Arianna licked her lips. If only he knew how much he tested hers as well. She'd never wanted anyone so much in her life. Aye, she may be a virgin but she knew that he'd ease the sharp ache in her groin. She knew that he'd touch her in ways that would give her intense pleasure. Best to steer things in a different direction however. "Have I passed judgment my laird?"

His pupils flared. Though he didn't like it he seemed to understand. "Aye, you may return from isolation." His tone lightened. "I expect you to steer clear of my man Arthur however."

Arianna enjoyed the easy camaraderie forming between them. She smacked her lips together and narrowed her eyes together in indecision. "I can make no promises."

~Fate's Monolith~

Chapter Nine

The sun sat high in the sky when they returned to the castle. Activity flourished upon the field as Iain left her and headed for the rock-throwing contest. He paused briefly and whispered something in Muriel's ear. She shot Arianna a sly glance and nodded.

Arianna watched families mingle together. Though most of the men were now in the lower field a select few remained. Some carried laughing children on their shoulders while others picnicked on the grass with adoring women and toddlers. Elderly folk intermingled and allowed grandchildren to frolic at their heels.

"Come sister, the day grows late. Let me show you to your new room so you can change," Muriel said, as she broke free from the thicket of people nearby.

"My new room?" This didn't sound good.

"Did you think you would be remaining in a servant's quarters?" Muriel rolled her eyes. "'Tis time for you to share a room with your new husband."

Uh oh. "Aye, that's what I thought you meant."

Arianna and Muriel made their way back into the castle and up the stairs. This time she led her up a smaller staircase Arianna wasn't aware existed. When they arrived at the top the two entered another hallway that sidled a long wall walk.

Small tunnels of spiraled staircases disappeared into the rock wall at random intervals. "Those lead to tower rooms."

Muriel gave a small wave to the men on guard. "Iain prefers his quarters on this floor versus any other because it allows easiest access to viewing the surrounding countryside. He's always on the outlook for enemies though he posts men along the wall walks"

"That's understandable." Arianna followed Muriel into a large, spacious room.

"This room will be yours now," Muriel said.

"Windows!" Arianna cried. *Thank God.* Thick wooden shutters and heavy animal furs hung from two windows located on either side of the room.

A long wooden chest rested at the end of a mammoth four-posted bed. Heavy drapes of bleached white wool hung like a canopy above the bed, tied back to the posts with long strips of blue dyed animal skin. A small oval table with two chairs cuddled in one corner in front of a fireplace carved into the wall. A warm fire burned in its womb. Huge, dark brown animal furs carpeted the stone beyond.

The walls were covered with a variety of tapestries depicting white-capped mountains giving way to steep cliffs that overlooked raging oceans.

"As well as your own hearth," Muriel stated the obvious. "You will not find another castle with such a thing in a chamber. Iain came up with the idea."

Muriel pointed at the top of the hearth. "That as well, pretty soon he will have one built for the hearth downstairs."

Arianna smiled. A hole above the hearth disappeared skyward through a tunnel of unseen rock. This allowed the smoke to billow outside. Little did Muriel know that eventually such a thing would become commonplace. Iain had created a crude chimney. Smart man.

"Such incredible tapestries," Arianna said.

"Thank you, my great grandmother wove them," she stated with pride. "The one behind you depicts the northwestern border of our land. She was especially fond of it."

Arianna turned. Her breath caught.

A long stretch of loch stretched across the horizon. Far beyond, a shadow of the distant shores shimmered with varying shades of jade. Half a sphere of sun set in the west and cast a warm glow over the water. Thin, iridescent wisps of mist crowded at the edges where the setting sun no longer burned the surface of the water.

"Are you okay?" Muriel said.

A tear rolled down Arianna's cheek.

"Aye." She wiped away the tear. "'Tis the loch my village bordered."

Muriel shook her head and mumbled, "Nay, 'tis impossible. You could only be familiar with the North Sea. The fever…"

Ah yes, the Arianna from this time period would not be familiar with Loch Fyne, would she?

"Your garment has been laid for you." Muriel waved her hand at the bed.

"'Tis but a sleeping gown, Muriel. Where is my gown for the night's festivities?" Did she really want to hear the answer?

"My new sister…that *is* your gown for the night's festivities." Muriel hid behind an impish grin.

"I'm not joining you at the bonfire tonight, am I?" She gulped and eyed the large bed.

"Oh you will. Eventually. The laird must be present." Muriel took Arianna's hand. "Are you so frightened by your husband?"

"No, you know I'm not." *I'm just not his real wife.*

Muriel sat on the bed. "He is not like other men. My brother is civilized and compassionate. His people come before him. When I was a child and my mother died I would sneak into his chamber at night and he would hold me as I cried."

Arianna sat down next to her. "I know what it feels like to lose someone close when you're so young. I'm glad Iain was there for you. My aunt was there for me."

Though Arianna couldn't recall how her parents died, she knew that she had lost them within a heartbeat. One day they were there, the next, they were gone. With them, they took Scotland. Home.

"Aye, I would have been lost without him." Muriel gazed at the floor. "She died giving birth to my sister."

Arianna took her hand. "I'm so sorry."

Muriel gave a sad smile. "'Twas meant to be. We're grateful for little Catherine none-the-less. She's a quiet child with a sweet soul."

"She appears fond of Helen."

"Aye, Helen has been like a mother to her," Muriel said.

"You have a strong family, that's a good thing." Arianna thought of her own family.

Muriel nodded and stood. She looked down at Arianna. "He will be gentle, have no fear."

"I'm sure you're right," Arianna replied. She had no reason to fear. She intended to leave.

"You should change now. Iain will arrive soon." Muriel's words trailed her out of the doorway before she disappeared down the hallway.

Arianna picked up the flimsy garment on the bed and held it in front of her. He would be gentle, no doubt.

She envied his true bride.

Minutes passed. Should she stay or go? Going was her only option. Things would only get harder if she stayed. Before she could second-guess her decision, Arianna tossed the material on the bed and left.

She would try to make it back to wherever she was when she arrived and hope that fate would bring her back home. Her chest tightened at the thought of never seeing Iain again but this was for the best.

Only servants speckled the great hall. No one paid her heed. She exited the front doors and intermingled with the throng of villagers. The field had far more people on it than before which made her goal easier than she would've imagined.

At the wood line Arianna turned and looked back. *Goodbye Iain.*

Choking back an acute surge of despair, she left him behind.

****

Iain walked up the stairs leading to his chamber.

Visions of his beautiful wife flooded his mind. The way she looked in his arms earlier, her long, damp fiery hair against smooth white skin; her large turquoise eyes so innocent and eager for him.

No woman could match her. Thoughts of her lying in his bed, waiting, aroused him to no end.

He stopped short at the threshold. Where was she? Muriel had assured him Arianna was here. *Bloody hell!* He turned and fled down the stairs.

"Michael!" He sought the head servant who kept close tally on what happened in the castle.

"Yes, my laird," Michael said from the far side of the hall.

"Where is my wife?" He towered over the man, furious.

"She is in your chambers, my laird." Michael's voice was weak.

"If she were in my chambers would I be here asking you where she was?"

Before Michael could speak a child's voice interrupted them.

"Excuse me, my laird." A small blond-haired child looked up at Iain. Brave lad.

"Speak child."

"Your pretty girl with the bright hair left a short while ago." The child appeared pleased. "She looked very nice."

Iain wasted no time. He patted the lad on his head and left.

Blasted lass.

He retrieved his horse and rode through the masses of clansmen around his castle. Many reported having seen her. In short time he knew what direction she'd fled.

Iain spurred his horse and flew into the forest. He caught up with her quickly.

'Twas easy enough to track her movements. The woman perplexed him. She made things far more difficult than need be. 'Twas time to clarify his intentions. He would see to it now that this behavior ended. Foolish creature. What did she hope to accomplish?

She was within sight now.

Her long hair streamed behind her in untamed ringlets of gold. The deep green spiked pines danced with her slim figure while she darted in and out of the trees.

She was his now.

He reined in his horse and slid from its sleek back.

Startled by the nearness of hooves, she spared a fleeting glance over her shoulder.

That was Arianna's mistake. He had her.

Iain grabbed her arm and whipped her around. Her high cheekbones were flushed, which made her smooth white skin resemble unblemished silk. He seized the other arm and pulled her up against his body. "Where are you going, Arianna?"

"Please. No. You must release me." Small hands came up to his chest in resistance. Fine eyebrows arched in wariness.

He leaned down until his mouth was next to her ear. "We had an agreement. Do you not honor your word?"

She swallowed the lump in her throat. "I'm sorry. We can't."

"We can and we will." A low moan escaped her when he spoke. He knew she wanted him.

Time stopped. Anger fizzled.

She was here. He was here.

Enough with waiting.

Arianna knew the moment it happened. She was trapped. *Thump. Thump.* Her heart beat so hard she was sure he could hear it.

Iain gazed down at her, his eyes transformed to that dangerous emerald green she knew so well. The hue was sharpened by a golden nucleus. His eyes shone bright like a Scottish warlock, which heightened his strong features into a staggering masculine beauty.

She tried to suck sparse, thin air into her lungs. If one moment could define a lifetime, her time on earth had finally fructified.

He smelled earthy, a rich and erotic scent that mingled spice with cedar. Her body shook. There was great power here. The land began to vibrate underfoot. It reminded her a lot of her experience at the stone. Was she traveling through time again?

Every bone in her body hummed. Her blood, thick and scorching, pumped rapidly through her veins. Soul-shattering warmth seeped up her legs into her stomach and chest, and then flowed down her arms to her fingertips.

The blaze rose up her neck and engulfed her face. Her lips sizzled like a volcano; easing smoldering lava heat back down to places she never imagined could feel such fury. Fierce, potent energy seized her body until she fell weak against him. She could no longer feel the ground beneath her feet.

He locked her within the massive wall of one arm and grabbed the back of her slender neck with his other hand. He grasped her will with ease as he lowered his lips to hers. As a ship to port, he governed her lips to receiving his with liquid control. Slowly, his mouth sipped from hers in ancient rhythm. Arianna had no choice but to give into sweet surrender.

Caught waist deep in the depths of him, her slender fingers curled and entwined the thin crest of ebony hair on his sun darkened chest. Iain's muscles locked. Even though she was an innocent, Arianna felt the feminine power she held over him. It was intoxicating. Pressing her breasts against his chest, she silently pleaded for him to take what he needed.

He didn't make her wait long.

His tongue slipped over her lips once in sleek enticement, then circled into her mouth seeking refuge. Sultry and searing, it wound around her tongue and invited hers to dance. She couldn't refuse him. His hand cupped her backside and pulled her tightly against his hard body. She felt his heavy, thick length pressing eagerly against her. A deep sigh poured from her mouth into his.

An eagle cried in the distance and tangled mystically with her primeval moan.

When he pulled his lips from hers, she felt only mildly alarmed by the raging lust on his face. His eyes dropped to her lips. "I like kissing your lips until they're red and swollen, lass." His thumb brushed her cheek. "You're out of time. I want you here and now. With the woods and mountains surrounding us."

Unseasonably warm wind rocketed through the silver shafts of woodland. Leaves spun to life around them. Caught helpless in a slow moving typhoon, they circled the intimate couple. Impassioned, the leaves continued to spin in wild circles.

Arianna stared in awe. What was happening? How could this be?

The wide silver and brown tree trunks circled magically in religious ceremony. High above, white pine and maple bent to entwine. Oak twisted with birch. Arms of succulent green ivory wound down the trees. Thick vines with less ambition hung loose between the thick trunks. They barely touched the woodland floor and created a forbidden nest.

"Magic, lass. My magic." He paused a moment. "And yours"

Arianna sunk into his vigorous, lust maddened eyes, hypnotized by his desire. She reveled in wonder as he summoned his Scotland to life around him. It was out of control now, their gifts whipped, unleashed and untamed. She felt strange. Lighter somehow. For a split second, she saw herself through his eyes. She was the epitome of Celtic mysticism. Her long hair drifted around her face as if she was under water. Her eyes gleamed bright with need and wonderful curiosity. How could she not realize the magic within herself?

"Come," he said gruffly and pulled her to the forest floor where he cradled her on his lap. He stroked her satin tresses and then firmly grasped the back of her hair so as to not hurt her and pulled back until her eyes were in intimate line with his.

"No more waiting," Iain whispered and claimed her mouth with savage authority. His fingers sifted through the plush curtain of wild, unkempt hair.

Time transgressed as she whimpered useless words born of pleasure and sweet anguish. Thoughts no longer formed in her mind as he ravished her mouth.

The sun fell into the distant horizon.

Her hand trailed along the swell of his forearm and slowed as it flicked over the thick ropes of muscle engulfing his bicep. Her fingertip skirted along his bronze shoulder to his neck. Her palm rested, intrigued by a vein that pumped under his skin, throbbing with heightened promise.

He ran his hands down her arms and wrapped them around her neck, running his thumbs along her jaw line. He made love with a kiss. His tongue entered and retreated in a slow sensual twirled rhythm.

Iain swung her from his lap to the soft, gold bed of wilderness floor. The wind billowed again with an impatient gust and created a hurricane of leaves to swarm around them like bees to a hive. His lips captivated her as he gently pulled down the top of her dress allowing her breasts to spill free.

Arianna shivered as the cool air touched her bare skin. She thrilled at the sight and feel of him touching her full breast. Arianna closed her eyes in pleasure as her nipple tightened in exquisite pleasure.

When his hot mouth clamped around the tight bud, her eyes shot open and she arched. While he suckled his hand gently molded to the other breast and his knee spread her thighs. *Lord, this feels good.*

After his lips traveled to the other nipple they slowly trailed up her neck to her lips. Groaning, she tried to assuage the building ache between her legs by pressing up against his thigh.

"Shhh," he whispered.

Arianna gasped when she felt his hand travel up beneath her skirts and cover the swollen flesh at the center of her need. Grabbing his forearms, she tried to fight the invasive touch but he remained immovable. Locked in place, she had no choice but to surrender to the terribly sweet feeling of his fingers spreading her hidden folds. When his feather-light touch circled her tiny hooded nub she cried out in pleasure.

"Iain. No, " she gasped. "Stop!"

But he didn't. Instead, she felt something slide slowly inside and realized it was his finger. Licking her lips, she instinctually thrust up pushing him further inside. This time he groaned and his lips once more focused on her overly sensitive breasts.

In. Out. In. Out. His finger...no, fingers moved in rhythm with her eager hips. Digging her fingers into his arms, Arianna tried to hold on as a wondrous coil of pleasure started to build and build and build. "Oh!" she cried when everything seemed to explode. Pure bliss rippled her belly and shot out to the tips of her extremities.

"Bloody hell," Iain said hoarsely.

Arianna was semi-aware of him pulling away, removing her dress and his plaid, then tucking it beneath her. Though her body floated on a cloud, her eyes soon became focused on his long, thick member jutting proudly. *Dear Lord! That will never fit inside me!*

Before she had too much time to contemplate things, he'd lowered his body over hers and spread her legs wide.

His soft kisses feathered along her jaw and trailed warmth across sensitive skin. Hot breath slid past her ear to touch her neck behind and beneath. Arianna's body quivered. Sizzling, naked flesh brushed against hers and caused even more delicious sensations to erupt.

"Iain." His name mixed with a moan and she laced her hands through his raven hair.

He groaned low in response, took her hands in his and pulled them taut above her head. His intense gaze seemed to hold her in place as she felt his rigid arousal press into her soft core. Alarmed, she wrapped her imprisoned hands around his and held on tight.

Too much. Too big. Arianna winced as he very slowly pushed forward. His mouth parted and his eyes slid halfway shut. She soon became arrested by the pure, untamed pleasure on his face and began to relax as he inch by inch, stretched her to accommodate him.

His muscles were pulled taught and veins bulged as he continued. Arianna knew he strained against thrusting into her. She felt his incredible need to bury himself to the hilt. Though she'd only taken half of his length so far and was still in pain, another feeling started to build inside and her hips bucked unintentionally.

Snap. That's all it took. He released her hands, braced himself and drove into her so hard her feet lifted from the ground. She yelped in pain and he froze. His eyes shot to hers in alarm as though he only just realized what he'd done.

Yet even as he realized it, Iain seemed unable to stop. When he pulled out, then pushed back in, she braced for pain. Instead, something else happened.

Friction. Wonderful, heart-pounding friction.

Arianna struggled to breath as his slow, even thrusts set her body on fire. A strong physical need began to claw its way into her womb and she wrapped her legs high and wide around him. Somehow this allowed him to go even deeper until she felt he'd rip her apart.

In response his breathing increased along with his thrusts. Grasping his wide shoulders she began to move with him, eager to feel the mind-blowing pull and push of his eager arousal. Faster and faster he thrust and her pliant body allowed it as quicksilver pleasure started to tighten in her belly.

Then everything exploded far more intensely than before. Stars flickered in her vision as Iain cried out and thrust deeply. The heavy throb of his buried member only intensified the flash flood of ecstasy that burst from her loins and pin-wheeled through her limbs until sending sparks of pain/pleasure to her extremities.

Her arms fell. Her legs fell. Arianna lay in shock as pure euphoria seemed to swamp her senses. Silver rays of new moonlight filtered through the thick canopy of trees. Leaves swirled no more. Left in their wake, humid, heady warmth engulfed them in a pool of damp heat. Warmth joined with crisp autumn air and caused fog to form around the edge of their enchanted sphere.

Iain's hand tenderly stroked her cheek. "Are you well, lass?" His finger brushed her thigh. "Is there pain?"

Arianna blinked and shook her head. *Does he have any idea what he did to me? How he made me feel?* Peering up into his emerald eyes she suddenly worried, *did I please him?*

He wiped away a tear she hadn't felt fall and whispered, "Aye, you pleased me, lass."

When he pulled her into his arms, she rested her head on his shoulder. Though she had much to say nothing came out. Instead her eyes slid shut. He held her that way for minutes, hours, perhaps longer.

But not long enough.

It could never be long enough.

~Fate's Monolith~

Chapter Ten

A light wind blew in through the glen and cooled her moist skin. Alarmed, she sat up. The sense of euphoria had worn off. What had she done? She'd lain with another woman's husband! Uncomfortable, she felt his eyes on her.

"We must return to the gathering, many other clans are arriving this eve." He stood behind her now.

"Aye." Arianna struggled to get the green dress over her kirtle. Her hands shook so bad she couldn't seem to get the garment pulled down properly. She froze when his warm hands clasped the back of her arms.

"Arianna, let me help." He turned her and his breath caught. She saw the admiration in his eyes, how lovely he found her. He touched her cheek and softly said, "You glow, lass."

Before she could stop him, he began helping her adjust the unruly skirts. His nearness caused her legs to shake. She took thin shallow breaths and closed her eyes.

"Arianna?" His voice sounded husky.

"Aye?" She liked the way he said her name, a heavy brogue rolled the R from deep within his chest. She opened her eyes just before his lips were on hers. She moaned and allowed him to pull her against him.

As quickly as it began, it ended, leaving her speechless.

Iain bent to task and rolled his plaid. His warhorse trotted from the forest. He tucked the plaid into the pocket of an unusual saddle and removed another. It was but a moment before he was dressed and his weaponry in place. Muscles strained beneath tan skin as he mounted the great beast.

"Efficient," Arianna said. Her blood had stained his previous plaid.

"I knew what I was coming for." Arianna cursed her weakness.

He took her hand and pulled her onto the horse. This time she sat astride the mount in front of him. "You will be the center of attention this night."

The warm intimacy she felt earlier between them now felt strained.

"I have felt such since I arrived here." Arianna tried to ignore his renewed arousal pressed against her backside. The man was insatiable. So was she.

"Aye, but this eve you will meet those outside your own clan. They will be very interested in what sort of woman you are. 'Tis important you act appropriately. There need be no talk of nonsense."

"To whom have I talked nonsense?" Anger replaced lust.

"Myself and my sister that I am aware of so far. I realize you suffered some trauma of the mind during the fever that took you. Muriel tells me it will take time before your wits are completely about you again." Iain directed the horse towards the orange glow shining through the trees.

"You don't say?" She turned the upper half of her body. "Perhaps you should have waited until my mind returned before wedding and bedding me."

If she weren't certain she would break a bone from the drop, she'd be off this horse and gone.

"You have a funny way of saying things, wife." Iain stared down his nose at her. "As for wedding you, I had no choice. As for bedding you, 'twould have happened either way lass." He laughed and caught her hand before it met his cheek.

"You give yourself too much credit, swine."

"Hush, lass." They left the forest behind and entered the clearing.

The fire sizzled against the black night. A cornucopia of colored wool plaids mixed together throughout endless clusters of people mingling upon the width of field. The light cast from the fire glinted off an endless stream of metal.

Hundreds upon hundreds of sword hilts poked at the night sky from the backs of towering warriors. Although peaceable at the moment, she sensed the bloodlust that coursed through the veins of these men.

"The MacLomain laird finally takes himself a bride." A stranger bellowed and came to stand before them with his arms crossed. The crowd cheered with agreement and held up their thick mugs in salute.

They swung down from the horse. Iain clasped the stranger's arm in such a way that their hands nearly clasped one another's elbows.

"Arianna, I give you David, Chieftain of the MacMillan clan, our strongest ally," Iain said.

"'Tis a pleasure to meet you David of the Macmillan clan," she said and stepped forward.

David smiled. His features were clean and even. He was tall and lean, his wheat colored hair curled down his back. What set him apart were his slate gray eyes. Sharp and intelligent, they appraised her.

"Nay, the pleasure could not be more mine, Arianna of the MacLomain clan, formerly of the Broun clan." He bent slightly from the waist and laid a light kiss on the back of her hand. He struck her a diplomatic sort. One who could comfortably converse with America's top politicians.

"Such kind words," Arianna said.

"'Tis good to see you well, my friend." Iain said.

"Aye, and you."

"The MacMillan clan resides well north of us Arianna, as do most of the clans here this eve." Iain walked them further into the crowd.

"Have you not heard o' my clan from your distant shores?" David asked.

"Aye, of course." Arianna met the man's inquisitive look. She had no idea whom they were, but instinct prompted her to keep that to herself.

"Apparently, you recall more than I gave you credit for my love." Iain's tone clearly hinted that he didn't believe her mind lost in the least.

"My wife suffered through a fever after her capture," he said when David shot him a curious look.

"Are you well, my lady?" David frowned.

"Aye." Arianna bit her tongue and glared at Iain. She stopped as three mountainous men intercepted them.

"Lady Arianna, allow me to introduce you to some fellow clansmen." Iain greeted them in similar fashion as he had David.

"Jordan, Chieftain of the MacLauchlin clan," Iain said in introduction.

"Pleased to meet you, my laird." She smiled and nodded her head. As tall as Iain, Jordan's features were fearsome. Pockmarked skin hung off harshly carved features and his eyes were hard, as though they'd seen too much.

"And I you, my lady." Jordan nodded his head in return.

"Alan, Chieftain of the Stewart clan." Iain placed his hand on the small of her back.

"I'm honored." Arianna was delighted when the man fell upon one knee and kissed the back of her hand. Long limbed and suave, this one surely broke hearts. With straight, black hair and high cheekbones, his chocolate brown eyes twinkled from beneath a deep brow. He quirked one eyebrow and offered a charming lopsided grin.

Iain cast a look of irritation at Alan.

"I believe the honor is all mine, fair lady." He winked and chuckled.

"Lachlan, Chieftain of the Campbell clan." Iain nodded at the third man.

"My laird." The man rivaled Iain with his handsome features save for the long jagged scar that ran down his left cheek. Dark blue eyes swept over her as he stepped forward.

"I only hope my future wife will be as breathtaking as yours, Iain." His lips grazed the back of her hand.

Arianna smiled. She couldn't help but notice that Iain didn't remove his hand from her back. Truth told, she liked the possessive gesture.

"My laird?" A small voice came from below. Arianna looked down and smiled in surprise. It was Catherine. Though ten years of age, she appeared a little cherub floating amongst the tall pillars of the Roman coliseum. The little girl's face reddened in exasperation as she tugged at his plaid.

Iain leaned over and picked her up. She wrapped her arms around his neck and kissed his cheek.

Arianna melted.

He whispered something in the child's ears. She nodded and grinned shyly at Arianna. He set her down and she came over and nestled her hand in Arianna's.

"We dance, us ladies that is, over yonder." She pointed to the cluster of women nearby. "Will you come join us?"

"I would love to. Excuse me gentlemen." Arianna curtsied to the men and gave Iain one last look. "I must entertain."

****

The minute she walked away, Iain felt the loss of Arianna's presence. Her hips swayed as her long hair disappeared within the circle of giggling women.

"Iain?"

"Aye." He redirected his attention to David. "We all come together again my friends."

"That we do," Alan said and scoffed a full goblet of whiskey from a passing servant. He eyed the crowd and drank. "It appears we all should have had our fathers make a marriage pact for us lads."

The other men agreed wholeheartedly and slapped Iain on the back.

"She is a comely lass if I ever saw one," Lachlan agreed. "What news is there?" Iain changed the subject.

"'Tis more peaceable than we have ever known." Alan yawned. "If no' a bit boring."

"What say you?" Iain noted the varying expressions of his fellow lairds. "We still have our ever feuding clans from the North and East."

"Aye, we will always have that," Jordan said.

"How fares the king?" Alan said.

"Skirmishing upon Scotland's southern border with Britain's King John." Lachlan's reply was sour. It had been the previous March that the former ruler of Britain, King Richard, took an arrow in the shoulder besieging the castle at Chalus. He died from the wound in April after appointing his brother John to the throne of Normandy. Rumor had it the new king crossed the border himself demanding William compensate for all damage done by the Scottish king's army to the English border.

"Bloody Sassenachs." Jordan scowled in a southerly direction. "Haven't they done enough damage?"

"Aye, they've made a run of it," Lachlan said. They had all witnessed the effects the Treaty of Falaise inflicted upon their country. The lairds were mere children when Scotland's king attempted to besiege Alnwick Castle. It was not a wise decision. They were severely outnumbered by England's garrison. It became a mute attempt when Ralf de Glanvil approached from the south with English reinforcements.

Within the thick mist of battle, William had the misfortune of becoming unhorsed. Attempting to stand, his horse rolled onto him, hence pinning him to the ground beneath. Captured, Scotland's king was chained and sent to King Henry II in Northhampton. Too busy to deal with William, Henry II sent his prisoner through England to the Kent coast, across the Channel to his castle at Falaise in Normandy.

Vexed, Henry II sent an English army to Scotland. Ravaging and destructive, the host took the castles of Jedburgh, Edinburgh, Roxburgh and Berwick, and then proceeded to plunder and tax the country. The spiteful Henry then extracted an oath of allegiance from William. The Scottish king held his country now only by permission of Henry II. Scottish soldiers were dismissed and replaced by England's own. The whole of the English garrison's smothering Scotland were demanded to be paid by the Scottish for English occupation.

The treaty lasted nearly fifteen years, raping the small wealth of Scotland. The country's dignity was ripped from its heart. When King Richard took throne he made a bargain with William. Eager to mount a third crusade, Richard requested ten thousand marks of silver to aid him to the Holy land. This he considered payment enough to extinguish the Treaty of Falaise. Scotland had suffered greatly and most clans remained bitter and acknowledged no king.

"Let us see how lucky our king gets this time," Alan said, annoyed.

"Time will tell." Iain was contemplative. "How old is his boy now?"

"Alexander is only three winters." David's voice was stiff.

"Young yet." Iain kept a concerned eye on David. After all, 'twas his uncle who battled with King William at the siege where he was captured back in 1174. His clan had recognized their king for many generations. Where David's allegiance took him nowadays, Iain was unsure.

"Birthed from King Henry's illegitimate granddaughter no less." Alan sneered and took a deep swig from the proffered mug of wine he now held.

"Just that," David said. His lips drew into a tight line.

"No doubt we will lose our country again." Jordan scowled and crossed his arms over his broad chest.

"Nay," David said, convinced. "William will not make the same mistake twice."

"Why are you not with him?" Alan's eyes locked with David's.

David shrugged and thanked the lass who gave him a mug heavy with ale. "He has not called upon me."

David's allied lairds had always treated his kinship to the king with passive indifference. He couldn't blame them for their anger for he felt it as well. Loyalty was foremost to David however and his clansmen knew as much. The devotion he showed his king was equal to that he had shown them over the years. He surmised they were not entirely discontent being allied with his clan, having fought alongside Scotland's king, though none would ever dare admit it.

"I see no immediate threat." Iain decided now was the time to interject.

"I concur," Lachlan said. "We have followed our ways for hundreds of years. We know who our enemies and allies are. If King William plays his hand wrong, 'tis irrelevant to us."

"Well said." Alan snickered. "I could fathom William gambling our country away."

"How is your wife Jordan?" Iain said. Further talk of kings would only continue to dampen the gathering.

"With child." Jordan beamed. Congratulations were offered as the conversation churned anew with talk of their clans.

"Let us salute to your new bride." Jordan raised his goblet into the air.

"To the mother of the next MacLomain laird. 'Twill be no hardship creating a son with that one." Lachlan grinned at Iain. The five men raised their pewter mugs high in the air.

"Tonight, we enjoy the last night of Samhain. Drink, eat and feast upon the woman available to you my friends," Iain said.

Pleased, the men departed in their perspective directions. Iain and David remained.

"You are wise." David placed a hand on Iain's shoulder. "'Tis how you led your clan so far."

"I'm only as wise as my actions." Iain cared for his fellow lairds. They had played together as children, before the weight of hundreds of lives were laid upon their shoulders. The future of Scotland must lay in unity if they were to keep their country. The constant bicker between his countryman's clans lent little promise.

"What will you do, my friend?" Iain said.

"Naught yet but watch closely as we all do. I will seek word actively however and if such is an option, my warriors will fight for William again," David said.

"I sense your eagerness in this and am glad to note you have become a patient man," Iain said.

And as he expected, David brought the conversation back to where he truly wanted it to be.

"Tell me, why did your wife suffer from fever?"

"Why ask a question that you already know the answer to?" Iain was no fool. Gossip traveled faster than wind.

"I'd like to hear your version."

Iain looked to the north. "Colin Cochran."

"Och." David sniffed in derision. "Ever the arrow in your side."

"The coward sent his men. His time is limited."

"You surprise me. The man I once knew would have already been at his castle's gate." David spied Arianna mingling within a group of chattering women.

"I've been distracted." Iain's eyes were on his wife as well.

"No doubt you have, she's very beautiful," David said.

"I'm glad she came."

Iain knew David referred to the rumor of her romance with her father's clansman. "As am I, friend, as am I."

"How fares your sister?" David enjoyed the smooth whiskey that a pretty servant handed him. "She looks lovely this night." His gaze traveled to the girl dancing gaily across the way.

"Taken with Hugh, I'm afraid," Iain muttered. He'd been watching his sister and Hugh closely. They thought themselves discreet.

It was always his plan to have Muriel married to David. The two Chieftains had discussed it the previous year and thought it a good match for the clans. Muriel was no longer a child and her beauty caught David's attention. 'Twas his hope the two would further acquaint themselves at this gathering.

"Hugh?" David saw Iain's man as he hovered near Muriel and eyed her possessively.

"'Tis a whimsy with him. She will marry you if you'll have her," Iain assured.

David wore a pensive frown. "Oh, I'll have her and a dance as well."

"I suggest you do." Iain nodded his head. David lingered a moment longer before he departed with a self assured grin.

Iain watched from afar as David intercepted Muriel. He had no doubt that the man would succeed. Once his sister spent an evening with him this infatuation betwixt her and Hugh was sure to vanish. Hugh had plenty of women to pick from.

Thoughts of Arianna returned and he scanned the crowd.

She wasn't hard to miss. Long beautiful hair swayed around her hips. She had a circle of admirers hoping for a chance to dance with her. Lachlan and Alan floated amidst them. 'Twas the way of the clansmen. The bride was not left unattended.

His mind drifted back to the forest. The way her body had felt and tasted. Ah, but he hadn't tasted all of her yet. Soon. Very soon. He couldn't wait to see the pleasure on her face when he showed her more of what men and women could do to bring one another carnal pleasure.

Still, no feeling would ever outdo the moment he'd taken her maidenhood. The pure bliss of entering her untouched body and feeling the tight heat surround his cock. He hadn't meant to take her so harshly but he'd lost control. How could he not with her beautiful body pinned beneath and her dewy eyes so curious?

Then her response... that unbelievable moment when pain turned to pleasure, her eyelids lowered, lips fell apart and she wrapped her long, slender legs around his arse, meeting him thrust for thrust. Arianna turned out to be far more sensual than he'd ever anticipated. Her orgasm would be forever entrenched in his mind. The rapid inner ripples, the heart-pounding clenches...

Och, his cock had long stirred to life. Time to stop thinking about this. He stared at her across the way and focused on thoughts of the babe who might already be growing in her belly.

If only.

He watched her with pleasure. Great spirit and laughter filled her eyes when she smiled. The lass had a way of making a man feel at his best. She was pure magic as she twirled. Her eyes sparkling as she danced amongst his kinfolk.

He had put that sparkle there.

'Twas his turn to dance with his wife.

****

I need a break. She was out of breath.

She'd danced with more men this single night than ten of her lifetimes put together. She rejoined the crowd of women eying their next victim.

"A rowdy lot for sure." Helen's cheeks were rosy from dancing. "Here."

Arianna took the mug from Helen and discovered it contained ale, not whiskey. Thirsty, she gulped it down.

"Careful. That can be just as bad as whiskey if you drink it that fast luv." Helen warned as her eye strayed to a tall warrior nearby. "After all, we're to be on our best behavior tonight."

"Trust me, I need this," Arianna said. She just lost her virginity to a relative stranger six hundred years in her past. She almost wished the liquid were whiskey.

"May I have a whirl, lass?"

A stranger stood before her. His long unruly hair was flaxen and his eyes were the pale gold of wheat under the sun. With a chiseled square jaw and bold features, he knew his own beauty.

Arianna had a moment to respond before he pulled her into his arms. Built tall and strong like most of the men around her, he differed from them in that his demeanor was one of not only arrogance, but stealth.

"I have never seen a woman the likes of you." His baritone voice rumbled slippery smooth.

A response hesitated upon her tongue as he spun her through the crowd.

Danger.

She had no idea how she knew, but this man meant her harm.

"Relax." He locked eyes with her.

She went flax in his arms. As they spun around, the fire became smaller and smaller. The stars overhead shone brighter. An indefinable smell assaulted her. Smoke mixed with melting sugar.

"Not much further." She was next to him but he sounded a great distance away. Trapped helpless in his arms they entered the wood line.

Arianna's legs dragged upon the ground as he pushed her against the scaly trunk of a pine tree. Chips of sticky wood pricked her skin. The stranger's hand clasped the hair at the back of her head and he pressed his body against hers. Why couldn't she respond?

His lips came down upon hers roughly while he lifted her skirts. He tasted bitter as he ran his tongue over her teeth.

"Help." Though she said the word, nothing came out. He lifted her off the ground and positioned himself between her legs. Was she dead? Was this hell?

No. She felt incredibly weak. Her limbs were thick and slow as she attempted to push him away.

"Not an option, lassie." He panted in her ear and hiked her legs higher. "I'm supposed to take you back immediately but you are too tempting. Has your laird had you yet, wench? I hope not. I want to make you bleed and mark the tree behind you with my lust. Colin need not know. I will tell him your Chieftain broke you in. Your word will mean naught where I'm taking you. Besides, after you've felt what I have to offer, you will want more."

Arianna heard something else. Something born of a distant memory. "Aye, my wee little piece of dung, there's a place for you in there."

A wicked monster of a man replaced the savage who held her. The mirage smiled and exposed brown, crooked teeth.

"Iain." Arianna's scream was nothing but a whisper. Her head dropped back against the bark. She watched in horror while the man made ready to claim her.

As she watched, as if through a film of dense fog, an arrow spear ripped through the brute's neck like a heated knife through butter. Two more whistled through the air and thumped into his side. He gurgled in protest as blood drizzled from the corners of his lips down his chin. It seeped in skinny tendrils down his neck.

His eyes bulged at her in silent accusation as his chin slowly dipped forward. He released her and slid down the trunk to the roots beneath.

The world spun in slow motion before darkness stole her.

Chapter Eleven

Iain lifted Arianna into his arms. Many of his clansmen surrounded him while others fanned out into the forest to hunt further prey. He nodded to Hugh who turned and strode away.

His fellow lairds appeared, their weapons drawn as they eyed the arrow-riddled man crumpled on the ground. His blood stained the needles dark red within the moonlight. Iain's arrow was lodged in the imposter's throat. He nodded at Lachlan and Alan in acknowledgment of the other two arrows. They'd been watching his wife as closely as he.

Jordan crouched over the man. He fingered the plaid with disgust then grabbed the man by the back of his head and yanked.

"He wears your colors." Iain did well to keep suspicion from his voice.

"Aye, he does. But I've never seen him before," Jordan said, grim. "He's in disguise. He did not travel here with us."

"One of our men is dead on the northwestern border." Hugh reappeared. Magic had its uses. 'Twould have taken hours to glean that information otherwise.

"My fellow lairds, please join me in the hall within the hour," Iain said.

He looked down at the body. The deceased wielded great magic to have accomplished what he did. Not even Iain sensed him. One second, the stranger took her into his arms to dance. The next, they disappeared. Either he possessed a new magic or a very, very old one.

"Stake the body and burn it." Iain strode through the curious crowd with his wife in his arms. He'd never felt such rage. He wanted to kill. Destroy. Annihilate every last Cochran clansman.

He entered the castle and climbed the stairs to his chamber where he laid Arianna on his bed and waited for Muriel. Methodically, he paced in front of the fire.

"Is she well?" Muriel raced into the room and went to the bedside. "Did he...is she hurt?"

"No. Yes. He should have never got to her."

"He did not compromise her, then."

Fury turned Iain's eyes from green to black. "He entranced her. I stopped him before he took her."

He clenched his fists and walked over to the bed.

"Poor girl," Muriel whispered.

"Iain," Arianna cried and sat up so fast that Muriel almost fell from her nearby perch.

Forgotten visions of her childhood bombarded Arianna.

A burning village stung her nostrils. Her mother and father screamed for her. Helpless, they were shoved into a small cottage with others. An avalanche of terror resurfaced. A man stepped forward with a torch and held it to the thatch roof. The flame caught and was fueled by the wind. Wails arose from inside as the fire swallowed the cottage.

It all came back. Ten years worth of repressed memories. Arianna had caused her parents death. Her sharp words made the evil men mad so they murdered. They killed everyone except her, Aunt Marie and a few others.

Iain grabbed Arianna and held her tight.

Sad for her, Muriel left the room.

Arianna sobbed against him as fresh pain tore her heart. Between tears she spoke. "I remember it all now, how could I have forgotten?"

"Aye lass." Iain pulled her head against his chest.

"I killed them." She cried harder.

"Killed who?"

"My parents." She tried to catch her breath. "In Scotland. The Highland clearances. I killed them."

"Your father is still alive that I am aware of Arianna," Iain said.

"You don't understand, the English came into my village and ravaged it. They destroyed everyone save a few of us."

"The English? Arianna, my sweet girl, you must be mistaken. We are our own country now."

She blinked. He was right. At the present time they were and he had no idea what she was talking about. Arianna had tried to tell him time and time again she was not who he thought she was.

Fresh pain overtook her. How she wished Aunt Marie were here. But she wasn't, he was. Arianna didn't care if he thought she was crazed. She needed release.

"The English were there and I instigated them and they punished my parents for it." Arianna sobbed.

"'Twas a traumatic event pushed upon you this eve lass. Your mind is dumbstruck. Know this though, wherever your mind is, words do not kill people. People kill people."

Years of guilt poured out of her. He was right.

She had only been a child. Violence and the hate that mankind could feel against one another was not something she could of possibly understood at the time. It still wasn't.

Arianna lifted her head from his body. She was exhausted. "What happened? Why am I in this bed?"

Iain stared at her. Why did he look so sad and furious all at once?

"Magic, lass." He frowned. "The enemy made it past our borders and tried to take you. Someone has repressed your memory of the event."

Arianna started to smile and realized he was serious. "You must be mistaken."

"I am never mistaken."

She had no recollection of anything except talking to Helen before the visions of her childhood surfaced. Fear flowed over her. *I don't think I like magic very much.*

"Thank you then—" Panic seized her. "Did he? Was I?" She looked down. There was no doubt the enemy was a man. Sore already, Arianna would never know if she had been raped.

"No, Arianna. No." He pulled her back against him. "I can assure you I have been the only man that you've known."

She trusted him. 'Twas a wonderful revelation. "Do you all have magic in this time?"

"Nay, 'tis rare." Iain sighed with exasperation, most likely because of her reference to time.

"You have a bit of your own as well, Arianna."

She removed herself from his embrace and walked to the fire. Lucky her. "How do you know?"

"Magic senses magic, lass. It lays untouched within you. Almost untouched."

"Almost?"

"Aye, you tapped it recently in the forest when we were intimate but more strongly than that sooner. However, it was... disoriented." Iain came to stand before Arianna and brushed a stray hair away from her cheek.

His finger trailed a blaze of heat across her skin. "Disoriented?"

He struggled for words. "As though it surfaced without you calling it and followed your subconscious lead."

"I'm confused."

"Aye, I'd gather you are. Look at it this way. Imagine you raced a blindfolded stallion across a meadow that ended in a steep cliff. You are mute and your hands are tied behind your back so you have no way to steer the horse away from imminent death. Your legs do not work; therefore you cannot clench your thighs or kick your feet in warning. What do you think your course of action would be?"

Arianna's brows slammed together. "Most likely, my only remaining option would be to use my upper torso to throw myself from the horse."

Iain chuckled. "So, most likely, you choose to break your neck."

Arianna shrugged in defeat.

"Do you not agree there may be a moment before, when you desire the animal to turn on its own without your command?"

"Sure I would, who wouldn't?"

"You did."

"Did what? You talk in riddles."

He took her hand. "Arianna, you turned your horse by will. Whatever magic you implemented of late, in the woods when we were together, was such."

"So I controlled my own fate with will alone?" Was that how she came to be here in this time? How she came to be with this man?

She laughed.

"In a way, yes. It happened on such a subconscious level that it was more the magic than it was you. It would be wrong of me to say you did it. The horse sensed your need and he did it. The magic sensed your need and it did it."

She shook her head.

"If you had control of the power inside you, you could scream, command. The bond holding your hands would have freed, feeling would have flooded your limbs and the blindfold would have been removed before the horse ever turned, ensuring certain safety. Instead, the horse slid to a stop very close to the edge of the cliff with you still bound and mute," Iain said.

She was too tired to wrap her mind around this.

"Well then, my sorcerer husband, pray tell me why I did not use it against my attacker this night?"

He walked away from her and leaned against the stone hearth. "Again, your magic has only been brought forth recently. Magic is something you have to be taught to use. It was strong magic used against you, lass."

"I see, so why bother with weapons when you could summon magic? Why could you not sense your enemy was with us?"

He walked back to her. "Good question. 'Tis a discreet gift in these changing times. Even if 'twas not, I prefer a blade in my hand. 'Tis more rewarding and honorable slaying your enemy with tactics and warfare. I am my country's man after all." He took her into his arms. "My magic usually does forewarn me when trouble lurks in the shadows but 'tis not always so acute as to show me the face marking danger. I depend on my wits and eyes for that."

"Thank you again." She touched his arm. "It seems you have saved me twice."

"'Tis my responsibility to keep you safe, Arianna."

"Aye."

An idea came to her. What if Iain was right and she did possess magic? Would she not owe it to her family to at least try to contact them?

"You need rest."

"Rest?" She eyed the big bed. This was the place they were to sleep together. Arianna's body warmed as she remembered their earlier intimacy. Her palms began to sweat.

"Just rest." Her thoughts played upon her face. He could feel her body temperature increasing and enjoyed the sensation. How did she know that? Ah, perhaps the 'magic'.

"You assume too much. I wasn't thinking..." She nodded at the bed. "About *that*."

Iain's eyes roamed her face with appreciation and he pulled her tighter against him. He trailed his fingers up her neck and over her chin where he skimmed his thumb over her lower and upper lip. His eyes hid within the shadows of his strong brows. She stared at his lips in fascination.

"Nay, 'tis not assumption my little vixen."

Her eyes slid closed and she tilted her head back in anticipation.

He kissed her cheek.

She opened her eyes and felt the fool.

"Rest." He repeated the word and pulled her lower half against him, just enough so that she could feel his thick, hot arousal.

Desire rippled through her body. Rest was the last thing she wanted to do right now. *Humph!* Stubborn, Arianna plunked into one of the chairs before the fire and curled into a ball.

Iain flicked his wrist and the fire renewed itself. As though she was as light as a bird, he swept her up from the chair. He ignored her yelp of protest and walked to the bed where he threw back the blankets and plopped her down. Before she could protest further he removed everything but her chemise.

"Rest." He pulled the blankets over her, winked, kissed the tip of her nose and left.

****

At long last, the lass was in his bed where she belonged. If she tried to run off again the men posted outside the door would greet her. But he highly doubted she would. They'd come far since she'd fled into the forest earlier. Further than he'd ever anticipated.

He worried for her though. What was this distress about her parents dying in some sort of Clearances? He'd heard of no such event. Had her mind truly snapped from fever? It didn't seem likely but how else to explain her confusion? Right now, he had more pressing matters to worry about.

Iain entered the main hall.

Hugh, Arthur, Ferchar and all four lairds sat at a trestle table. Iain strode to stand before the fire and clasped his hands behind his back. He appraised the clansmen. Content with the loyalty he saw in each of their eyes he spoke.

"As I'm sure you all understand, I'm displeased the enemy made it past my men into the festivities this last night of Samhain." No clan took pride in such a breach of security.

Iain understood, as they did, how this man got through. His clansman on watch would have been dead before he knew the enemy lurked so close. Such was the magic his enemy wielded. Though his arrow was shot under the cloak of magic, Iain had been surprised it met its mark. Such was the beauty of Arianna.

The man had let his guard down.

Still, Iain did not know why the enemy clansman was so brazen as to infiltrate his land, he had to be well aware that Iain himself knew magic. Typically, such false bravery was aided by the over arrogant. Mayhap, he had an enemy within his clan.

Time would tell.

As the years rolled on, magic had become almost a secret society within the Scottish clans. Magic was of the old Pagan ways and the new Christian religion

~Fate's Monolith~

they followed now did not smile upon the two being combined. He nodded his thanks when Ferchar handed him a mug of whiskey.

"My belief is that this is the work of clan Cochran, Laird Colin Cochran. Anger still consumes their hearts at my ancestors who rightfully claimed the whole of this land. It was many generations ago that our forefathers began their hatred. My entire life their maggots have chewed upon the edges of our land. They've raped and murdered the women and children of my clan, killed and tortured our warriors of past. They have scoured the lands and lochs for over a year waiting to steal Laird Broun's daughter, my betrothed, as she passed to the MacLomain clan. I willnae subject my children to an ageless foe." Iain took a deep swig from his goblet. "Clan MacLomain goes to war."

Silence followed. Only the spit of the fire and the distant sound of celebration could be heard.

"As does Clan MacLauchlin," Jordan said and stood. "Although having had little dealings with Clan Cochran, we have been purposefully dishonored this eve. For that alone, I long to sink my axe into the lot of them."

"'Twill be a long siege played out during the winter months. I dinnae call you here to ask for you to fight my friends but to let you know the intentions of your allied clan." Iain accepted Jordan's alliance and nodded once at the Chieftain of the MacLauchlin clan.

"A full out battle betwixt clans you say." Alan rubbed his palms together in delight. "What of the Laird of the Isle?"

"What of him? He has naught to do with this," Iain said, though he understood why the laird was mentioned. "I consider this a small matter, and once it is finished there will be our clan left or theirs. We've no qualms with the Laird of the Isle. He will care naught about this unless we lose, for his eye is always upon the land that borders his waters."

The truth was that the Laird of the Isle had more magic than the lot of them put together. His great-grandfather long ago made a peaceable pact between the two clans.

"The Cochran clan numbers many and their location borders to the north of our land." Alan's brow furrowed. "Our clan would suffer the worst if you were to fight and lose."

"Aye, my friend. 'Tis why I let you know my intentions," Iain said. Alan eyed him long and hard.

"Count us in." Alan chugged down the remnants of his drink and slammed the empty goblet upon the wooden table.

That left two.

"You have me." A telltale glint sparked David's eyes.

All turned to Lachlan.

"Well, where would my clansmen be if we turned from our allies at this crux in history?" Lachlan said. "But what of their allies? There is much to consider."

"The Cochran clan is not well liked, for they have proven themselves to be meddlesome. They will, however, find an ally with Clan MacEden in that their clans are generations upon generations of intermarriage as are ours. They count a few smaller clans allies as well." Iain sat with the men. "Clan Cochran will expect war having been so bold this eve. I believe they goad us intentionally for just such an outcome."

The men nodded their agreement, each of them lost in thoughts of strategy.

"Assuming 'tis just the two clans, how many warriors are we dealing with?" Jordan was eager for his enemies' blood.

"Clan Cochran's warriors nearly equal my own," Iain said. "Clan MacEden is as large as yours, Lachlan, which is half the size of mine."

Iain continued. "With all of our clans unified the advantage will lie in numbers. The disadvantage will be location. The Cochran's dwell high within the mountains. Their Chieftain has fortified his holding well these past few years. However, the man, like us, enjoys a good battle. It could be he has no intention of fighting from his castle at all. What fun is there for him in a long, drawn out siege?"

"Aye," David said. "Yet we must take care to think like the enemy. He is clever and has magic at his disposal."

Commotion clamored outside the door of the great hall. Iain stood and touched the hilt of the dagger at his waist when the doors were flung open. One of his men entered and shoved a boy to the floor before him. He tried to recover his footing when Iain kicked him back to the floor. Within seconds, he entered the lad's mind, interested to see and think things from his point of view.

"You wear the Cochran plaid. The odds are against you, lad," Iain said.

"He was found with a steed in the woods north of us.

He's the enemy's squire," his clansman said, then turned and left.

The boy looked up at the warriors surrounding him. The man who had kicked him back to the floor stood with his legs apart and his arms crossed over his wide chest. He was more intimidating than three of his own lairds wrapped into one man.

This must be the great Chieftain of Cowal. Shaking, he felt warm fluid run down his leg. Stories of this man traveled far and wide.

"I give you two choices." Promise dripped off every word. "Talk or die."

"If I do talk, what will become of me?" His voice quivered. Why bother betraying his clan if he was going to die anyway?

"Your words are braver than your actions." The Cowal Chieftain nodded to the urine pooling beneath him. "Take comfort in the fact that if I do decide to kill you after you talk, it will be a far quicker death than if you do not."

Disturbed by the dark glint in MacLomain's eyes, he pondered the threat but a moment. "What do you wish to know, my laird?"

He thought it best to bestow the giant warrior his proper title for the mercy he offered.

"Who is your laird?"

As if he didn't already know. He gulped. "Colin Cochran."

"What is he planning? Dinnae tell me you dinnae know because you are merely a squire for I'm no fool." The Chieftain pulled a dagger loose and held it by his thigh, allowing the fire to glint off its slick edges.

He licked his dry lips and wished he'd never eavesdropped on the warriors in his clan and truly knew nothing. Something dark and unfathomable lay within the great Chieftain's eyes. As though he could clearly see within a person and would know if they lied to him.

So he told the truth. "My laird intends a battle betwixt your clan and ours."

"He invites a siege upon his castle, then?"

"Nay, my laird. He intends to fight upon the open fields north of the Clan Stewart territory." He cringed as one of the other men with long black tresses sneered at him.

"Is he there now?"

"Nay, my laird. He will be there in a month's time. A messenger will arrive soon with the challenge."

"'Twould appear your laird saved himself the effort upon your capture." He was confused. What did he mean by that?

As if the Chieftain could read his very thoughts, he offered an explanation. "'Tis my belief you are the messenger."

He dwelled on that chunk of information. *Och. Laird Colin knew that I would be captured.*

'Twas not a good feeling to be betrayed by your clan, to realize your life had been forfeited. He withered under the wall of warriors and waited for the hammer to fall.

"'Twould appear Cochran had little faith in the magic man who now burns upon your fire outside." Alan gave Iain a devilish smile and chuckled.

"Does your laird intend to fight alone?" Iain asked the lad, though he already knew the answer.

"This I know naught, my laird."

The truth behind the lad's words confirmed him merely the enemies' messenger. "You will not die this night, lad." Iain motioned to Ferchar. He would not murder the boy. He'd been made to run a fool's errand.

"You will be held here and we will speak further at a later date." He turned away and left the boy's mind as Ferchar led the squire from the hall.

"I believe many questions have been answered this night comrades. There will be no long months waiting outside walls that spit arrows down upon us. No lines of provisions and supplies. No battering rams or hot oil poured over flimsy shields. 'Twill be clean fighting made of bloodlust and revenge." Iain turned back to the men. "My instinct tells me their numbers will be greater than anticipated...or they'll have stronger magic."

Iain again joined the men at the table. "We must wrap our minds around this before we proceed."

He laid his dagger on the table. One by one, the men followed suit and crossed their daggers over his.

Hours stretched as they talked strategy over the good omen asterisk of battle worn blades. Ferchar fetched more whiskey and ale. Highlanders relished the planning of a good battle.

The celebration continued outside as the Chieftains parlayed ideas off one another. When the midnight hour crept upon them they ended their discussion, content with their plans.

"My clan will leave this eve to journey home," Alan said. "My holding will be ready to receive you in less than two weeks time." He stood, clasped arms with his fellow lairds and then departed the hall.

People began to filter into the chamber to resume their festivities for the great bonfire outside was extinguished at midnight. Iain sent Muriel to check on Arianna. He craved to do so himself but this eve now demanded his presence more than ever.

Clan MacLomain and its allied clans would be going to war together.

Chapter Twelve

Muriel crept into the room to check on her sister.

"Hello." Arianna sat up in bed.

"You're awake." Muriel sat on the edge of the bed. "How do you feel?"

"I'm alright."

Muriel scowled. "Good, you've had a rough time of it here so far."

"'Tis not been that bad." Arianna grabbed Muriel's hand. "I need to speak with you before you rejoin the festivities. How are they keeping down there?"

"Ha. They're all blutered to be sure." Muriel chuckled. Scotsmen were a rowdy bunch when they consumed alcohol. She thought it best not to tell Arianna about the private conference the Chieftain's held and what was going to transpire. She'd been through enough this eve.

"Aye." Arianna chewed the corner of her lip. "I've a favor to ask of you."

Muriel nodded. "Of course. Anything."

"I need to speak with the Shaman."

"Why?" Muriel had a bad feeling. What could her sister possibly want with Adlin?

"'Tis not of import to you, my friend. I ask only that you trust me." Arianna seemed genuine.

Muriel twisted her lips. What harm could there be letting her speak with the Shaman? Adlin was Iain's mentor after all.

"Well, I suppose that I could arrange such."

"Would this night be possible?" Arianna said.

"This night?" Her sister asked a lot of her. "'Tis not for me to say if it can be done. People would question his absence. He is Shaman. I will tell him that you wish to speak with him. However, I make no promises. 'Tis the last night of Samhain."

Arianna threw her arms around Muriel. "You have my eternal gratitude."

Muriel straightened. "'Twould not be appropriate for him to come to this chamber, Arianna."

"What's at the top of the tower at the end of the hall closest to this room?" Arianna asked.

"At present, nothing." Muriel understood the implication and stood.

"I will ensure the guards posted outside your door slumber but go quietly none-the-less for there are more posted on the wall walk."

Iain would crucify her for this. What harm could come of it though? The enemy was in custody and besides that, she wasn't pleased with her brother. She thought of Laird David dancing with her earlier. She knew what Iain intended. It wasn't going to happen.

"Thank you so much, Muriel," Arianna said from across the room as Muriel closed the door behind her.

Time to deal with the guards.

****

Arianna dressed and went to the door. She opened it a crack and peaked out. One man slept against the wall on either side. She waved her hand in front of one of their faces. Out cold.

Muriel knew magic too. She would've never guessed.

Arianna kept to the shadows and made her way up the narrow, spiraling stairway to a small room bathed in moonlight. She closed the door behind her. A single cot was snuggled into the far corner and a simple wooden chair stood beside it. She crossed the room and stood before a window with a rounded top and flat bottom.

Arianna waited and enjoyed the glorious view. Cowal was encrusted in silver shards of ice. The loch slithered beneath the white moon and digested flat wisps of clouds on the horizon. Tall pine trees swayed in the wind. From here they looked black and muscled, as though they were the shadows of the warriors who dominated this land.

"My child."

Arianna gasped. Aldin stood beside her. Long, alabaster hair floated weightless over his floor length white robes. His timeless gaze was afire with sapphire flame within the darkness of the stone chamber.

She felt in the presence of a god and lowered her head. He was a man worthy of kneeling before.

He took her elbow and shook his head. "Do not kneel before me lass. I am naught better than any other."

"Nay, but you are," she said. "I've thought so since meeting you."

"For one who just ken the existence of magic, I am pleased by your ready acceptance. Most would think themselves daft."

His voice sounded musical and young. He must've been beautiful in his youth.

"I was well sought after by the ladies." He chortled.

Heat rose to Arianna's face. He read her every thought. She breathed deep and tested the waters. *"So we can converse this way?"* She spoke in her mind.

"But of course my child, if that would please you."

"It's much more discreet." It felt strange not using her mouth to communicate. His words echoing within her mind were as real as her own thoughts, yet carried their own unique impression. His individual essence.

"I've asked you here because I have a request."

"I know, lass"

Startled, she narrowed her gaze at the wizard. A wizard to be sure.

"Yes, my girl, 'tis a most appropriate description." White eyebrows arched over the twinkle in his eyes.

There were no secrets here. *"Then you know why I requested you?"*

"Aye." Serene in countenance, his thin, vein-ridden fingers clasped over his robe.

"So you understand where I'm from? You understand I'm from a different time?"

"I ken my child." His simple words eased her.

"Good." Arianna leaned against the stone wall. How wonderful it was to know at least one person in this world understood her plight.

"Dinnae fear lass. 'Twas all meant to be."

"Meant to be? I have traveled back in time to a land and way so unlike my own." She was sure she must have screeched mentally.

"You have traveled back to your own land, no?" He placed a warm hand on her arm in reassurance.

"Aye, but I'm in my own past." It was time to talk aloud. Tears began to fall.

"Indeed, you shimmer upon the waves of time. Travel such as yours is rare. Ken this, though you are in a time you were not born into matters little. You are alive. You continue to live your life as was told before your birth. Being here is part of your time among mortals. 'Tis just the present for you, part of the pre-destined life you were meant to live."

Befuddled, Arianna gazed out the window and contemplated the old man's riddles.

"Write what you will upon a scroll and place it on this window sill. I will do what you wish. 'Twill come to pass when you make a prayer to the god of the ocean for its safe passage. He will hold it safely within his coral pocket. When the time is right he will roll it through the mighty waves of his salty fingers until it lands in the hands of whom you seek."

He knew her plan. "Will I return home?"

"'Tis not for me to divulge, my child." His long, bony forefinger grazed the sill as he spoke.

"What of Iain if I do?" Arianna felt helpless, frustrated by the wizard's passive response.

The door to the small room whipped open and smacked off the rock wall. Arianna spun.

Iain ducked through the entranceway, obviously enraged, his arms akimbo as his gaze swept the room. He spied her and narrowed his eyes.

Arianna looked to the old shaman only to discover he'd vanished. She moved, but not quickly enough. Iain closed the distance between them, grabbed her arms and pushed her against the wall. "Talk fast. Explain."

"I was restless." She turned her head from the wrath in his eyes.

He turned her face back to him. "So you wandered to the top of my tower? Tell me lass, who did you seek?"

"No one, I but strayed with curiosity." *He looks so furious!* She could smell the whiskey on his breath. His eyes burned her. The lower half of his face was encased within the shadows. Though he released her face, his strong fingers continued to both strangle and caress her arms.

Iain searched her face searching for truth. She jutted out her chin. This time she knew his mind touched hers. It felt far different than Adlin's. Far more sexy and ruthless. She knew he found nothing there. Her memories of meeting with Adlin were hers alone. How interesting.

"I came to check on you. You were missing." If possible, his expression turned stormier. "My guards slumber within magic. Someone will suffer and I've a good idea who."

Arianna started to defend Muriel but stopped. Perhaps he spoke of someone else? Before she had a chance to ask who, Iain lifted her upon the sill of the window. He spread her legs and placed his body between them. Wrapping his hands around her slender waist he pulled her close. An instant sweet ache rose between her legs.

Arianna put her hands to his chest and struggled to move. Locked within his well-muscled arms, his lips crashed down on hers. His tongue crawled inside her mouth, seeking and searching as his talented hands pushed up her dress. She moaned as heady sensation poured thick, hot lava down to her core. His liquored lips violated her with sugared ecstasy. His hard member burned against her inner thigh.

"My Arianna," he murmured between kisses. Riveted, he trailed them along her jaw then nibbled her earlobe. "How you affect me."

"Iain." She pushed at his chest but spread her legs wider. "No."

He returned to her mouth and kissed her so deeply any protest vanished. Wrapping her hands around the back of his neck, she pushed against his arousal. He pulled his lips away and trailed them down her neck, his hot breath leaving a trail of pure fire.

"Too soon," he murmured.

Before she realized his intent, he'd fallen to his knees and pushed her dress up further. What was he doing? Mortified, she cried, "Get up. No!"

But he didn't listen. Leaning forward his tongue flicked out and lapped her center. *Oh, sweet Heaven!* Vaguely aware she sat in a window hundreds of feet above ground she clasped the stone walls on either side.

"No," she repeated, only to realize she whispered her denial. His lips and tongue were swiping, licking, tickling her private place in such rapid succession, Arianna moaned in pure pleasure. The man had talent. When his hot slippery tongue found her core, her head fell back. It almost felt as though his needy tongue sought to sooth away the last remnants of slight pain left behind from losing her virginity.

In. Out. Up. Down. Swirling. All the while returning to her precious little nub. Digging her nails into the stone surface, she grinded her teeth together and arched.

So close. So very close.

With one final thrust and twirl he pushed her over the edge. This time the feeling ricocheted straight from her core to the tips of her breasts, to the tips of her toes and fingers. Her eyes rolled and she fell backward, unable to resist the pure rush of perfection riding over her body.

The last words she heard were, "Bloody hell, no!"

Instantly sober, Iain jumped up and grabbed Arianna as she fell backward.

What had he done? Lifting her now slumbering body into his arms, he turned and leaned back against the wall and hung his head. *I almost lost her!* Indeed, she'd almost fell right out of the window. *Och, but I've never tasted anything so sweet.*

He lifted his head and stared down into her face. Not once in his life had he acted so impetuously. He was laird, the Chieftain of one of the most powerful clans in Scotland, and this wee lass had brought him to his knees, made him want to please her so much that damn the consequences.

But he'd done it in a rage. He'd done it while drunk.

Watching the way her eyelashes fluttered in her slumber and the way her lips murmured useless words made him feel weak. As though he was no longer in control of himself. *No, I'm not weak. This is but lust.*

Standing tall, he carried her down to their room. What if she told him the truth? What if she were from a different time? If magic existed, why couldn't time-travel. Though he'd sworn to himself he wouldn't, Iain briefly touched her mind. He found nothing there unusual. In fact, she was rather closed off. Some people were. Yet had she traveled through time he'd know. Such an event would surely remain. He fully intended to teach her how to open her mind to him as the years went by.

He gently laid her in bed and covered her still form. How could he have done such a thing this eve? Frowning, he turned and left the room.

****

Once she knew he'd left the room, Arianna slowly opened her eyes. What was Iain thinking? She'd spied the sad look on his face when he left the room. The man of her dreams. The mighty Laird of Cowal. The fierce warrior.

She could admit she craved more from him now. Everything snapped into focus after she spoke with the Shaman. If this man was meant to be her husband in the life God pre-ordained that she live, Arianna wanted everything. She would accept nothing less than his heart.

The truth left her on guard. She wanted everything and there was a woman coming who was supposed to be his wife. Arianna knew when she arrived the situation would turn catastrophic. She couldn't stay for that.

She was in love.

If Arianna stayed she would lose him. If she left she would lose him. She lost either way. Why stay and face some horrible punishment? The indecision wracked her with remorse. She turned onto her side and curled into a ball. She could only pray for an answer to her plight.

What seemed like mere minutes later she awoke to the sound of heavy rain. Arianna opened her eyes. Dismal light flooded the chamber.

She stared at the canopy overhead. *I'm in his bed. Our bed.* Rolling over, she gazed at the tapestry of loch Fyne. The fire was fed at some point and crackled brightly across the cool, damp room. Wind blew against the castle walls and caused an eerie howl.

She was alone in the bed. What would it feel like to have a man sleep beside her? Arianna pushed the blanket aside and sat up. A light blue dress lay on a massive trunk by the door.

She dressed and stepped into the hall.

The men posted outside her door nodded. The holding was silent. As she passed the tower walk she spied the men that faithfully kept their posts. Like ancient marble statues, they stood regal. Sheets of rain carved their strong, chiseled stances.

She made her way down to the hall. Many men slumbered at random on the trestle tables. Arianna stopped at the threshold of the hall. She had nowhere to go. Rain consumed the countryside.

"My lady."

She turned to Ferchar. "Good to see someone awake down here."

"Aye." His smile didn't quite reach his eyes. "I can do naught but offer you a seat by my fire, 'tis located in the warrior's quarters."

She was allowed in the warrior's quarters?

He placed a hand on her shoulder when she blushed.

"I can assure you that this day, not only do they all sleep, but they are well attired."

"I see." She really didn't *see* but wanted to find Iain, needed to talk to him. "Then I accept your offer."

Ferchar waved a servant over. "We will need a plaid."

The servant nodded and fled. He returned in short time. Ferchar took the plaid and held it over her head.

"Please walk with care, 'tis very slippery." They left the hall and walked quickly to the building not fifty feet out. By the time they reached the quarters the plaid was drenched, as was Ferchar.

When they entered the door she stopped short. Iain slumped; sound asleep in a chair amidst his slumbering clansmen.

Ferchar led her to a chair before the fire where she welcomed a mug of warm, spiced wine given to her.

"I knew you would come." Ferchar's voice was so soft she barely heard him.

Arianna frowned. She'd heard the gossip about the woman named Arianna Broun from this time. That she loved her father's warrior. Ferchar had apparently believed in this girl's devotion to her clan and not the rumors. What should she say?

"I'm most grateful that you had such faith in a stranger." That sounded good.

He gave her an odd look. "You dinnae ken."

Arianna met his eyes. "What do you mean?"

He seemed to reconsider what he was going to say.

"Naught, my lady. I mean naught. You are meant for my laird, 'tis all." His eyes returned to the fire.

"Does that displease you?"

"Certainly not. You are a treasure." His cheeks reddened.

"Indeed she is, lad."

Iain suddenly stood behind them. Black whiskers darkened a chiseled chin. His eyes were bleary but exceptionally green. Tousled black hair and a sleepy look only enhanced his natural sexuality. And those amazing lips...

It became hard to breathe when he stood directly behind her. He rested his hands on her shoulders. Caught by the feel of his touch, Arianna closed her eyes. She didn't want to make him upset again. But she would.

"My laird." Ferchar greeted him.

Iain gave no response to Ferchar but ran one finger along her jaw. He leaned forward and whispered in her ear. "You are so very... sweet, my lass. I'd prefer another taste of you to break my fast."

"My laird." Overwhelming heat infused her body and beaded on her skin in response to his very private, very provocative words. He obviously wasn't upset any longer. With a crooked grin and a slow wink, he accepted a mug from a servant.

"Scoundrel," Arianna said.

"Well, I do." Iain went to stand before the flames.

"Wish what you like, my laird." She graced him with a teasing smile and her body filled with sudden longing. Arianna turned her attention to her mug save he see how he affected her. The man had the devil in him.

"Will we ready the hall and bunkers soon?" Ferchar asked. He did well to feign indifference to the sensual banter between the laird and his wife.

"Aye, lad." Iain's expression remained impassive.

"For what?" Arianna glanced from uncle to nephew.

Something was amiss. Ferchar shot her a concerned look and then excused himself. She'd never seen anyone move so fast.

Iain gazed beyond her at the men sleeping.

"Iain?"

He met her inquisitive gaze. "I've been up 'til the wee hours with my men, lass. I'm weary. We'll speak of this later."

Clear as day, she heard his thoughts. *It bothers me to tell her this. I hope she drops the subject.* Frowning, Arianna said, "Tell me now."

Iain contemplated her for several long seconds before responding, "I will be leaving soon."

"Leaving?" Arianna threw the word in his face as she stood. "And where will you go after I have come so far to be with you?"

It mattered naught that she thought to leave him. Let him think that she had traveled across the whole of Scotland for all she cared. He was leaving her?

"'Tis a war long overdue."

"War?" She spoke loudly. "You've got to be kidding me."

Men raised their heads from slumber in interest. Iain grabbed her arm, held a plaid over her head and led her outside. Before they got to the door of the castle, she pulled away. She struggled to gain footing in the slick mud underfoot and refused his aid.

"What war?" Arianna wouldn't take another step.

"This is no place to discuss this." Heads poked out from the surrounding buildings, eager for gossip.

"This place suits me just fine," she said. His black hair was soaked and plastered against his head. "It'd probably do your cloudy head some good anyway."

Random snickers emanated from the shield of rain.

"Feisty wench of a woman," Iain muttered. He lunged forward and threw her over his shoulder. Her legs flailed as he brought her through the doors of his castle and plunked her in front of the fire. A servant handed him a blanket and he threw it over her shoulders.

Arianna shoved the blanket away. The last thing she wanted was comfort. The hall was clear of slumbering men in an instant. How convenient it must be to have the world at your whim.

Iain picked up the blanket and handed it back to her. "Don't aggravate me, lass."

He appeared more concerned than angry. With a shiver she took the blanket back and patted her hair.

"Hear me out." His statement sounded heavy with compassion.

Anger deflated, she sank into a chair while he told her his tale. Tears welled but didn't fall. Iain would leave in a week. He was going to fight. He was leaving her. She stayed silent after he finished and watched the fire ride the logs. Her nineteen years suddenly felt elongated and stretched.

Life had too many facets.

"I dreamt of you. Long before we met. In a different time than this." Though she whispered the words, he heard her. Iain's expression remained blank and his gaze far away as he stood before the fire.

"I love you." Arianna wasn't sure if she thought it or said it.

Iain didn't look at her but left.

How could he? Iain had walked away when she'd given him her heart, as though her words meant nothing. Perhaps the love had always been one sided. After all, he had been with her for so long and been there when she remembered the truth about her parents. It its own way, it felt as though he'd saved her from the guilt she felt she should suffer. He had freed her.

But had she done anything for him to truly love her?

There was no way of knowing. Yet the thought that her feelings weren't reciprocated hurt deeply. Still, she would not cry. The time had passed for tears. Arianna accepted a goblet from a lone servant boy who appeared before her.

"Fear naught, lass," the blond haired servant boy said. Lost in thought she gave him an absent glimpse.

When he turned away Arianna could have sworn she saw the Shaman in his young profile. She sat up and looked around.

The boy had disappeared.

Chapter Thirteen

Iain wasn't sure how long he sat before the small fire in his chamber. His clan would be going to war within the week but all he could think about was Arianna.

Instead of contemplating the numbers his enemy would host, he imagined her soft hair in his hands and her languid eyes as they seduced him. Instead of considering provisions for his warrior's journey, he remembered the pain in her gaze when he told her he was leaving. What had become of him? She was naught but a lass. She knew nothing of *love*.

Any more than he did for that matter.

He couldn't sit still any longer so he joined his men on the wall walk. Sheets of rain continued to pour down. Pleased to have their laird join them, they voiced their approval of the up and coming battle. Iain knew none desired to be left behind to guard the castle. The taste of war was already upon their lips.

He took a few minutes and spoke to them of sure victory. When he left, new men appeared to reprieve those who had stood watch through the eve and morn.

Down in the hall, Arianna sat with Muriel and Helen in front of the fire. Little Catherine was at their feet while they taught Arianna how to create a tapestry. Odd she would not already know how to do such a thing.

Their eyes met for a moment before he sat at one of the tables. He accepted a mug of ale and continued to watch his wife. Her hair was braided and wrapped about her head. None of the women adorned veils. He disliked them. What was the point in hiding beauty?

He made it known long ago he did not expect the women of his clan to wear them if they did not wish to. Scottish royalty could do what they would. He didn't have to.

Muriel's midnight hair covered her face as she leaned down to whisper something in Catherine's ear. The child's laughter peeled across the room in merriment. Her brown curls bounced when she jumped up to point at a patch of Helen's tapestry.

"My laird." Hugh sat down across from him.

Iain's mouth watered when a wooden platter full of thick slices of beef and venison was placed between them. When had he last eaten? He grabbed a piece of beef and sank his teeth into it. Chewing, he contemplated the man across from him. Hugh was Iain's best man. Devoted, loyal and quick of wit, he'd earned his place with good reason. Iain drank from his mug and waited for Hugh to make his move.

"I must speak with you" Hugh grabbed a slice of Bannock still warm from the fire.

"Aye." Iain met his eyes.

"'Tis regarding your sister."

"What of my sister?" Iain pushed his food aside.

"I wish to marry her."

Iain's brow shot up. "Marry her?"

"Aye," he said.

"Why?" Iain noticed that the women had quieted. "It better be an excellent reason."

"I love her." Hugh looked at Muriel.

"Love?" Iain laughed. "That is no reason to marry."

Muriel stood abruptly and flew up the stairs. Arianna pursued her.

"'Tis the best reason that exists. Do you not wish your sister to be loved?" Hugh looked troubled. 'Twas obvious he had not expected this.

"I have no doubt she will be when the time is right. You are too young mayhap to understand the difference between love and lust." Iain dug into the newly presented porridge.

"Nay, I know the difference," Hugh countered. "I believe I'm the same age as your new bride. Do you think her not capable of loving you? 'Twould be a pity if she was too young to return the love you feel for her already."

Iain stopped, his food half way to his mouth. "Muriel is intended for someone else."

There was not shock, but a touch of defiance on Hugh's face at this news. "David?"

"'Tis not your concern," Iain said.

Hugh stood and excused himself.

"'Tis for the best, Hugh. You will thank me in the end," Iain said when Hugh reached the door.

Hugh turned slightly. "You are wrong about that, my friend."

Before Iain had a chance to respond, Hugh left.

Iain lost his appetite. 'Twould be a better match, Muriel with David. He held Hugh in the highest regard but it was just youth at its best betwixt him and Muriel. This planned marriage thickened the tie the two clans already shared. His fellow laird would have his sister. It only made sense.

He went and sat before the fire. Helen and Catherine had left as well. Iain closed his eyes.

"How could you?" He groaned and opened his eyes. Muriel stood over him, her hands planted on her hips. He should've seen this coming.

"You are but a child." He sighed and sat up.

"Am I? Old enough to marry but too young to fall in love?"

"Muriel, you dinnae—" His words were cut off.

"Nay, brother, I'll hear none of it. I will not marry David. I love Hugh." Muriel leaned closer. "Hugh; your first in command, your closest friend, a man far closer to my age than David. How could you not approve of him? He has been naught but loyal to you always."

"What do you know of love, Muriel?" Time to be shrewd with his sister. "I seem to remember a time you thought yourself in love with Alexander, Fergus and Kenneth."

"Irrelevant. I was a mere babe." She glared with fury.

'Twas just a summer ago." Iain laughed.

"This is different, 'tis Hugh." Muriel stopped him before he spoke further. "Don't throw your own fate upon my shoulders. Don't marry me off to a stranger. Allow me to marry who I wish."

Anger surfaced. Do not throw his fate upon her shoulders?

"Do you not see what has come of my fate? Arianna? A beautiful woman who will share a future with me. Do you think my fate so bad?"

"Nay brother. Your fate served you well because you love one another. I can never love David when I will always love Hugh."

Iain snarled. "I do not love, Arianna."

Muriel looked at him with pity. "You are a fool, brother."

"You will marry, David."

Muriel stood tall. "I will not. I will marry Hugh. With or without your consent."

Iain clenched his jaw. Ignorant youth. Hugh would not betray him.

Muriel walked to the door of the hall and stopped at the threshold. "Mayhap, David might not want me now."

Iain spun. "What, pray tell, do you mean by that?"

Muriel shot him a triumphant grin. "I think you ken."

Before he could reach her she was out the door and lost within the dim dreariness of a rainy twilight. He stood in the rain. It fell like a waterfall and masked everything beyond.

This day had gone from bad to worse. Blasted Scottish lassies.

He did not love Arianna. How could Muriel say such? No doubt because she was a lass with romantic ideas. The trouble with romantic ideas was that they didn't stand up well in reality. They didn't keep a warrior safe in the battlefield or ensure their bairns a Da if they died while fighting.

The best answer was always lust, affection and stability...never love.

****

Arianna almost felt bad for him... almost.

"You just continue to swim upriver, aye?" Arianna sat on a stair, elbows on her knees and rested her chin in her hands.

Standing in the rain, obviously unwilling to chase after his sister, Iain narrowed his eyes. "If there was ever a time to hold your tongue lass, 'tis now."

He stepped inside, removed his wet tunic and strode to the fire. Arianna followed. She'd heard every word. He did not love her. Pain ripped through her at his earlier declaration but she couldn't change what was. To love someone who did not return that love was a true travesty.

"You're wrong you know." She tried to keep her gaze on his face but failed miserably. A light trail of black hair trickled down his bronze chest. His blue and green plaid hung low on his hips. Sinewy muscles were carved by firelight.

"Your opinion in this matter is irrelevant."

"That's the problem, amongst many others."

Arianna tossed her braid free hair back, amazed by how calm she felt.

Iain ran his hand along the back of his neck as he faced the fire. "Have at it, lass, seems the day is ripe for it."

"Okay, shall I start with my opinion regarding your sister or that regarding us?" His muscles flexed when he stretched his arms toward the flames.

"Well, you may as well start with Muriel because once you speak of us there will likely be little talk."

She tried to ignore his sidelong smoldering look. "She loves him, Iain. Though you may not understand nor care, her feelings are genuine. I've watched them both, as have you. Having done such, you must surely realize that the two will act upon their love, preferably with your blessing. They will marry without it if necessary. Time will take care of the details, but if you force her into something she does not desire, she is lost to you forever, one way or another."

Arianna touched his arm. "I have perceived in my short time here that your relationship with your sister deserves more than what you presented tonight."

"Well said." He peered at her intently. "But there is more to this than the whimsy of two people lusting after one another."

"So you will force her to marry someone she cares nothing for?"

"I will do what is best for the clan. Muriel is too young to understand the dynamics."

"Just as our marriage was best for the clan?" Arianna pulled her hand away. "So you subject your sister to the same prison your Da did you."

"I think we make a good match, lass." He snapped. "'Tis not so bad a prison."

There was no more painful prison than to love and not be loved. "So you say but we are closer in years."

"Years?" Iain yawned. "Age means nothing."

"Perhaps not to you but Muriel will be forced to marry someone nearly twice her age." Arianna grimaced. "That may mean naught to you, but I certainly wouldn't want to be in her position."

"She will adjust. He is not so old his seed is not good."

Ugh. Men. Arianna took tally. "'Tis my belief that this has more to do with you going back on your word. You promised her to him years ago, didn't you?"

The flicker of approval in his eyes told her she'd made a valid point. He reached over and played with an escaped curl teasing her cheekbone. "What of us?"

This wouldn't do. Her wits separated into fragments when he touched her. She turned away. "We cannot be."

"Look at me woman when you say such things and remember that we are married so we *will* be." He turned her back.

"Why did you leave earlier when I told you I dreamt of you?" *And I told you I loved you. But that would not be voiced again.*

His intense eyes flared for a moment before he softly said, "Because I have done the same, Arianna."

Taken aback, she stared up at him. "You have?"

"Aye."

The fire snapped louder on the hearth, eager to drown the silence of the huge hall. The many torch flames on the walls narrowed into elongated needles of orange. Living smoke caressed the ceiling far overhead, then stopped its flow and waited.

Iain peered at her, his gaze far away. "We sat upon a small bed in a wooden room with a low ceiling. The windows were covered with clear stone. The furnishings were foreign and fanciful. Your hair was wet as you sat with your family plaid strewn across your lap." His eyes fell to her lips. "I wanted to kiss you. Cover your lips with mine until we were but one person."

Breathe. Just breathe. If Arianna ever needed a breath, it was now. She stumbled backwards and landed in a chair. Her heartbeat increased. "You then told me I was meant to marry a MacLomain while you fingered the plaid upon my lap and pulled me closer, aye?"

He nodded. "'Twas magic of course."

"When did you have your dream?" Arianna was perplexed.

His lips thinned as his mind worked. "I believe it was the day before you arrived. Was that your chamber in your Da's holding?" He sat in the chair next to her.

"'Twas my chamber, but not where you think. This dream of yours must help you to understand I'm not who you think I am?"

"'Twas very different in appearance," he conceded. "But you are not from these parts Arianna. No doubt the living structures are not the same. What was that clear stone? I'd like some for the castle."

"Iain, you traveled to my time." Arianna shook her head. "As I have traveled here many times in my dreams. It matters naught, unless you've had another of us, have you?"

"Nay, just the one," he said. "As strange as this may seem, luv, 'tis all explained easily enough through magic."

"I do not dispel your notion of magic being behind this. The dream you had of me was real, that was my bedroom in America. The clear stone is called glass."

She thought it best not to tell him how it was made. Things were created when they were created for a reason. Of that, she felt certain.

Iain crossed his well-muscled legs out in front of him and clasped his hands behind his head.

"America." His thick brogue shredded the word to such a comical degree she almost laughed.

"Aye, that's right. I was born in Scotland, but in the year 1780. I moved abroad in the year 1790. You visited me in the year 1799."

One eyebrow shot up. "I've not heard of such a land Arianna, where is it?"

Well, this was certainly more of a response than she'd ever got from him!

"Far across the ocean to the west." She dared not hope he was serious. "There is a great stretch of land yet uncharted."

Iain shook his head and frowned. "'Tis well known there is nothing beyond the great ocean."

Sensitive to his reaction, Arianna thought before she spoke. She wanted to tell him so much of her history and the future but she was wary. What good would come from telling him that Scotland would eventually succumb to England? How could she tell him that the clan system that was his life would be destroyed?

Besides, it would be impossible for someone from this century to be able to fathom mankind roaming the whole of the planet.

"I'm not the Arianna Broun born into this time," she repeated. What else could she say? "She is still out there."

"Och, Arianna, how could you exist in two places at once?"

"We are not the same person. I am, perhaps, a descendant." Arianna realized how ridiculous she sounded.

Iain groaned and leaned forward. "I would like to know what happened when you traveled here from Lothlian." His eyes pleaded with her.

"I cannot give you that. If I could I would. Do you wish me to make up a story based on rumors? I will not lie."

A length of silence ensued before he spoke again. "I see."

"I'm sorry," she said.

The two sat in silence for a long time watching the fire. Mystery shrouded them from one another, a particular confusion born less from distance but from fine tuned evasiveness. Yet, she knew deep down inside that Iain was more comfortable with her than any other person he had met in his life. She felt the same.

Soon enough, lulled by the fire and the easy comfort of his company, Arianna felt herself nod off.

When Iain looked back at her, Arianna's head had dropped to one side in slumber. His heart twisted at the sight of her sleeping face. So angelic.

Standing, he lifted Arianna and carried her to their bed where he laid her down then simply gazed at her. He could look at her forever.

'Twas indeed strange that they'd shared a dream. Iain could not deny she struck him out of sorts at times. Her reaction to his fellow clansmen was unusual in that she was raised around such. Her accent had a strange bite to it but that could merely be normal in the eastern lowlands. He'd touched her mind and saw nothing.

It mattered naught.

Arianna was his now. She slept in his castle. Crawling into bed, he pulled her close, watched her through drowsy lids and realized something.

I'm content for the first time in my life.
****

For the remainder of her days, Arianna would remember the first time she awoke next to Iain in his bed. How tenderly he watched her.

"Hello." He lay on his side with his head propped on one elbow. His eyes caressed her face.

"Hello." Arianna pulled up the blanket, embarrassed. "How long have you been watching me?" *Say you just awoke.*

"Does it matter?" Iain grazed his thumb along her eyebrow.

She must look horrible. Heat scorched her face. "Do I strike you as that immodest?"

"You are lovely, Arianna. Even more so when you sleep." His thumb continued over her other eyebrow. "Besides, to my greatest regret, you're fully clothed."

Arianna pulled the blanket tighter against her.

"Well, then, I suppose you're not a complete blackguard."

Though it remained horrible to realize he didn't love her, being near him like this seemed to make the heartache vanish.

His eyes fell to her lips and then down lower. "Are you so sure?"

She met his eyes when they returned to hers. *Oh!*

"I'm not ready for—"

His thumb fell to her lower lip and held the next word at bay. "Were you ready the other day in the forest?"

Her heartbeat quickened when his thumb left her mouth and he slowly pulled down the blanket. When he leaned over and fastened his wet mouth over her nipple, her eyes fluttered and she raised her knees.

His sure hand cupped her mound and he kneaded the tender, wanting flesh with the heel of his palm. With little whimpers of pleasure she bit her lower lip. He left her nether region to skim his hand lightly up beneath her chemise and over her stomach. When the tips of his weapon-toughened fingers grazed the ultra-sensitive underside of her breasts, she sighed in bliss.

The slow, easy way he seduced her had her pulse skittering and her mind swimming. "Iain," she whispered.

"Aye, lass," he responded softly. "Tell me what you want. What you like."

Dreamy, eyes half closed, she wanted to give him some of what he gave her. Slowly, Arianna slid her hand over and down until she found the hard length she knew would be there. She liked the way his entire body stiffened and a low moan escaped his lips when her fingers brushed the soft, weeping tip of his member.

"Iain?" Arthur's voice boomed along with his fist on the other side of the door.

"Bloody hell." Iain growled. "Not now, man!"

"Aye. Now," Author repeated.

Arianna pulled the blanket over her as Iain frowned and left the bed. It appeared this was an unusual thing for Arthur to do.

Something was wrong.

Chapter Fourteen

Still in his clothes from the previous day, Iain crossed the chamber and swung open the door.

Arthur's face was as red as his hair. "We have a problem. Follow me."

"Stay here, Arianna." Iain flung the command over his shoulder and fled the chamber.

She bolted out of bed. His intended bride must be here! Arianna couldn't stay. In fact, she intended to be far from here when Iain discovered the truth.

Unfortunately, there was only one way out.

Stealth was her only hope. Thankfully, there were no guards outside the room and very few men on the wall walk. This may be easier than anticipated.

Unless, that is, everyone is in the main hall.

When she reached the next landing, her fear was confirmed. A great many people were down below. What she saw there was the last thing she expected.

The door was ajar. Wind driven sheets of rain formed a puddle at the entranceway. About thirty servants and clansmen stood frozen. Arthur and Iain had stopped halfway down the stairs. Helen and Catherine were huddled at a table.

Oh no. Her heart stopped. She gripped the stone balustrade.

Malcolm had Muriel pulled up against him with a dagger to her neck. Hugh stood mere feet from the two.

"Don't bother with your magic," Malcolm barked at Iain.

"This blade is protected, as am I."

"I gathered as much," Iain drawled.

Malcolm looked composed despite the situation. Muriel kept her gaze on Hugh who held a knife at his side.

Malcolm smiled when he spoke. "'Tis a shame it had to come to this so soon. I'd hoped to sample a taste of your lass first." His eyes traveled up to where Arianna stood.

"She widnae have had you if you tried," Muriel choked.

His knife dug deeper into her throat.

Hugh took a step forward.

"Step back." Malcolm rolled his eyes. "If you manage to kill me be quite sure I will take Muriel along."

"What do you intend to do, Malcolm? You'll never make it out of here with her," Hugh said, though he took a step back. "And know this, when I kill you, which will happen very soon, you willnae be bringing my lass with you."

Malcolm laughed, and then turned serious as his attention again focused on Iain. "I intend to see this clan smothered. Extinct."

"And what of you Malcolm?" Iain's brows shot up. "Do you think Colin Cochran will let even one MacLomain live? Are you that invaluable to him?"

A muscle twitched in Malcolm's cheek. "I am a Cochran now. Two weeks ago I was married to Laird Colin's niece."

If Iain was shocked by the news, it didn't show. "Well then, I guess you're right. Clan MacLomain is surely doomed."

Malcolm sneered at Iain's sarcasm. "Not entirely. That is where you are wrong. Not all of your clan is doomed. After all, Muriel will soon be the wife of Colin Cochran and my mistre—"

A dagger slammed into the back of his wrist and the knife fell from Muriel's neck. The next dagger lodged itself deep within the center of his forehead.

His mouth fell and his eyes popped wide with shock.

Muriel flew into Hugh's arms as Malcolm slumped to the floor.

Iain walked down the stairs, crossed the hall and knelt over Malcolm. Arianna and Arthur were close behind.

He removed the daggers Hugh had thrown, stood and turned back to where Muriel stood within his clansman's embrace. With practiced ease, he wiped the blades clean and handed them to Hugh.

One side of Iain's mouth inched up a fraction and his eyes held pride. "Well, my friend. I'd say it's time that you married my sister."

Muriel ran to Iain and embraced him. "Oh, I knew you'd come around."

Arianna was amazed by how calm everyone seemed. Then again, she supposed in this era they were well used to violence.

Iain smiled. "Hugh won you fairly, sister. He saved your life."

Iain turned his attention to his first in command.

"How did you manage to get your weapons past him?"

Hugh's face broke into a wide smile and he nodded toward the door. "I had a little help."

Everyone turned to look as Adlin materialized from the curtain of rain. His hair and robes were dry. "A fine day to do away with a traitor, wouldn't you say?"

Iain nodded. "I'd say so. To you I'm most obliged."

"'Twas nothing at all." Adlin looked down at the lifeless body at his feet. "Scandalous fellow, aye?"

"'Twould appear so." Iain turned to a nearby clansman. "Have the body tied to a horse and sent to Colin Cochran. The corpse should be ripe by then."

"What was it between you and Malcolm?" Arianna asked when they commenced before the fire. All thoughts of fleeing were gone for now.

Iain took two goblets from a servant. "Simple jealousy."

"Ahhh." Arianna took one of the offered goblets. "And what was he jealous of?"

"My brother's position," Muriel said and sat on the edge of a table closest to the fire.

Hugh stood behind her with his hand on her shoulders, his voice low when he spoke. "When one is raised to be jealous, the emotion is only intensified."

"Without a doubt." Iain looked at Arianna. "Malcolm's father, my eldest cousin, who died years ago, sired his son at the mere age of twelve. 'Twas always his strongest desire to become laird of this clan. When he realized there was no hope of that happening he became bitter, resentful. He taught his child only hatred and malice."

Arianna shook her head. "Such a shame."

"Well, 'tis over now. Malcolm had no children to ruin, as his father did him," Muriel declared.

Arthur grabbed a huge mug of ale, held it high and grinned at Hugh and Muriel. "Here's to the end of one generation and the beginning of another!"

The MacLomains raised their cups and saluted the future.

Rain gushed from the skies for three days. The loch swelled and the land sunk into great murky puddles of mud. Autumn's colors were glossed over and dull.

The women and children of the clan remained hidden within their homes. Warriors came and went from the great hall to eat. The bulk of time was spent in preparation for war.

Arianna passed her days with the women of the household. She spent her nights talking with her new husband and was pleased by his profound intellect. He could read and write, which was a great feat in this day. His passion lay within the structure of leading such a large clan. Endless hours were spent in front of their chamber fire as he told her the clan's history. Every tale told was recounted with great pride.

Each day she woke and decided that this would be the day she would flee. Day turned into night and then into day again. Still, she did not go.

Arianna decided to tell him the bits of her life he could understand. She described her family. Iain never asked her to speak of her father, whom he thought was the Broun clan laird. She talked of her horse and her love for the woodlands of her home, which of course made sense to him. Arianna allowed his imagination to picture her accounts taking place on the eastern shores of this time.

He respected her desire to wait before intimacy took them again. After all, didn't she owe his real wife that at the very least? As the days passed, however, her longing grew, as did his. He persuaded her into many a stolen kiss. Tempted her with arousing touches. He would curl around her protectively when they slept. How had she ever lain alone?

Two days before the MacLomain warriors were to depart on their journey the sun peeked around the corner of a train of retreating clouds.

The saturated birchwood and pine trees shook themselves off as a cold wind blew. Sunlight burned away the mist and ignited the prisms of foliage like a peacock spreading its tail. Warriors spent their afternoons practicing weaponry upon the field.

One of those last nights, Arianna found herself once more sitting with Iain in their room when he said, "It's time you learn a bit more about magic."

"You want to teach me?" Arianna smiled.

"'Twould be an honor," he replied.

She sat forward, eager. "How does one teach...learn, something such as magic?"

He pulled his chair closer and took her arm. In one hand he held her elbow. In the other her hand, palm up as he caressed his thumb over the pad of her palm. She relaxed beneath the lull of the gentle stroke.

"Have you ever daydreamed, Arianna?"

She allowed him a tender smile. "Aye, who hasn't?"

"How do you feel when you daydream?"

Arianna thought about it. "I suppose that I don't really know. I'm usually more aware of the way I feel when I'm caught daydreaming."

He smiled. "And how is that?"

"Discombobulated. Confused. Shy," she said.

"Why shy?" He was intrigued.

She shrugged. "I suppose because I feel vulnerable when I'm caught daydreaming. As though my soul had lain bare for all to see."

It occurred to her that he'd stopped moving his thumb. She loved to mesmerize him.

As if caught in a daydream himself, he shook his head and continued talking. "'Tis that place in your mind where daydreams dwell that magic is accessed." He lightly ran his thumb from her palm up the tender flesh of her inner arm. "As the blood flows through your veins beneath your skin, so does magic flow through your subconscious just beneath the conscience."

Her sultry eyes followed the path of his finger. "So my magic exists where my dreams exist."

"Not exactly, but very close." Burning need flared to life between them but they ignored it. "I will teach you how to manage that place of daydreams. How to call forth the magic from within and direct it as you wish."

Arianna's eyes rose to his. They yearned for her. "'Twould be wonderful if you would. I accept your offer."

"Och, I will lass. I will."

They both knew that while magic lay ahead something far more exciting threatened to happen first.

The next day, Adlin left on an unknown mission. He claimed the weather befitted it for a brief time. Arianna stood with Iain as the old man wobbled away through the woods. His long white hair and robes blew behind him as he left.

"Does he not wish a horse?" Arianna frowned with concern. "Or an escort?"

"Nay lass, he willnae travel the way we see him now."

"Really?" She squinted at the old man's distant form and then spared a glance at Iain. When she looked back, the wizard was gone.

Iain slid an arm around her waist and pointed above the tree caps. Arianna spied a magnificent white eagle beating its long wings in ascent. It lifted higher into the air and flew in a wide arch until it passed directly over their heads. With a glorious cry, it flew westward into the sinking sun. She clasped her hands together in delight and laughed. He did it. Adlin, dear wizard, had retrieved her scroll.

Iain seized Arianna and pulled her close. "You incite my needs, Arianna." He leaned down and kissed her, pleased when she melted against him enjoying the delicious shivered he invoked.

Reluctant, she pushed back and removed herself from his embrace. "Nay, my laird." She lowered her eyelashes. "We're out in plain sight."

"That never stopped you before." He grabbed at her skirts as she twirled away from him.

He was right. She'd displayed little modesty with him amongst his clansmen.

"I need you." He caught her and pulled her back against him. "I cannae wait any longer."

"We can't. Every time we do it's wrong." She closed her eyes when he leaned down and ran his lips along the side of her cheek and neck.

"The time is always right for the taking of you. And rest assured, every single time I take you it will be the furthest thing from *wrong*."

She opened her eyes and spied Arthur walking toward them. Arianna attempted to unlock herself from Iain's grasp. "I'm trying to do the right thing by your wife. Let me go."

"No." He continued to hold the lower half of her body against him. "Besides, you *are* my wife!"

"My laird. My lady," Arthur said. He looked happy as always.

"We begin the battle axe throwing before that next storm brewing reaches us my laird." His eyes twinkled. "It being your favorite pass time, I figured I would let you know but I see you may want to indulge in a more favorable endeavor."

A fresh batch of dark clouds rolled across the sky. Distant thunder rumbled within their tall, blackened bellies.

"Aye, he will surely join you, Arthur," Arianna said.

"Nay, I willnae." Iain allowed her to break free.

"Aye, you will."

"Nay, lass." Iain pinned Arianna with an implicative look. "You must excuse me in this Arthur, for I will indulge in that more favorable endeavor you speak of."

Arthur nodded.

She'd held Iain at bay for days without too much of a fight. It'd made her urge to flee all but vanish. Truth told, it was easy on the conscience talking and kissing and flirting. Even though they were married with consummation, Arianna had managed to convince herself that she'd done right by the woman meant for him. While she'd allowed him use of her body, she hadn't stolen his heart. Why did he now grow so persistent?

Arianna knew the answer. War loomed on the horizon. Iain was a man. She was a woman. He desired fulfillment before he might die.

Fresh pain seized her heart. War. Soon. Whether the other 'Arianna' came or not, he would be riding off to certain death.

Arianna shook her head in denial and answered, "I will not have you. Therefore, Arthur, he will be joining you."

Arthur's barrel laughter filled the field. "She will not have you? Smart lass."

"Will you have me, instead?" Iain said to Arthur and drew his sword.

"I would be honored." Arthur pulled free a small dagger, his face a mask of mock terror. "I dinnae know. Yours is much bigger than mine."

The two men spared. They met blade for blade. Iain fell to his knees when Arthur's dagger slid beneath his sword. "I am defeated."

He shook his head in shame and arched one eyebrow at Arianna. "Are you sure you willnae have me? You can plainly see that I'm harmless."

Her heart hurt. She found no humor in it. Their fun seemed like mockery. "You're both ridiculous."

They laughed as she stalked back to the castle.

She wanted nothing to do with Iain and everything to do with him all at once. Aye, he might not love her yet but he could eventually. What was she thinking?

They had no 'eventually' together. Everything they shared was a lie. But her rational didn't make it any easier. Groaning, she shook her head.

Could Iain not wrap his mind around the fact that she cared? Did he not realize that she was petrified of him dying? Tears streamed down her face but she wiped them away.

He didn't care. Why should she?

Within minutes, Iain found her on the wall walk. With one look from their laird his watchmen left.

"You dinnae know a bit o' fun, lass," he said when they were alone.

She spun and glared. "Fun? How is any of this fun for you?"

Iain leaned casually against the castle wall. "Have I irked you, wife?"

Arianna strode over to him. "You're a bloody arse, making such a mockery of me down there when I've made it endlessly clear that we cannot be together again." She swallowed the lump in her throat. "I've given you all I am able."

"I am laird of this clan. 'Tis my right to do as I please." Swift, before she could dodge away, he yanked her into his arms. Black storm clouds roiled overhead and a single, swollen raindrop hit her cheek. Leaning down, his tongue flicked out and lightly licked the drop away.

"No," she whispered.

"Aye," he whispered. Wind whipped hair across her face. Distant thunder rumbled. His hands rode down to her backside and gently squeezed. She struggled halfheartedly. "Please, we're way past this, are we not? Lass, you create your own problems."

He scooped her up into his arms.

Arianna pushed against his chest as though that would accomplish anything. "Put me down." *Don't put me down.*

He said nothing while he strode down the hallway. They entered the bedchamber where he paused long enough to throw her onto the mammoth bed.

"I don't want you." She should have left by now. She knew this would happen.

Iain came down on top of her. "Is that really how you feel, lass." He ground his urgent erection against her. "Truly?"

She couldn't move as his muscled body pressed against hers. Too aware of every hard, aroused inch of him, Arianna stilled.

"I am of my own mind." He was too close. Too perfect. "I should always be free to act however I choose. I won't be controlled."

"Aye, luv." He ran his lower lip along her jaw line, sweeping just below her lips. "And I liked the way you acted on the field. Nothing like a Scottish lass with a temper."

He called me love. He did not say he loved me. She longed for breath as his lips hovered over hers. "You're willing to accept that?"

"What?" He pulled his lips away and pressed them tenderly between her eyes and then her forehead. "Anything, luv." Iain used his weight to pin her and rained kisses on every inch of her face. Hungry, he traveled down her neck. He wrapped his arms around her lower back and pulled her slightly off the bed, exposing the shear plane of neck he now dominated.

Air came to her in short sporadic wisps. She breathed as though she'd cried for hours. Vulnerable to his aggression, she slid her hands up to push him away. They met bare, muscled flesh.

I have one more chance to stop him. Salvage this beautiful man for the woman to whom he belongs. She had to stop him. What if she became pregnant? Was already pregnant? Under different circumstances, she'd be thrilled. Regrettably, their situation was far too precarious. The woman coming, the 'real' Arianna, did not deserve such a situation. Nor did Iain.

With ferocious resolve, Arianna lashed out. She pushed his chest away and managed to wiggle out from underneath him.

Iain protected himself when she attacked. He shook off the slap she'd dealt him. "What fire burns in your belly?" Anger combined with lust. "I have done you no wrong, lass."

Aye, but you have. You don't love me. You only wish to lay with me! Hell if she'd ever tell him that though.

"I have told you before and it appears I will have to say it again. I'm not the woman you think I am." Arianna ran to the door and gave it a quick tug. It was locked?

"Bloody hell." This is silly. Why was she doing this? Arianna could admit that she continually yanked him in different directions when it came to intimacy. Right. Wrong. Right. Wrong. It was simply a tug-of-war within her mind. She turned to confront her husband. Thinking he was still on the bed was foolish. Before she knew what hit her he had her backed against the door, his wolfish eyes mere inches from hers.

His voice was low and dark. He clenched his jaw. "You make no sense, lass. You never have, so lose this tired tale and know that you're mine, completely and thoroughly *mine*."

He must've seen something in her eyes he didn't like because the next thing she knew he turned, strode to the hearth and flicked his wrist. A fire sprang to life. He leaned his forehead against the stone and stared deep into the flames. "I'm sorry. I didnae mean to scare you. You vex me."

Arianna didn't move. Scare her? She'd never heard such tormented words when he spoke. Did he really consider her his? Aye, as a possession of course, not as his love. Closing her eyes, she tried to find solace in the burning need she'd heard in his voice, the unabashed need in his gaze when he'd spoken. Opening her eyes, she ignored the tears that fell from her eyes and accepted the truth.

She was lost in time. Lost in him. Misplaced by fate.

What would make this right? There was nowhere to turn for answers. Nothing left to say to the one person she most needed to understand her situation. How could one ultimately explain something that they themselves did not understand?

It was all over. Arianna gave up. She loved him dearly and as much as she loved, she felt betrayed. Betrayed by Iain because he had another wife, betrayed by this other 'Arianna' because she'd never shown up to claim such a prize. Betrayed by herself because she hated this other 'Arianna' for truly belonging to Iain. Deflated past the point of return, she started to sink to the floor.

Iain flew across the room and took her into his arms. She trembled and buried her face against his chest. He wrapped his arms around her and didn't move. Pain. Way too much pain.

He stroked her hair. "I didnae mean to sound cruel. Please forgive me?"

"No. Not cruel," she murmured. Her breathing became shallow, her body unresponsive to his touch. Iain pulled her closer to the warmth of the fire and continued to hold her.

Time became non-existent.

Seconds turned to long minutes before he looked down into her face. "You fly with the angels, my heart." He wiped an escaped tear from her cheek with his thumb.

Arianna crumbled under the beautiful words and the way he looked at her. She couldn't stop this. It was no longer within her power. It never was. When his intended bride arrived, she would simply flee. Whether she was with child or not. She may not have his heart but her soul would not deny his touch any longer.

She would pay the price later.

But hadn't she come to that decision a million times already? No matter. Arianna met his opaque gaze and relaxed beneath the hypnotizing effect he had on her. Heavy drops of rain poured on the castle as they swam in the languid pools of each other's gaze.

With extreme tenderness, he ran the outside of his finger along her cheek. She knew he didn't want to lose her. Slowly, he combed his fingers through her hair.

Arianna stared up at him.

He encased one hand around the top of her collarbone and dragged it, ever so lightly, up her neck until he encased her jaw and tilted her head back. Her eyelashes fluttered and her tongue flicked briefly over her lower lip.

Transfixed, he gazed at the moisture left behind and ran his thumb over it. He pulled back his hand and laid his lips to the nub of his thumb where her moisture lingered. The golden firelight enhanced his masculinity creating a visage that could only be described as a fabled and ancient demigod.

Muscles wrapped their way down his body, rippled and slick, constricting as though ready to go into battle. His face was so well formed that the light cast alluring shadows with one purpose in mind, seduction.

His eyes drifted back to hers.

Arianna didn't waste another minute but raised her mouth to his. Her tongue entered his mouth and she pressed her body against him. Blazing need roared up. So fast and furious, Arianna hoped he understood. Hoped he felt the same.

She needed him now.

With a low growl, Iain pushed her against the hearthstone, mere feet from the billowing flames. Her heart slammed painfully in her chest. Warm fluid wet her thighs. *I can't touch him enough, feel him enough.* Desperate, she ran her hands over his shoulders and arms and torso. Blood roared in her head.

"Arianna." He buried the word in her hair. With surprising swiftness, he pulled up her skirts, and as though she weighed nothing he lifted her against the wall and came between her legs. Panting, desperate, he yanked up his plaid and gave one hard thrust, penetrating her fully.

Giving her no time to adjust, he began to pound into her as if he was determined to convince her they were one. That they'd never be separated. Impaled, thrilled, gloriously filled, Arianna wrapped her legs around him and held on for dear life.

Sweat made his skin slick beneath her hands but the firm grasp he had on her backside made it irrelevant. He'd never drop her. Never let her go. She cried out with every thrust, reveling in the feel of him being so very deep inside. She heard him grunt her name over and over. Other muffled endearments came out but she couldn't hear them. Couldn't focus on anything but the feel of his hot body turning hers inside out.

The fire flared. The wind howled.

She felt wild and free, alive and enlightened. All she could do was *feel*. Her body, heart, and soul were thrown into a state of ecstasy. There came no tenderness, but urgency. Wonderful, untamed, pent up urgency. She cried his name. Demanded more.

Lightning sizzled across the night sky and filled the large chamber with splendorous, corner consuming light. A cold wind hammered the outside walls and blew down the shutters and wool over the windows like a bear mad with rabid disease. Flames spat defiant sparks at the intruding gusts of icy air.

Iain held her as though she was a lifeline. She tightened her legs around him and crushed her fully clothed breasts against his chest. *Sweet Jesus*. This time there came no slow build up but a sharp shove straight off the cliff. He howled. She screamed. His knees started to buckle but he used her and the wall as a brace. He throbbed so strongly inside of her, Arianna whimpered from the untamed sensual overload of her body's response. It felt as if her innards clamped down so hard on him that they might never be able to pull apart.

He held her tightly while she floated in his arms, torturous sweet ripple upon ripple washed over her. Her body shook against him and he continued to throb within.

"Never. Anything. Like. This," he panted into her hair.

They stood that way for some time, both struggling to catch their breath, trying to understand their tsunami of emotions. As though a mammoth sledgehammer crashed against the side of the castle an angry clap of thunder roared around them.

Startled, Arianna squeezed his shoulders and held him tighter. He sucked in his breath and she felt him once more grow within her.

In a violent storm of motion he swung around and brought her down to the plush fur carpet in front of the fire. Impatient, he removed the clothes separating them without losing intimate contact.

"Love me, Arianna." *She looked down, unsure. I'm straddling him!* When he thrust his hips, pleasure shot straight up through her body. Her mouth fell open.

Though he'd led the way, the seductive gleam in his eyes told her... She was in control.

Shy, she trailed her fingers down his chest. His eyes never left her face. Arianna knew little about arousal but that's not really what she wanted to show him right now anyways. After all, he was already rock hard inside of her. Leaning forward, she covered his body, her heart against his. She closed her eyes and relished the feel of his strong, sweat soaked body against hers.

Slowly, she turned her head and flicked her tongue, relishing the taste of salt on her tongue. He bucked, his arousal anxious and impatient against her womb. Perhaps she should have continued to seduce. Perhaps that's what he wanted. But...

She lost control.

Sitting back, encouraged by his half-mast eyes and the moan that escaped his lips she began to rock her hips very slowly. As she began to move, Arianna realized that each little shift of her hips created a different feeling.

"Aye, lass," he whispered.

His attention was solely focused on her body, on where they joined. Perhaps she seduced without meaning to? *I can do this. I can control him without meaning to.*

Hands on his chest, she started to move with more assurance. New pleasure began to burn. It started in her thighs and crawled into her stomach. Eager, interested, she rolled her hips.

Grunting, he grabbed and guided her. The expression on his face was pure lust and need. Like a banshee havocking in the turbulent thunderstorm she met him and rode. The more he responded to her the more excited she became.

"Arianna." He groaned her name over and over. She continued to guide him. Enraptured. Humbled. He was hers. Sensation built and built until... *Ohhh!* She had no choice but to fall forward as her body shook uncontrollably. Iain pulled her close, thrust up hard and groaned low and long.

Time passed while they lay that way, unwilling to move or let go. Eventually he murmured against her ear, "You are full of surprises, my little dove."

She gave no response but remained encaged in his arms listening to his steady heartbeat. What was there to say? Her life was utterly perfect at the moment. It was not long before he sought her lips again and carried her to the bed.

Chapter Fifteen

Iain was up with the sun and broke his fast with his men. He spent the remainder of the morning exercising his swordsmanship amongst fellow clansmen.

Hugh had never seen his lord look so well. Iain was in fine form and challenged many to swordplay. Iain even made a point of splitting Hugh's arrow in two when they practiced their marksmanship.

"It was owed you my friend," Iain said and Hugh laughed.

The men returned to the great hall for the afternoon meal. Spirits were high as everyone conversed on the journey and war that lay upon the morrow. Iain spied Arianna and joined her.

He pulled her close and kissed her long and hard. To his delight she returned the affection in front of everyone. His pearl had finally popped from her oyster.

They sat with Muriel, Hugh and Helen but Iain couldn't take his eyes off the lass beside him. Her skin glowed from their loving. Again and again he thought to take her back to bed.

"My laird." Ferchar entered the hall. Helen rose, so great was the distress on her son's face. "Someone has arrived."

Iain rose. "Bring him in."

"Nay my laird. 'Twould be best if you receive his message elsewhere." Ferchar cast a worried look in Arianna's direction and she frowned, alarm flickering in her eyes.

Iain nodded and departed the hall. A stocky clansman stood impatiently in the courtyard.

He clasped arms with Iain and gave his name as William Broun of clan Broun. *Ah, at last one of her kinfolk makes an appearance.*

"I have grave news, my laird." He shifted his feet. "Regarding your betrothed."

Iain caught Ferchar's eye and understood the need for discreetness. The lad knew something already. Ferchar went back to the hall. Iain waited until the door was shut behind him.

Once alone with the Broun clansman he said, "Go on."

"My lady...your lady, has run off," William said.

"What?" Iain felt uneasy.

William sighed. "It shames my clan to deliver such news but 'tis only right that you know. We traveled far, ninety men strong, to deliver her safely to your door. Well into the journey we camped on the shores of Loch Lamond."

Iain scowled. His gut clenched. "Go on."

"Regrettably, as word may have carried even to your own ears, Arianna was quite taken with Stephen, my laird's first in command. Speculation and rumor fructified that eve at Loch Lamond."

The man before him squirmed. "What transpired?"

William cleared his throat. "We woke the next morn and they were gone. We searched them out to no avail for Stephen is very clever."

"Nay, you are mistaken. She is here." Iain shook his head.

"Arianna is here?" He looked incredulous.

"Aye."

"'Tis impossible."

"I tell you she is here and we have been married so as to honor your laird's arrangement with my father,"

Iain said. "I was curious why she appeared unescorted."

Careful, William continued. "When did she arrive my laird?"

"'Twas nine nights before Samhain's eve." Did the man doubt him?

"Something is amiss, my laird." The clansman stood taller. "For my lady disappeared but five nights past."

Iain stepped closer. "You must be mistaken."

"Nay, I'm not." William took a step back.

"Then who did I marry?" *A girl from another time?* Iain's shoulders tensed. Anger started to bubble up. This was impossible! The lad was wrong. Or was he?

"I know naught, my laird, but it could not have been our lady Arianna Broun." William broke into a sweat under the rage churning in Iain's eyes.

"So you doubt my word?" Iain stood half a foot taller than William. He knew the man spoke the truth but felt the need for intimidation to appease his own discontent.

"Nay, perhaps this could be easily solved if I could see my lady again." William's eyebrows arched in question. "I fear trickery may be at work here."

"Aye." Iain wanted to throttle the clansman. As he led the lad back towards his hall, Arianna's words echoed in his head. *I'm not the Arianna meant for you.* Was she an imposter? Fear made logical thought a slippery thing.

The door opened before they reached it.

"Where's my wife?" He barked.

"She slipped out after you, brother," Muriel said, concerned.

Damn them all too hell. "How is it she slipped out with all of you oozing from my door like sap from a tree?"

"I know naught." Muriel shook her head and stepped back.

"Search the area," he ordered his men. The damn lass liked to run off.

William stood quietly nearby. Upon Iain's invitation, he warmed himself by the fire and accepted a mug of whiskey from a servant.

"My laird, there is more."

"Have out with it." Iain eyed the door. Conviction flooded him. Arianna had heard everything they said outside. A small nucleus of belief sprang to life within. Could it be that all the nonsense she'd spoken was the truth? He himself detected she'd recently executed her magic for the first time. He'd touched her mind. How could it be he hadn't seen the truth? He choked on his ale as a thought struck him. Adlin! God above, no. He had a hand in this.

"I believe I was followed by a small band of men," William said.

Danger. Arianna.

Angered magic boiled in his blood.

"I covered my trail well so as to not lead harm straight to your door. They number only ten men, but they are out there, beyond your northern border."

"My laird." Arthur burst through the door. "She is gone."

Clan Cochran. "Hugh, Arthur, round up twenty of your best men. We ride," Iain said.

"I will join you my laird." William was in hot pursuit as Iain headed for the door.

"Nay, rest. You've traveled far."

"She has been my lady since I was a lad and she a lassie." A stubborn nature defended his words. "I'll not have harm come to her."

Iain nodded and left. There was no time. He adorned only his axe and mounted his horse. Spurred into action, his steed flew across the field. She was out there somewhere, vulnerable. He entered the woods and quickly picked up her trail.

Iain ordered his men to fan out. He would travel alone.

He halted his horse at the base of a tall pine and jumped down. It could not be. Iain studied the pine needles underfoot. Many hooves had been here recently. At least three horses had headed west. The other three went due east. Whichever direction Arianna went her trail had been covered.

Iain tried to touch her essence. Nothing. Magic.

He sent his horse away. Animals were uncomfortable and skittish around magic. As he stood alone in the forest he closed his eyes, called upon Mother Earth and chanted in a language long forgotten by mankind.

A wind ripped through the tree trunks and blew at his face. Iain opened his eyes and looked up. The pines far above leaned over as though they looked down at him. Judged him.

The trunk of the tree he stood nearest to glowed green on one side. She'd gone west. Iain put his hand on the tree and nodded. He removed a small pentacle from his side and tucked it alongside the tree trunk. "Thank you, my friend."

"Uncle Iain?" Ferchar emerged from the forest. "Let me fight with you?"

"'Tis a fight I must battle alone, lad." Iain grabbed the reins of Ferchar's horse.

He well understood his nephew's eagerness. He'd been the lad's age once.

"Have you need of another weapon?" Ferchar unsheathed the small knife at his waist.

Iain pulled his axe loose and handed it to the lad, hilt first. "I will need no weapon." 'Twas time for magic.

Ferchar frowned.

"I must go." Iain ran into forest. He could already smell his enemies stink upon the air. He was close. A small meadow lay ahead.

He stayed low and watched. She was here. Iain scanned the area and saw nothing. Then she burst free from the wood line on the opposite side.

Arianna! Iain had never spoken to her through the mind.

Her head whipped in his direction.

A single clansman emerged from the trees behind her and held a bow and arrow to her chest.

Iain stepped forward. Be careful. He clenched his fists at his side and summoned his magic. Wind soared down from the mountains. The grass underfoot bent and the trees stood ready for battle behind him.

He heard them clearly. Everything happened very fast.

Arianna's back was stiff. "Have you the courage to kill me?" What a woman.

"Aye." The man pulled the bowstring tight. Iain's world stopped.

"You have an enemy," she said. Iain met the man's eyes. *You will die.*

Iain flicked his wrist to turn the bow and arrow to ash.

Nothing happened.

He tried again. Still nothing.

Arianna looked at him, her heart in her eyes. *"I love you."* She spoke into his mind.

"Evil," the man said and muttered a prayer under his breath.

"Arianna! Nooooo!" Iain started to run.

The arrow released and sunk into her chest.

Arianna fell onto her back, stunned. She wrapped her hands around the arrow protruding from her chest. When her head turned and their eyes locked he knew he was losing her.

"God, no. Please, Arianna, no." He slid to the ground and pulled her limp body into his arms. Cupping her head, he kept pleading, "Don't leave me. Don't go." Blood trickled from the corner of her mouth as her body began to disappear. Transparent now, Arianna's glazed eyes looked up at him. There was so much pain there.

"Arianna! *Arianna!"* He called to her aloud and in his mind.

Then she was gone and his arms were empty. Iain's mind went blank. Arianna was gone. As he knelt on the ground his world turned black and white. His heart went numb and his soul shriveled. All that he could do was shake his head in denial and stare down at his empty hands.

Chapter Sixteen

"Arianna, wake up."

"Mama?" Arianna awoke and looked around. She was snuggled in her bed in her childhood home. The small cottage nestled by Loch Fyne in Scotland.

"Aye lass." Her mother stroked her hair. "You've grown into a beautiful woman."

"I'm so sorry, Mama." Arianna closed her eyes.

"You've naught to be sorry for, lass." Her mother kissed her forehead. "'Tis time to go home now."

Arianna smiled. Iain.

"Arianna, wake up." Her mother's voice was urgent. She opened her eyes.

Her mother was gone. The monolith from Pattee's caves gazed down at her. Its sharp head blended with the gray sky. How did it get here?

Arianna blinked and raised a shaky hand to her face. She sat up and leaned her back against the cold rock. Bare branches splintered the dismal sky. An icy snowflake fell in slow motion and settled upon the bridge of her nose.

She looked around, confused.

Icy blobs of snow fell heavier as she hunkered against the stone. Arianna had to find Iain.

She had to tell him that she was well. She attempted to stand and staggered back. Perhaps she would lean against the rock for a few moments.

Everything blurred.

"Walk, Arianna. Walk." She looked around. Who had said that?

"Now." It was as if she was a puppet on a string when she pushed off the rock and began to walk.

Arianna didn't know where she was or where she was going but she walked anyway. Snow fell heavy now so she concentrated on the ground and put one foot in front of the other.

She grew colder by the minute but continued on. *"Iain, I'm here."* She called again and again to him in her mind.

Finally, she could walk no more and fell to the ground. Where was he?

"Mama, mama!"

Annie? What was she doing here? Where was she?

The child's voice echoed from somewhere far away before everything turned dark and she heard no more.

****

"I love you." Arianna woke with the sweet words on her lips. She kept her eyes closed and rolled over to cuddle against Iain. He wasn't there. He must have gone to the field already. She yawned and smiled. Everything was perfect.

Then she opened her eyes.

The stone walls of the castle chamber had turned to wood. Where was she? The canopy overhead. The beautiful tapestries. The fireplace. All were gone.

Somebody tapped nearby.

Arianna couldn't orient herself and blinked to clear the fog.

Tap. Tap. Tap.

She frowned at the old oak tree beyond the window.

Oh no. She sat up and looked around at her bedroom. *Lord no.* Soft snow rimmed the outside panes of the windows.

Then an avalanche of memories crashed down. The Broun clansman. The fury on Iain's face. She'd stumbled through the Scotland woods, heartbroken with little thought as to where she intended to go.

Her dream became reality.

Detail by painful detail, it all came back. Iain was there. He caught her and held her as she vanished. The pain on his face had been unbearable.

Iain was gone forever.

Had it all been part of the same dream? No.

Of that she felt certain. The sudden wash of pain she felt didn't make that knowledge any kinder. Arianna sat on the edge of her bed and hugged herself. She trembled. She didn't want to be here without him. Her numb mind tried to wrap around things. She had to find reason in this.

She was back in Salem. Back in New Hampshire. America. A place so very far away from Scotland. Arianna should be grateful for she'd known that she couldn't stay there much longer. She was back where she belonged. This was good.

This was horrible.

For all she had thought she'd stay and face inevitable persecution, Arianna had run. She'd turned coward.

All was lost.

She rolled her head around on her neck. Her body ached. The oak tapped on the glass again as if urging her to open the window and acknowledge her homecoming.

Arianna stood, her legs unsteady and walked to the window. She'd changed so much since the last time she stood in this very spot.

The world was white. Clean and pure, the previous slews of colors were slathered in cotton drifts. A thick layer of newly fallen snow defined every pinstripe branch on the oak tree. A deep blue sky shone beyond.

She positioned her palms beneath the ledge of the bottom eve and slid the window up. Bits of stacked snow tumbled inward. It melted on her hands as Arianna leaned her head outside. She inhaled sharply and then released. Warm breath met frosty air in a billow of fog.

"Arianna?"

It was if she woke from a dream when she turned. Aunt Marie. She cried in delight and flew into her aunt's embrace.

Marie sobbed happy tears on her shoulder. After a long while, Arianna pulled back and attempted a wobbly smile. Marie's teary blue eyes turned sorrowful and she shook her head.

"I wasn't sure if you would return. I've been so worried about you, lass." She hugged Arianna again.

At least now she knew it hadn't all been a dream. She'd really vanished.

"Sleeping beauty finally arises," Liam said from the door. Arianna welcomed his embrace.

"Aye, you must've been frantic. What day is it?" Arianna felt confused. They appeared shocked not angry. "Why do you stare at me so strangely?"

"You're speaking in Gaelic." Liam cleared his throat. "And quite fluently."

Arianna touched her mouth.

"I'll answer your questions once I get some food into you." Her aunt took her elbow and led her out of the room. She circumvented the stairs and then allowed Marie to sit her at the table. The house she'd spent the last nine years of her life in seemed foreign. Small.

The next few minutes were spent nibbling on a muffin. It had no taste. After a few bites she resolved to sip from the hot tea provided her. The kitchen looked angled and distant.

"It is November third. You were missing but a night and slept for two days." Liam sat down at the table.

Arianna choked on the tea. One night? She shook her head as her aunt patted her on the back. Her coughs finally abated. Blood rushed to her head. Arianna closed her eyes and sucked in a deep breath. *Am I going to faint?*

"Are you all right lass?" Both her aunt and uncle asked with concern.

The feeling passed. She nodded and took another careful sip from the teacup. "I'm fine, thank you." *I'll never be fine again.*

"Are you sure luv?" Marie wrung her hands.

"Of course I'm sure." Arianna switched to English. *I'm sure that I've lost him.*

Marie snatched the near full cup of tea from in front of Arianna and turned to add more hot water from the kettle over the fire. She looked grim when she set the beverage back down in front of Arianna.

It occurred to her that they hadn't asked her where she'd been. Arianna didn't know what to say next. The truth? They would think her insane. Tears blurred her vision as she twirled a finger around a knot in the wood tabletop. A light hand fell upon her shoulder. She looked up into Marie's eyes.

"All is well now," Marie said before she continued to bustle around the kitchen. She stirred batter with too much vigor then poured it into a pan. She proceeded to chop another hot loaf of bread into slices as though it were a tough carrot. Then she whipped back around and heated more water for another round of tea.

Uncle Liam ate quietly and shot Arianna a curious glance every so often. Arianna smiled when the children entered. Both came and embraced her.

"I'm so sorry," Coira said and looked at the floor.

"You have naught to be sorry for," Arianna said. The girls wanted to know where she'd been. Arianna had no answer to give them. Marie shushed them with fresh muffins and talk of a future snowball fight. After a time, the children pestered to go outside and play.

"I believe that I'll join you girls." Liam stood and gave Marie a peck on her cheek. The three of them bundled into warm clothes and disappeared outside.

Arianna frowned into her mug. *I love them but I want to go back to him.* Everything reminded her of him. The way Marie and Liam looked at one another. All the places that she'd stood in this house, thinking of the man from her dreams.

She closed her eyes.

Arianna couldn't push the heartache away. Her eyes shot open when a thump sounded. An old yellow bottle sat on the wooden table. Her aunt sat across from her now, arms placed with care in her lap. Silent, Marie waited.

A shiver ran through her as Arianna studied the oblong bottle. Dim and worn with age, it was obviously ancient.

As though she pushed her hand through water, Arianna reached out and grabbed the vase like thing and pulled it closer. Miniscule cracks lined the surface. Green algae sunk deep within their recesses. Arianna's tongue felt thick and swollen. She swallowed hard when Marie unveiled a glass-encased paper from under the table.

"I got your message." Marie laid the object on the table. "It nearly fell apart in my hands so I had it framed."

Arianna's hands shook as she lifted the ancient scroll. How could she have forgotten? Tears again blurred her vision and her throat constricted as she remembered the white eagle, Adlin, taking flight into the distant horizon just yesterday.

No, not yesterday.

Six hundred years ago.

The night that followed his departure resurfaced and squeezed her heart. The passion of the storm that raged outside and the passion that ravaged them within their chamber. Arianna strangled back a groan of anguish and read the words she'd written...

Dear Aunt Marie,

I hope this finds you on the shores of Boston, Massachusetts. I chose Boston instead of England for I knew that you would walk to the shore of your new homeland. If you are reading this then my memory serves me well.

You will never receive a stranger missive. I write it in hope to save you from worry in the future.

On October 31, 1799, I will disappear from an annual party held at the Huntington's house. I do not know how long I will be gone but please know that I am well.

Now I will tell you. Since we arrived in New Hampshire I have had a reoccurring dream. In this dream, a Scottish warrior plagues me. On All Hallows' Eve, I see him in a mirror in the Huntington's basement.

In the future, you can confirm this if necessary. It was a silly game I played with...well, a child. In the end, it was not so silly.

That night I ran into the woods and ended up at Pattee's caves. Somehow, I traveled back in time.

I write you now from Scotland in the year 1199. He is here, Aunt Marie, the man who I've always dreamt of. The story is long and strange. I do not have the time for details.

I will give this scroll to a Shaman and he says it will find you as I desire. I can only pray this is true for I do not want you to worry.

I love you. Be happy.

Most sincerely, Arianna

Arianna bit her lower lip. What a struggle it'd been to write this without anyone finding out. To make sure that she didn't mention Coira who hadn't even been born yet.

It was even tougher getting back to the small chamber in the tower where she was to set the seal.

Arianna had prayed fervently to the god of the sea as was instructed. As an afterthought, she left a lock of her hair, if only to prove to her aunt it was she.

"Are you alright?"

Arianna's thoughts were so far away that her aunt's words startled her. "Aye."

"I found the bottle washed up on the shore when we first arrived in Boston Harbor. We've much to talk about." Marie gave Arianna a pointed look.

Arianna nodded and sat back. Where should I begin?

"Just start at the beginning," Marie said.

Arianna jolted upright. "Did you read my thoughts?"

A merry twinkle sparked Marie's eyes. "Of course not silly child."

Not altogether convinced, Arianna began her tale. First, she described the dream that had plagued her for years in more detail.

"You could have confided in me." Marie took her hand.

Arianna gave a small nod. "I should have. I just thought...well, I thought it was merely a dream."

"Aye." Marie urged her to continue.

Arianna told Marie of the mirror and the monolith at Pattee's caves. Then Arianna weaved the story of recent events in medieval Scotland. Her aunt didn't interrupt once. Instead she appeared to relish every detail. Many times she questioned her about scenery, clothing and the people.

"I'm married." Arianna blushed and frowned. "Was married."

Marie's eyes rounded in astonishment.

"The man from my dreams. His name is Iain. He is...was Chieftain of the MacLomain clan."

Marie's back straightened more if that was possible.

Arianna squared her shoulders. Don't cry. "We were married at the edge of a stream in a forest not far from the southernmost point of the Cowal Peninsula in Argyll shire."

Marie's expression went dreamy while she listened to the details. "It sounds very romantic."

"Aye. It was." Arianna sighed. Magically romantic.

"So, you are a woman now." Marie's expression was unreadable.

Heat burned her cheeks. Very much so. Marie waved her on, obviously not having need of an answer. Grateful, Arianna continued.

By the time Arianna finished, Marie was sitting forward. One elbow rested on the table and supported her chin. The other hand was braced on its edge where she methodically cracked one knuckle at a time, over and over again. She stared straight through Arianna she was so deep in thought.

"Aunt Marie?" Her aunt continued to stare into space. "Aunt Marie?"

"Hmmm?" Marie finally responded. "Sorry, I was just absorbing your story, sweetie."

"Aye, it is quite the tale," Arianna said. Did her aunt believe her? Arianna contemplated this while Marie appeared indecisive about what to say next. When she did speak, Arianna almost fell from her chair.

"I do believe everything you've said. It appears that magic controls your destiny."

"You believe in magic?" Arianna gripped the edges of the table.

"Aye lass." Marie sat back. "How else could you have traveled through time?"

She made a good point. "What do you make of it all?"

"There are no words that could describe what you must be feeling right now. In light of what you've told me I only wish I spoke with you sooner." Marie disregarded her niece's inquisitive look and continued. "You should not have been told by a stranger you had magic."

Arianna's mouth fell open.

"Aye, you know now, that's clear. It was always my intention to tell you sooner but—"

"But...but what?" Arianna was disturbed. Magic existed here? In this time?

Marie met her niece's eyes. "You've been through so much in your young life, girl. Such knowledge as this is staggering. I prayed that this day would never come to pass. I prayed that some twist of fate would keep you from leaving us three nights ago. I never dreamed such strong magic still existed in our family." She squeezed Arianna's hand.

"But, tell me Arianna, what would have come of things if I had told you? Do you think things would have transpired as they did? What motive did you have when that missive was sent to me? Some part of you must have thought I would understand, aye? Or did you send it thinking I would assume I had lost my mind? Really, luv, think through all the aspects of this situation. On some subconscious level, you must have hoped that I possessed magic as well."

Arianna bit her tongue. Marie was right. Everything that had happened, returning to Scotland and meeting Iain would most likely never have transpired had she even contemplated magic existed. Let alone that she possessed it.

"Well, lassie, no need to be tongue tied. I can see you have the right of it now."

Arianna stood and walked to the window. The day was full of white ground and gray sky now. A steady wind blew at the bleak landscape. The human eye could strain for hours for a speck of color and come up bereft.

Laughter bubbled forth. It sounded insane to her ears. "Funny, that's why I sent a lock of my hair."

"What lock of hair?"

Lost in her own mournful reverie, Arianna shrugged. "The lock of hair I sent you. It was merely to convince you it was truly me who sent you the letter. What real authenticity would a lock of hair lend a missive sent from six hundred years in the past? I only thought the hair would make the letter seem more real, how could it? Silly notion, really."

"Your line of thought was not so silly sweetie. Before this, neither you nor I would have ever even contemplated time travel, let alone its many dynamics. You should know, however, I never received any lock of hair."

Arianna turned and smiled in direct contradiction to her mood. "That makes no sense." As if any of this did.

Marie crossed her arms over her chest. "Truth told, I received no lock of hair. That said, it's never been like you to be crass with another."

Arianna faltered. Her tone had been rather snide.

"Aunt Marie, I'm scared."

Marie's features softened. She crossed the room and took Arianna into her arms. "I know."

She released Arianna but continued to hold both arms. "Again, I'm sorry that a stranger had to reveal magic to you."

"He's not a stranger." Arianna's shoulders slumped in defeat. "He is my husband."

Marie nodded and led Arianna back to the table. "I know, I didn't mean it that way honey," Marie assured. "You're right, he's not a stranger. It was my responsibility to tell you before October thirty-first."

Arianna merely nodded. "What do you know of magic?" She was not surprised that her aunt had withheld such knowledge. It was the eighteenth century after all.

"That we of the Broun clan possess it. Have always possessed it. Passed on, generation after generation, magic is in our blood."

Marie retrieved two fresh cups of tea.

"There is another thing I don't quite understand." Arianna said. "What of the ten day lapse? I traveled back on October thirty first, but that day did not come to pass in 1199 until ten days after I arrived."

Marie shrugged. "I wouldn't begin to understand the dynamics of time-travel dear."

For a brief time the women talked of the past. She told Marie about her repressed memories of their frightful experience in Scotland when she was a child.

As secrets were uncovered and history traversed, Arianna had a short reprieve from the empty and soulless place she was doomed to dwell without Iain in her life.

~Fate's Monolith~

Chapter Seventeen

Arianna didn't dream anymore.

Instead, she fell back into her timeless routine. She arose, dressed, milked the cows, collected eggs and helped prepare breakfast. Then, she would groom and feed the horses, clean the stalls and lay down fresh hay. After that, she retrieved buckets of water from the well, heated them over the fire and washed laundry.

Beeswax candles were to be made once a month but took two full days worth of work. Spare time was spent either mending linens and clothing or making them. Every day ensured hard work for the women of the household. Spare time was valued.

Four days after she returned home, Beth came to visit.

Arianna laughed when Beth ushered her up to the bedroom, shut the door and turned to her with her hands on her hips. When her friend spoke, she was all business. "Two questions. How are you feeling and what is going on between Edward and you?"

Arianna was glad those were the only questions. Marie told the partygoers on All Hallows' Eve that she had fallen ill and walked home.

Arianna smiled. "I feel better, thank you and nothing is going on between Edward and I."

Beth burst into laughter and walked over to the small collection of books stacked on a table in the far corner. She leaned over to eye the titles. "I don't believe you."

"I can assure you, I feel much better." Arianna sat on her bed.

Beth stood and stretched. "Don't patronize me."

It was Arianna's turn to laugh as she sat back against the oak headboard. "Come now, would I do that?"

"Without a second thought." Beth plopped down beside her. "He was discreet with me as only a gentleman would be. I'm your best friend and he is like a brother. Let's just cut to the core, shall we?"

Arianna rolled her eyes. "I have absolutely no interest in Edward. I never have and never will."

"What's so bad about Edward?"

Arianna almost laughed again but saw something in Beth's eyes that stopped her.

"You're serious?" Arianna said.

"He's attractive, intelligent and ambitious. What else could you ask for?" Beth laced her hands behind her head.

Love. "You're right. It's just that I don't have those sorts of feelings toward him," Arianna said.

"He kissed you, didn't he?"

Arianna cast her friend a sidelong glance. "Yes."

"I figured as much. He's had his eye on you for some time." Beth stood up from the bed. "Give me the juicy details."

Arianna sat up. "It was pleasant enough."

"Just pleasant?"

"Aye, just pleasant," Arianna said. She may not be much older now but she was certainly wiser. She now knew what feelings a simple kiss should ignite.

It was apparent Beth didn't believe her. She switched topics none-the-less. "I got the scholarship."

Arianna smiled and braced herself. "No?"

"Yes." Beth stood proud. "I found out yesterday."

"Congratulations." Arianna screeched and jumped from the bed to hug her friend. "I knew you would."

Beth had worked hard. She was an exceptional writer and now she was going off to college, all expenses paid. Arianna was amazed her friend had been granted money, it bespoke well of her talent. She was a woman ahead of her time.

Beth pulled back. "What will you do?"

Wish I were with Iain the rest of my days. "Without you? I'll be simply lost."

Beth was serious. "Really, I'm worried about you."

"Don't be," Arianna shook her head. "I'll marry someday and I'm skilled at making clothes. Perhaps I'll have a career as a seamstress." Her plans sounded boring even to her own ears.

"Perhaps you'll marry Edward." Beth adjusted her skirts as she said this.

Arianna shook her head. "I'm not ready to marry." Besides, I'm already married. How she wished she could tell her friend everything. That she traveled back in time, discovered magic existed and she was capable of using it. How she fell in love with an incredible Scotsman.

"We'll see." Beth gave Arianna a tight grin. "Just so long as you're happy."

Arianna forced a smile. "I'll miss you. When are you leaving?"

"After the New Year," Beth said. "I really do have to be going."

Arianna walked Beth downstairs. At the door the two embraced again.

"I'll see you soon," Beth said.

"Aye." Arianna helped her with her coat.

Beth leaned in close and spoke soft. "Don't give up on Edward, he'll be lost once I'm gone."

Arianna giggled and watched Beth walk down the drive toward her carriage. Only once Arianna shut the door did she realize the truth behind the words.

Edward would be lost once Beth was gone.

Although he'd asked about her, it was a month after she returned home that Edward appeared at the front door. Arianna was upstairs changing into evening clothes when Marie appeared at her doorway to tell her. She collected herself and followed her aunt down the stairwell.

The men stood at the bottom of the stairs in casual conversation about work. When he turned her way Edward's eyes lit up. "Arianna." He smiled. "It's so good to see you well."

She allowed him a quick kiss on the backside of her hand, as was the English way.

"It's so kind of you to check on our Arianna, Edward." Marie rested her hand on Arianna's tense shoulder. After she received his overcoat, Marie steered them towards the parlor. "I'll prepare some tea."

Arianna sat on the deep blue settee facing the fire. Please don't let him sit next to me. He sat down in the velvet-winged chair opposite the one Liam sunk into.

"There will obviously be more men needed," Liam said.

"Absolutely." Edward crossed one leg over the other.

Edward was dressed to perfection in brown trousers and a crisp white shirt. He laced his fingers together on his knee and smiled with confidence. "This venture cannot be done without the proper manpower."

"Have we men available that are eager for work?" Liam said.

"But of course, the surrounding towns are growing. Hampstead and Derry host many interested men unable to find work in their own towns. Then of course there is Methuen."

"Methuen?" Liam appeared shocked. "There are men inquiring from Massachusetts?"

Edward grinned and accepted the proffered cup of tea from Marie whom had entered quietly. She served Liam next, then Arianna and herself before she sat down beside Arianna.

"Does that really shock you? We are the future after all. The day is upon us that we, this United States of America, come together, unify. Why not have folk from bordering states work in ours?" He sipped his tea and cast an appreciative glance in Arianna's direction.

"Aye, lad, you're right. It's the only way a nation can progress." Liam set his teacup aside and leaned forward. "But what of protecting our states commerce? If we give our jobs away, will they do the same?"

"How will it ultimately benefit them if they do not?

Trust me, diversification is essential," Edward said.

Liam loved to talk politics and drew Edward into further debate. Arianna disregarded their incisive talk and focused on the fire in the small hearth.

Memories bombarded her.

She recalled a fire that burned magically in a land and time far away. The night before Arianna left medieval Scotland.

After hours of making love, Iain had carried and placed her before one of the two windows in their chamber. He allowed the fire to extinguish and the room remained cloaked in darkness.

The storm had retreated and the view was spectacular. A black wave of cloudbank stretched far and wide on the distant horizon, carried with haste upon the steady eastbound wind. Left in its wake was a quicksilver loch sparkling beneath the voluminous moon. Distant mountains melded with the black of the sky. Loch Holy was one glorious looking glass.

"Very soon the stars will stand with their king and you will see something far more wondrous then this."

Arianna was enthralled by Iain who now leaned out the window. He breathed in the salty air and threw his head back. One would've thought he sought to warm his face in the sun.

She leaned forward and waited for him to continue. Many minutes passed before he spoke. "Can you feel it, Arianna?"

"What?"

"The energy left upon the air. 'Tis more powerful than any magic that exists." He took her hand and held it out. He turned her palm skyward and released his grip.

"Close your eyes." His request was soft in her ear. "And just feel."

She obeyed and almost jumped when sensation washed over her skin. It felt as though tiny, heated raindrops fell, but softer. Arianna rubbed her fingers together, but felt only dryness.

"Now, open your eyes love."

When she did, Arianna was humbled.

His arm slid around her waist and pulled her close while she gazed at Scotland. The mountains had turned the same shining white shared by the moon, their jagged edges scorched vivid against their obsidian backdrop. The loch turned from molten silver to a fathomless black. In its depths the moon swam amidst a thousand shiny flecks.

"I've never seen anything so beautiful and rare."

"Nor have I." When he turned her, Arianna realized he no longer spoke of the landscape. She shivered when he ran his hand through her hair.

"The magic of Scotland, lass. 'Tis my gift to you." His lips grazed hers so softly she barely felt them. Her eyelids lowered when his hands caressed the outer curves of her breast, when his fingertips rode lightly down either side of her stomach until he held her hips.

Body heat burned between them they stood so close. "So bloody beautiful," he whispered.

Lowering his head he kissed her hard, deepening the exchange second by second as he lifted her upon the rough stone ledge. Her eager heart pumped with anticipation when he positioned himself between her legs.

He wrapped one strong arm around the back of her waist and dipped her back enabling the wind to whip her hair. She thrilled at the feel of hanging so high above the land with only his arm to keep her from falling. Burning fire blazed through her. He trailed his tongue down the valley between her breasts and pushed his hard member deep inside...

"What do you think, Arianna?"

Startled, she ripped her eyes from the fire and tried to redirect it at whoever had spoken. *I think that I should pay attention.*

"Arianna?" She turned to her aunt and sat upright. Marie stared at her with expectation and nodded toward Edward. "Edward asked you a question, dear."

"I'm so sorry." Arianna had the good grace to blush. What had he asked? She thought quick and flashed him a smile.

"What would you imagine I think?" Arianna took a sip from her teacup and tried to will away her arousal. The thought of Iain always make her feel this way. "As you know, I'm fairly liberal minded." She licked her lips and prayed.

"That you are." Edward gazed her way with admiration.

"Arianna would, of course, support the hiring of Ms. Phillips," Marie provided.

They'd been speaking about hiring a woman to do a man's job.

"Absolutely." Arianna nodded at her aunt. "Ms. Phillips is a good woman. It is a progressive move. No doubt the gristmill will be marked in history for its forthright thinking."

"Yes, and she is a hard worker to be sure," Edward said. "Well, I must be leaving soon as mother and father will be expecting me for the evening meal."

"Very well, lad." Liam and Edward stood, shook hands and they all commenced at the door to bid farewell.

"May I call on you, Arianna?" Edward asked. He was formally requesting to court her.

No. I'm married. Arianna nearly said so but was interrupted.

"I see no reason why not," Liam said.

"But—" Arianna's words were cut short.

"Of course you can." Marie threw Arianna a curt look.

"Superb." Edward pinned Arianna with a promising gaze before he departed.

Arianna ground her teeth and waited for the door to shut.

"Why?" She tossed an infuriated glance from her aunt to her uncle.

"Well, I see she's feeling better." Liam walked back into the parlor.

"Aye, that she is." Marie followed her husband.

Standing at the entranceway to the room, Arianna's temper escalated. What were they thinking?

"Do you really want to know what we're thinking?" Marie said as she stood before the fire. It was apparent that Liam knew everything.

"Ha!" Arianna placed her hands on either hip and narrowed her eyes. "I thought so. You can read minds."

"Well, you're right." Marie was too calm. "When enough emotion is involved."

She walked back and stood nose to nose with Arianna. "I'm sorry I lied about it before. Right now you're far more emotional than you need be, so much

~Fate's Monolith~

so I doubt it would take one to read your mind to understand such."

"How could you do this? I'm already married, yet you and Uncle Liam are allowing another man to court me?"

She almost wilted under Marie's smoldering evaluation.

"Girl, there is no reason for you to be having such a fit. You know how much we love you and it pains us to see you this way." Marie took Arianna's hands. "Come sit and let's talk this through."

"If it pains you to see me this way and love me as you say you do, why pursue Edward on my behalf?" Arianna sat down and tried to reign in her temper.

"Exactly for those reasons, Arianna," Liam said and stretched out his legs in front of him. "You've been like a ghost walking around me house since you returned from your expedition. You've no life in ye, wee one. Me thinks the Devil himself must be having a good laugh just watching ye skirt around with a soul as barren as his homeland down below."

Arianna's lips quivered with the truth of it. She pulled her hands free from Marie's and made a show of adjusting her skirt.

"It breaks our hearts to see you this way, child. You've fought enough battles in your short life and made it through with a smile still on your comely face. Now, it seems, the final apple's been bobbed for and you're done for. Let me tell you this, I'll not allow it. That's right. You've come too far to give up now." Marie's face turned pink with frustration.

She stilled Arianna's fidgeting fingers and continued her tirade. "I cannot imagine the grief you are experiencing but you simply must move on. It's been nearly four weeks since your return. It saddens me to point this out my sweet, but you sent me no other correspondence from the past. Don't you think you would have by now, telling me all is well if you had ever returned there, that you were with him again?"

Arianna sat forward, eager. "I've thought of that as well. Perhaps, you simply have not received it yet, but will in the future."

Perhaps," Marie said on a sigh. "No doubt, time travel is a dynamic and complicated thing. Irregardless, you cannot continue to live this way. We refuse to allow it. Besides, my girl, you're not getting any younger. It's only the natural order of things that you consider starting your own family."

Arianna knew Marie didn't enjoy having to say these things. Interrupted only by the obtrusive spit of the logs on the hearth, tension lay thick within the room.

She'd known for some time this moment would arrive. Regardless, Arianna felt misunderstood and rejected. She knew she had no right to. Her aunt and uncle had taken good care of her. They did nothing but love her and provide a wonderful home for her to grow up in.

"I do not wish to re-marry." Arianna walked over to the fireplace. "You cannot force me." Could she sound any more like a child?

"Think about what you're saying niece," Liam spoke softly. "Please don't put us in such an uncomfortable position, we don't deserve it."

She rolled her shoulders in an attempt to release the tightness and turned back to face them. Both wore miserable frowns. Despite an unfounded sense of spite, Arianna's heart went out to them. Why couldn't everything go back to the way it was before?

She wasn't the same person. That's why. They were right. It broke her heart, but they were right. Whatever may come, she was stuck in 1799. She lived six hundred years later than her beloved.

Arianna couldn't stay here. It was time to move on.

"You're both right, things need to change. I will leave."

Marie crossed to Arianna and placed her hands on her shoulders. "We have no wish for you leave. You are part of the family."

Whatever hope she saw flood Arianna's eyes, Marie disregarded. "However, it is time for you to allow a courtship."

Before she could deny her, Marie silenced Arianna with a finger to the lip. "This is not merely a request."

"We welcome you to stay if you allow Edward the chance to spend some time with you." Liam came to stand beside his wife.

"Why Edward? There are other bachelors." Arianna already knew the answer.

"He is the one most interested and will be able to provide amply for you. Not only monetarily but also in social standing. Besides, rumor has it no other man is willing to surpass him in regards to you, Arianna. His position in society has become most prominent."

"What of love?" She whispered. "I don't love him."

"You don't know him." Marie was tender. "You may have as children, but that has come and gone."

"If this is my only option, then I will leave Salem." Arianna turned to the fire. This was the only option left. As much as she feared such a thing, she would do it. She'd go to Boston. There, she could board somewhere until she had enough saved...

Marie murmured, "Please don't be upset with me for intruding on your thoughts again, but that's a horrible idea. Have you any idea what happens to women such as you in Boston in this day and age?"

"Arianna, what on Ireland's green Earth are you thinking about?" Liam's tone turned dry as he stepped past her and stoked the fire.

"I would do just fine in Boston." She'd done just fine in twelfth century Scotland. Arianna looked at Marie. "You made it in London just fine before meeting Uncle Liam."

"That was London, not Boston. Do you know how fortunate we were to work in that bakery? You know as well as I do how lucky it was we walked into that place when we did. If it wasn't for the fact the owner was miraculously Irish with a thick distain for hiring the English we would have never had it so good." Marie reminded. "Besides, London is a very different city than Boston. It's not half the melting pot. Every day immigrants arrive off ships to begin a new life here. If you don't have an established position in that city it'll eat you alive."

"There would be only one trade they'd make of you there," Liam agreed. "A naïve Scottish country lass such as you."

"Don't be foolish." Marie put an arm around Arianna's waist. "Besides, I'll need you to stay close, what with the babe coming and all."

Arianna cast a suspicious glance at her aunt.

"You must not leave Salem for I'll need your help here still," Marie said.

"So I'm to understand that I must marry, therefore staying in Salem so that I may be available to continue on here with household duties?" Arianna said.

"Aye, lass, you have the right of it." Liam came to the aid of his stunned wife. "You cannot deny the need for some extra help."

Arianna didn't know how to respond. Most of what she was inclined to say was downright rude and ungrateful.

"So, I'm trapped." She sat, numb, in a nearby chair.

"What words do you utter under your breath?" Before the full fury of Marie could accost her, Liam intercepted.

"I would highly advise you to apologize to your aunt readily, for you owe her that at the very least."

Arianna couldn't stop the overflow of silent tears. She'd made a mess of everything. She hadn't meant to say that. Her poor aunt, the one who'd done everything for her since her parents passing was the last person that deserved such treatment. She felt deflated and hollow. Arianna shook her head with regret and met Marie's angry eyes.

"I'm so sorry." What more could she say?

"Are you? I realize you may very well feel trapped at this moment but your lack of tact baffles me. Who is this selfish creature you've become? You've wounded me, Arianna Lilias Broun, and I do not receive it kindly." Marie put a protective hand to her stomach. "I'm going to bed."

Arianna stared after her, stung by the use of her name without O'Donnell. Ironic, it was not long ago she had resented the name. What was the matter with her? Everything.

"'Tis ill bode, lassie." Liam followed his wife from the room.

Alone, Arianna closed her eyes.

Ill bode was a grave understatement.

Arianna sat alone for a long time. As her tears dried she stared into the fire. Time dwindled with the flames in the hearth.

She felt the magic before it came.

Vibration surrounded her, combined with blurred vision. She closed her eyes. Don't panic. After several moments, she opened them.

The wizard Adlin sat beside her, nearly transparent. His long white hair floated amidst the curved feet of the chair. White robes dusted the floor.

His icicle eyes didn't look her way. Her heart thrummed wildly. *He's here for me! I'm going to see Iain again!*

"Nay, say not a word, my child." The foreboding words floated into her mind.

"Why? Adlin, are you here to take me back? Adlin?"

Slowly, he raised his hand and pointed at the diminished fire.

A gold mist drifted from his outstretched finger to the hearth. Enchanted, she followed it until it settled on the blue embers. Unable to look away she watched as the embers flared to life, erupting into hungry flames fueled of magic.

Oh! Arianna leaned forward.

Inside the flames she saw, as an eagle would from high above, hundreds of horses burst free of a forest onto a plain of rock and moss. Snow fell heavy.

She dropped from the chair to the floor and crawled closer. A cold wind pushed at her face from the riotous fire. Mesmerized, she watched the furious line of horsemen plummet forward.

Then Arianna had wings and as she flew closer she realized there was another line of horses erupting from across the way. She swooped lower and began to understand what was happening.

There was no mistaking the Scottish Highlands. Uneven slopes of sharp mountaintops penetrated the sky above and below her. Deep gray rock rolled in and out like a dizzying waterfall. Stoic pines grouped together to keep warm.

Unburdened by the human form, she reveled at the feel of strength and power rippling through the feathered wings that spanned out on either side of her. Free and uninhibited, she pumped her wings and learned the feel of the noble body at her disposal.

How she yearned to soar over the highest steep and fly where fate took her. However, the pull of curiosity and something undefined overtook her and she continued to careen towards the battle unfolding below.

Thousands of horses pounded upon the ground and caused an earsplitting thunder. Eager hooves mixed with the sound of battle cries. Vengeful clansmen growled and roared their way towards the enemy.

She coasted within a stone's throw of the two vicious fronts when they clashed together.

Time became sluggish as she soared over the front warrior. He whipped his gleaming battle-axe in a wide arch. His battle cry was loud and fierce.

Bloodlust. Iain.

Enraged, she screamed as she soared past him and beat her wings viciously to gain height. By instinct alone, she stopped beating on one side and continued to pump rapidly on the other.

Her nimble body whipped around. Caught slightly off balance she evened out by pumping both wings simultaneously. The wind caught her and she began to glide back down.

Blood shot towards the sky and spiked the fresh snow as mortal men battled. She flew so low that the smell of sweat tinged the nostrils.

Nothing mangled the soul such as war like this.

Overwhelmed, she made a wide circle overhead. Where was he? How could she possibly find him again in the evil unfolding below?

As the cries lessened far below, she dove again. One clan had more left standing than the other, but which one? She rode the wind and sailed downward.

A horrible feeling arose.

Then, out of the swirling flakes, he appeared.

Iain.

He lay on the ground with an ogre of a man standing over him. His horse lay still beside him.

No! Iain! She pumped her wings harder. *I'm coming!*

Time stopped as the swordsman above her husband lifted his blade. Iain lifted an arm and draped his hand over the forehead of his horse.

Iain. Roll away. Fight. Don't give up!

But the blade fell. Arianna wailed as the long sword broke through his chest. Strangely enough, when his chest arched she could have sworn his eyes sought hers.

For a moment, they transgressed time.

"I loved you." She heard his voice from far away.

His eyes turned back to meet the vacant eyes of his horse.

Then he was gone.

She felt him pass deep within. As her body drifted slowly over his she watched his hand slide slowly down the animals head until it rested lifeless on the ground.

No. Please, sweet Lord above. No.

Arianna wept as the frigid snowflakes whipped her feathered cheeks. A biting wind turned to a sizzling flame and a heavy, unwelcome feeling overtook her. She looked down and saw not majestic, uneven mountains but the stark even lines of a hardwood floor.

Another sob wracked her body. Arianna turned to search out the wizard. There was nothing there but an empty chair. She knelt, laid her head where he had sat. Please come back, Adlin. Please. He was all that remained of that brief life.

Iain had died defending his clan.

Chapter Eighteen

Arianna opened her eyes then immediately squeezed them shut. Sunlight blinded. Rubbing her swollen eyes, she eventually stared out the window. What she wouldn't do for a small slit of a window in a servant's chamber.

He was gone. In every way possible.

Tired of the sick game fate played with her, she spent most of the previous night soul-searching.

Do I stop breathing?

Forego hope?

Take my own life? No.

She had to move on. She couldn't bring him back.

Fresh pain twisted her gut. Arianna dismissed emotion and shoved the blanket aside. It was time she started to act like an adult. No more fairy tales. No more handsome Scotsmen with heart-wrenching green eyes.

The December day was radiant. November hadn't existed for her. She realized that there was a cup of tea steaming on her bedside table. Despite her bad behavior the prior evening, she was forgiven. For that alone, she knew it was time to return to the living.

Arianna dressed and hurried downstairs. The house was quiet. Distressed, she hurried into the kitchen. A lone plate heaped with freshly baked muffins sat on the table. She searched room to room until it occurred to her that it was Sunday. Church.

Then she heard voices.

Arianna ran to open the front door. "Aunt Marie."

She rushed into her aunt's arms. "I'm incredibly sorry, can you ever forgive me? I'm the most undeserving creature you've had the misfortune to be related to. Please don't hate me."

Before she could utter another word, Marie quieted her with a fierce hug.

"Shush child, you're forgiven. It was just your young heart at work." Marie pried Arianna from her arms. "Come. Let's get in out of the cold."

Arm and arm, they went inside and sat down at the kitchen table.

"All right me little lassies, why don't we go warm our fingers and toes in front of a fire," Liam said to his daughters.

Alone, Arianna and Marie clasped hands across the table.

"I did a lot of thinking last night," Arianna confided. "I'll do whatever is necessary. I'll permit Edward to court me if that pleases you. Just allow me to disengage myself from all I've been through. There is a life that exists in which I'm with my true love. He's gone. I'm here and intend to be available to help you. It's the least I can do for all you have done for me."

Marie's eyes turned moist. "Thank you."

"There's something I'd like to share with you."

"Aye?" Marie said.

Arianna sipped her tea and ignored the well of sadness within her. "I had a visitor last night."

"A visitor here? Last night? You mean after your uncle and I retired?" Marie's asked, concerned.

Arianna nodded. "Not in the sense you might expect. It was the wizard Adlin that I told you about. He simply materialized in the parlor."

"Oh my!"

"Aye, his arrival initially filled me with hope. Regrettably, the sentiment didn't last long. He'd only come to show me something."

Her voice was thick with anguish. "I've got to let Iain go."

"He died," she whispered. A hot tear rolled down her cheek. "I saw the battle in the fire. Through the eyes of an eagle I watched history unfold."

Marie squeezed her hands. "I'm so very sorry, lass. I truly am."

Nodding, Arianna pulled her hands free and wiped the tears from her eyes. "I know you are." She sighed. "I'll get better with time. I suppose I'm just happy that I had the time I did with him."

"You've matured, lass." Marie scooped her into a hug. "Time will lessen the pain. I promise."

The next morning she kept Marie's words in mind when Edward came calling. They sat in the parlor together with Marie as a sporadic chaperon who checked on them rarely. Had they been younger, their courtship would've been different.

"I'm so pleased you agreed to this, Arianna." Edward sat in the chair across from hers. A fire burned in the hearth.

"As am I," Arianna lied.

"I must say that it was a pleasant surprise, your willingness to accept my favor."

"You are persistent." Arianna smiled and practiced at formal flirtation. It felt terribly fake.

"Why wouldn't I be, you're very beautiful and still wonderfully available." He smiled.

"Thank you, I suppose I just blossomed a bit later than the other girls." But I blossomed, just not with you.

"What matters is that you blossomed." His eyes locked on hers.

~Fate's Monolith~

Arianna blushed at the innuendo and set to examining her tea. It appeared that their courtship before marriage was going to be a short one as far as he was concerned.

"Have I embarrassed you?" Humor laced his voice.

"Not at all, you say what you feel. I can relate to that," Arianna said.

"I know. That's what I've always enjoyed about you, even as a child. I seem to remember a certain afternoon many years ago when you did just that, right before pushing me into the Spicket River." He laughed and he set his teacup back upon its plate.

"I remember," she chuckled. "You must admit, however, you had that coming."

"It was just a bit of mud," he said. "I think you over reacted."

"A bit of mud shoved right into my face," Arianna said. She could do this.

His eyebrows came together. "I landed backwards into the water, you little scamp."

Arianna laughed. "You got what you deserved."

"I always do." He shot her a predatory glance.

Suddenly, all Arianna could see was Iain. His crooked grin. The arched eyebrow when he was set on teasing her. How he flirted. The way he'd made her heart race and her breath catch. Edward incited none of these feelings.

"I'm not so bad, you know?" Edward said.

Arianna stared at the fire. "I never said you were."

"Why the tense body language and the faraway look then?" Edward's gaze was both shrewd and speculative.

She tensed. "I'm just new at this." *No I'm not.*

Edward shifted in his chair. "Fair enough."

Arianna inwardly groaned. "Just give me time."

Edward got up and came to stand before her. She looked up into his face as he took her hand. "Arianna, I've already given you the past nine years."

Indeed he had and for that she would try harder. Be the woman he thought he saw when he looked at her. It was the very least she could do…wasn't it?

And so she did.

The next few weeks of December passed in a blur of activity. Between household chores, her courtship with Edward and preparing for Christmastide, Arianna had little time to think.

Despite her best efforts she would, on occasion, be subject to memories. Late at night when the moonlight glazed the thick snowfall she thought of them. Muriel's smile, Arthur's endless good humor and Hugh's kind jests. Helen's whiskey and Adlin's mystery.

Then there was Iain. Always Iain. It seemed the more she was with Edward the more she compared him to Iain. Edward's shoulders were nice. Iain's were broad and strong and dependable. Edward smelled of citrus cologne and starch, Iain of spice and woods and dark sensual nights.

Yet the next morning would come and it would be Edward she'd see, never Iain.

As was tradition, the night of Christmastide was spent at the O'Donnell's home. The Huntington's as well as many other prominent Salem families would be in attendance. Marie was in top form. Not only had she and Arianna tended to their normal chores but they readied the house for the evening's festivities.

Fresh garland was strung. Candles were placed on the tree as food and spirits were set out. When the hour came, guests were received well. The Huntington's were the first to arrive since their son courted a member of the household.

Edward positioned himself by Arianna's side to receive further company.

She found little thrill in the formalities until her friend Beth arrived. Clad in a gown of deep red velvet, the garment was fashioned to her advantage.

With a snicker Arianna leaned over and whispered in her ear. "Who are you trying to impress?"

Beth stood back, eyed the ceiling and fanned her face with one hand. "You, my dear. You," she said with her best southern accent. "Who else?"

Arianna laughed. "Well, I'm quite taken. You look splendid."

Edward frowned. "Since when do you dress like that?"

Both women turned their heads in shock. Though their banter had always been the behest of a joke, Edward's tone sounded a little too serious.

He appeared to realize his folly. "Not that it's a bad thing. You just don't look like your scholarly self."

Beth rolled her eyes. "Would you prefer that I'd sewn some books into the hemline? Maybe fashioned one as a hat?"

"It would add a curve or two," Edward said, his English accent dry.

They were back to normal.

"Scoundrel."

"Hussy." He gave Beth a quick hug.

"I must mingle. My fans are waiting." Beth raised her chin and vanished into the parlor.

The evening progressed with finesse. Eventually, everyone made his or her way into the parlor to gather around the modest piano.

Arianna smiled as Liam and Marie sat down together on the bench. Their voices were beautiful as they sang carols. When they finished everyone applauded. Edward had remained with her by the fire the entire time and offered Arianna his hand at the closure of the music.

"If you all would excuse my heartfelt interruption, I request but a moment of your time," Edward said, loud enough for the room to hear.

The crowd turned to them as he pulled her closer. Edward released her and fell down on one knee.

Oh no, no, no! What is he doing?

"Before all of those with us on this Christmastide, I ask you, Arianna, to consider me in a fashion beyond what we are this night."

Arianna stared at him. Consider him in a fashion beyond what?

He took her hand in his and continued. "You have my heart. No woman is as beautiful or graceful as you."

Aye, there are plenty of other women.

Memories of a river encased by a rainbow and a tall, dark Scotsman filled her vision. Her knees threatened to buckle.

Edward squeezed her hand.

"Arianna Lilias Broun O'Donnell, would you give me the extreme pleasure of becoming my wife?"

An anxious silence smothered the room. Seconds passed with excruciating slowness. She owed her aunt this.

"Yes." Nothing came out. Arianna swallowed and licked her lips. What would Iain make of this? Would he be pleased she had someone to care for her in his absence? Of course he would.

"Yes." This time the word was loud and clear.

The room erupted in cheers. Before the crowd moved forward, Edward halted them with a brief raise of his hand.

Still on his knees he reached into a pocket. "Please accept this as a symbol of our promise to each other."

He slid a beautiful diamond onto her finger. The cut was exquisite, set into an elegant swirl of gold.

Arianna could only stare at the lovely jewel upon her hand.

The crowd would wait no longer. They surged forward and flooded them with heartwarming embraces. Marie brought forth an influx of tears and kisses. Liam gave her a fierce hug and shook Edward's hand. Her future mother and father-in-law were equally pleased and didn't hold back their enthusiasm.

"Welcome to the family," Richard Huntington declared.

Edward slipped an arm around Arianna's waist and pulled her closer. He felt strange against her. Although he was a strong man, his build was much slighter than Iain's. She also noted that though he was one of the tallest men there, he was shorter and far less imposing than Iain.

The remaining hour passed in a light and festive mood. At last, the crowd began to leave. As they were the first to arrive, the Huntington's were also the last to leave. With fond farewells, the family departed for their carriage.

"I'll follow in a moment," Edward said to his father.

Well aware that he hoped for a bit of privacy with their niece, Marie and Liam made themselves scarce. Edward smiled at Arianna and buttoned his jacket.

"It's been a wonderful evening," she said.

"Yes, the best I've had." Edward pulled her up against him. A blond lock of errant hair fell over his forehead as he lowered his head. "I long for the day that we are official," he whispered. "And yearn for the night."

Not sure how to respond, Arianna placed her hands on his arms. Edward placed a hand beneath her chin and tipped her head back. Then his lips were on hers. It was a soft kiss. She closed her eyes and allowed his mouth exploration.

A small sound came from Edward and he pulled her tighter against him. Patient, she waited for a flood of emotion. Nothing. No weakness of the knees. No quickening of the heart. Instead, she contemplated whether she wished to take Fyne out for a quick trot in the morning before she began her chores.

When he ended the kiss, Edward brushed the back of his hand down her cheek. "I look forward to seeing you for the New Year."

Arianna nodded in agreement and stood at the door until he reached the waiting carriage. She wouldn't see him for another week in that he would be traveling out of town on business.

She closed the door and leaned back against it. Was this it? Perhaps, in time, things would change. She'd learn to love him, learn to feel passion at his touch.

For now, it was time to clean.

Arianna joined Marie in the kitchen. Her aunt was silent as they executed their duties. Liam sat before the fire and smoked a pipe in the other room. Only when the last candle on the tree was blown out and the house was as it should be did Marie speak to her.

"Come with me, I want to show you something."

Arianna trailed her up the stairs and paused as Marie lit a candle. She was shocked when her aunt unlocked and opened the attic door. This was a place that had only ever been reserved for Marie and Liam.

Coldness enveloped as they transgressed the steep stairs to the next level. The distinct mustiness told of an area not lived in. Arianna peered around in an attempt to discern what the dark corners concealed. The lone candle did nothing to aid her.

"Don't bother," Marie said. "I've used magic to cloak everything but what we're here to see."

"You can..." Arianna's words trailed off when Marie set the candle on a small wooden table and flicked her wrist. Just like Iain.

An oval swath of swelling candlelight poured from the wick's flame. Arianna was speechless.

Her aunt was a wizard.

"A witch, luv, as are you. We are not wizards. A great power lives within you. Eventually, with assistance, you will learn how to use it."

Magic. Two months ago, she never would've believed such a thing existed outside of fairytales.

"Witch." Arianna rolled the word around on her tongue.

This couldn't be good. After all, this wasn't the twelfth century. "It's not such a safe thing. What we are in this time."

"No, it is not." Marie met Arianna's eye, her tone serious. "You must always remain discreet. Only with me, here in this room, should you ever even think of it."

"What of the rest of the family? I gather Uncle Liam knows. Is he a witch as well? What of the children?" Her mind reeled with curiosity.

Marie cocked her head. "You're full of questions, aren't you child?"

A small smile teased her lips as Marie pulled a simple unfinished wooden chair from the shadows. She sat down and remained silent for a time.

"Liam knows but carries no magic of his own. Coira is free of the gift, but Annie and her brother are not."

"Brother?" Arianna was confused until she saw that Marie gazed with love at her swollen belly.

"Oh, Aunt Marie." She kneeled before her aunt and gently placed her hand on her little nephew. "I'm so happy for you."

"Thank you. His name will be Calum." The women shared a space of comfortable silence to contemplate the little wonder yet unborn.

"Look." Marie broke the quiet when she pointed behind Arianna to the soft ellipse of light carpeting the wooden planks underfoot.

Arianna gasped.

An oak treasure chest sat alone. It sparkled in the candlelight, dappled with marble sized emeralds. It was at least four feet long and two and a half feet wide. Unbelievable! Drawn to the magnificent fixture, she ran her fingers over the smooth surface. Although they gave the appearance of protrusion, the stones were set into the wood.

"Open it." Marie knelt beside Arianna.

Arianna was careful as she braced her hands on the wire-thin stems of rose shaped emeralds that acted as handles. They warmed under her touch and the pedals became as supple as worn leather.

"How very—" Again, Arianna's words broke off when the handles turned to plush white roses in her hands. A light breeze passed through the attic and carried the sweet smell of flowers. Had she just heard the sound of a bagpipe in the distance? As quickly as it came, it was gone. Click. The trunk slowly opened of its own accord. Arianna's breath caught at the sight of its contents.

An incredibly beautiful dress.

One might call it crème, another gold it was such a unique shade. She reached down and lifted it up. The long, elegant sleeves tapered down to triangular points that would fall over the hand and stop at the apex of the index finger. Beyond this point were circles of petite pearls meant to anchor the sleeve in ring fashion. The same pearls ran along the deep point that was the dress's bodice and the low neckline.

Parallel to every polished line of pearls was a glorious stream of glistening emeralds. Right before the pearl rings, the end of the sleeves hinted at the exotic and mysterious with their unusual star shapes that weaved within the emeralds.

Arianna ran a finger over the emerald stars. "These are magnificent."

"Aye," Marie said. "The pentacle. Pagan. The oldest symbol known to man."

Arianna gave a slow, contemplative nod. "These are incredible as well." She touched the glossy surface of one of many pearls.

"Every single pearl on this dress was hand selected from oysters born of the North Sea long ago. She was a woman of our bloodline. We descend beyond the Eastern shores of Scotland and the Northern shores of France," Marie said.

"France?"

"Every clan of Scotland traveled from somewhere, sweetie." Marie expected the next question.

"What of the MacLomain clan?"

"Ireland. The origin of the greatest magic in the world."

"Ireland." Arianna repeated. That she could understand, but France?

"Every country has its secrets. France has theirs. But our heritage merely passed through France. In that, I mean we were there for about two hundred years. Before that was Austria, back further into Hungary. Before Hungary was Romania. The very first of our blood resided on the Black Sea. All of the hundreds upon hundreds of generations now run through your blood."

"Incredible, isn't it?" Marie nodded at the dress.

"Aye." Arianna sighed with worship.

"It was your mothers."

"My mothers?"

"It was her wedding gown. Before that, it was the wedding gown of every woman of your lineage."

"I've never seen anything more lovely." She imagined her mother in this glorious garment.

Marie patted her on the shoulder and then lifted a magnificent veil from the trunk. "This, my niece, is part of the ensemble."

Arianna was in love.

From a crown of heavy emeralds, silky crème gauze hung in a sheet of velvety softness. A mere three inches from the bottom, thirteen fragile Celtic crosses of pinpoint emeralds were sewn across the width, touching arm to arm.

"I can only fathom how much this is worth," Arianna murmured.

"It is worth the generations of the women in your family."

"It appears so new," Arianna said with a rueful smile.

"Of course it does, it's been preserved well."

"Aye."

"May I?" Arianna looked with longing at the ring of jewels in Marie's hand.

"It is your right."

Eager to hold what'd once adorned her Ma and so many before her, Arianna reached out. As her hand clamped around the ring of emeralds she was yanked forward.

Then the floor fell out from beneath them.

Chapter Nineteen

Marie's eyes narrowed.

When she spoke her words sounded as though she stood far away. "Great magic is coming. Do not release the headpiece. Do you understand me Arianna? Do not release the headpiece."

Petrified, Arianna stared at her aunt. Marie's eyes were alert yet calm. Her mouth formed a straight line and her skin glowed to the point of transparency. What struck Arianna most was the pale gold window of film that clung to them as a cobweb would its master's prey.

Marie chanted in a strange language. Her words were an echo. Arianna sucked in her breath and continued to focus on Marie. Through peripheral vision, she knew that the attic was gone. The ring of emeralds turned to a ring of white, crème and pale pink flowers.

The very same headpiece she'd worn that wonderful day not so long ago. Her heart thundered against her chest.

A small stone room with a slit for a window materialized. It was the servant's room she had slept in. Scotland!

Arianna saw herself sitting on the bed in the wedding gown she wore the day she married Iain. Muriel stood before her and placed the ringlet of flowers on her head.

"Oh God, Muriel! It's so good to see you. Muriel?" Arianna said. Nothing came out of her mouth as she went to release the ring in her hands.

"Do not release the headpiece, Arianna. If you do, you will be forever lost in a rift between times. You will not exist either in the twelfth century or the eighteenth century." Marie's urgent words crashed into her mind.

Startled, she clamped her hands.

Arianna heard her other self speak as she fingered the flowers on her head. "The flowers are beautiful, if not a bit elaborate?"

"Nay, 'tis tradition," Muriel said to the twelfth century Arianna. "Now let me show you this great land that is your home."

Muriel turned and headed for the door. She came to an abrupt stop when she stood in the very same spot as Marie.

Marie disappeared within Muriel's solid form.

"Child, do not release the headpiece. Though you cannot see me, I still hold the other side of the ringlet." Marie's words soothed Arianna.

Then twelfth century Arianna stepped into her body. She stared down in baffled awe. Her solid body of the past held her arms by her side whereas her transparent arms stayed forward as she held the ringlet.

"Muriel?" Her own voice emanated from her solid form.

"Aye. I just had a strange feeling overcome me," Muriel said.

"Are you feeling well?" This from her solid form again.

Arianna swayed as the scene split into tiny fragments and left only herself and Marie as they continued to hold the ring of flowers.

The room twisted them. A kaleidoscope of color swirled past them. Then everything turned white. Arianna clearly heard Adlin say, "Iain's soul tries to pull Arianna back. She must marry on the last day of December or all is lost."

Iain! Was he still alive? Could it be? Suddenly, Marie and Arianna stood alone in the cold attic with only the candle to see by. The trunk, chair and small table were gone. Arianna now held the gown and veil over her trembling arm. Her aunt stared at her intensely.

"Did you hear that?" Arianna's heart swelled. "It sounds as if he's..."

"He's what?" Marie asked, confused.

Arianna blinked. A funny feeling rolled over her.

"Who do you speak of, lass?" Marie prompted.

Shaking her head, Arianna frowned. I've no idea what I was about to say. The last thing she recalled was holding up the veil. How odd. "I'm sorry, I lost my train of thought."

Marie's voice was melodious when she looked into Arianna's eyes and spoke. "It is time to move on. You will marry at the end of the year."

"What?" Arianna felt slightly light-headed. "The end of the year?"

"Aye, the end of the year."

Arianna felt detached as Marie took the dress from her arms. The end of the year? Hmm. Well, why not? "That sounds acceptable."

"I thought you'd think so." Marie hung the dress and led Arianna down to her bed.

"It's time for sleep, lass." Marie pulled the covers up over her niece. Arianna's eyes were closed before her head hit the pillow.

What felt like mere seconds passed before she awoke. Bright sunlight filled the room. Morning already! With a wide smile, she sat up and stretched.

She was getting married this week! By the time she made it downstairs the family was waiting eagerly for her.

"Congratulations!" Liam caught her at the bottom stair where he hugged her tightly. His sky blue eyes were as merry as ever. The girls and Marie flittered around her like humming birds.

"I've spoken with Richard and the matrimony will happen Sunday, the day after Edward arrives home. We shall have the ceremony here. The wedding will precede the New Year celebration." Liam's excitement was ill concealed.

Arianna laughed when Marie placed a hand on Liam's shoulder and shook her head. The message was clear, stop rambling. Resolved, he allowed others to chatter and plan alongside him.

And so they planned and prepared and the week flew by. She'd never been so happy...had she? The time spent with her family before the wedding day was wonderful. Her daily chores seemed less tedious. Everything seemed perfect. Absolutely perfect. Not once did it occur to her that this all seemed to be happening too quickly. Not once did she think about Iain.

At long last, the wedding day arrived.

The day was bright, clear and bitterly cold. Several new inches of snow fell overnight. When evening fell, the house was ready. Marie joined Arianna when the time came to retire to her room to get ready. Downstairs, guests began to arrive. Slipping into the wondrous dress, she tried to tune out the voices that floated up the stairs.

"It fits you perfectly," Marie said.

Arianna ran her hands down the satiny front. She felt very feminine, almost sumptuous. When she ran a finger along the bodice her mind became strange. It almost felt as though Iain stood before her. He was tall and broad and hungry. His finger grazed where she now touched, half on the material and half upon her sensitive skin.

"Arianna." Marie frowned.

Marie took Arianna's hand and rubbed her thumb in slow circles over her niece's palm. "Iain is gone. Edward is not."

As though she awoke from a dream, Arianna's face softened. "Edward is not."

"Aye." Marie confirmed, "Edward is not."

"Now for your hair. Let's see." She sat Arianna down on a stool in front of the full length, oblong mirror and fiddled with different styles. "We want to keep your hair as free as possible I think."

"I agree," Arianna said.

"Perhaps a few parts from the front pulled back into the veil's crown. This will show off your beautiful features better." Marie grabbed the brush and ran it through the long glorious hair. Once the fiery waves shone, she pulled some strands back from Arianna's cheeks and pinned them on top of her head.

"Here we are." Marie crowned Arianna with the ring of emeralds in such a fashion that the front of the ring covered the pins and made it appear that the jewels alone held back her hair.

"You are a vision."

"I feel like royalty." Arianna reached a single hand up to the glittering gems afloat her head.

Marie circled her niece while she pulled, tucked and made pointless adjustments to a dress that already looked perfect.

"But what of this?" Arianna turned halfway from the mirror, bent an elbow back and touched the end of the veil, which fell shorter than the length of her hair.

Marie stood behind Arianna and ran her hands down either side of the material. She laughed with delight when the veil lengthened with the touch until it ended at the bottom of her back, falling even with the locks. They smiled at each other in the mirror.

"I think you are ready. How do you feel?"

"Calm, actually. Is that normal?" Arianna twirled a lock of hair.

"No. No it's not," Marie whispered.

"What?" Arianna frowned.

"I said nothing, dear."

She shrugged. "Hmm. I could've sworn."

Marie paused at the door. "Godspeed child." Then she vanished downstairs.

As she stood at the top of the stairs, Arianna surveyed her surroundings. Simple cherry wood wall sconces lined the wall opposite the banister. Tall beeswax candles burned bright and lit the stairwell. Spruce wrapped down the banister held by intermittent pink bows. The home smelled like cinnamon and evergreen. A violin played from the parlor.

Dressed to perfection in a black suit, Edward stood at the bottom. The only other person in the foyer was Liam. Edward looked up at her and gasped. The violin stopped and people drifted into the foyer. They filled the small room but left a path open to the parlor beyond. All fell silent.

The violinist broke the silence with a sweet, soulful melody. Arianna descended the staircase, slow and graceful. At the bottom, she looked up into Edward's warm blue eyes. For but a flicker of a moment, she yearned for Iain's cool emerald eyes.

Then she yearned no more.

Arianna accepted Edward's extended arm and allowed him to lead her to the fireplace. They would be married where he proposed. Marie and Liam came to stand beside her. Edwards's mother and father were beside him.

The priest shuffled forward and stood before them. Bent with age, Father McGregory's hair was dull gray and his long robe needed hemming.

"Welcome all. We come to—" Father McGregory coughed and Liam stepped forward to pat him on the back.

His coughing spell ended and he looked up at Liam with appreciation. "Thank you, son. Thank you."

Liam nodded and resumed his place next to Marie while Father McGregory continued. "We come together to join in holy matrimony Edwa—" He started to cough again.

This time, before Liam could step forward he raised a hand and shook his head. Someone behind him handed him a glass of water and he drank from it as the crowd waited.

Wind began to howl.

"Are you well, Father?" Marie stepped forward.

Father McGregory set the glass of water down. "Yes, thank you. Shall we continue?"

Everyone nodded.

"Very good." The priest opened his bible.

"We come together in holy—"

A loud crash sounded from the foyer. Fierce wind blew into the parlor and extinguished the candles. Only the fire cast light.

"Fyne!" Beth yelled from somewhere in the back of the room.

Liam lurched into the crowd toward the entryway. Arianna and Marie turned and ran the other way. Though they ran through the dining room, study, hallway and kitchen they arrived at the foyer at the same moment as Liam.

"Fyne." Arianna ran forward as Liam tried to get the animal under control. Her horse ran in evasive circles while wind driven snow blew in the door.

Arianna jumped in front of the horse, raised her hand muzzle level and met Fyne's oncoming eyes. "Stop."

Fyne did.

With a sigh of relief, Arianna ran her hands along either side of Fyne's muzzle until she was able to scratch behind the ears and calm the sweaty horse. Her eyes were wild when they met Arianna's.

"What's the matter, girl?"

"She's in season," Liam said.

Crash. Something fell. That's all it took

Fyne pulled away from Arianna and ran out the door. Liam went to the closet door and pulled it open. "I'll get her." He pulled multiple lanterns out. Edward and Richard were amongst the men who took a lantern and fled outside.

Beth shooed Arianna into the kitchen while Marie shut the door and invited the baffled crowd back into the parlor for some piano music.

Arianna sat down at the table. Poor Fyne.

Beth sat across from her and pushed a cup across the table. Arianna took a sip. Whiskey. "Thanks."

Beth took a sip from her cup. "It's the least I could do."

"Welcome to my wedding." Arianna gave a small laugh.

Beth quirked first one brow, then the other. "You're getting married?"

Arianna smiled and glanced at the doorway. "Why is she behaving like this?"

"She's in season. Just like you will be later tonight."

Arianna returned her attention to Beth. "You really are a scamp."

Beth tipped back her head and downed the contents of her cup. "Me? Never."

"I know she's in season but why did she do what she did? How did she get out of her stall?"

"No doubt the wind had something to do with it. Do you hear it out there?" Beth got up and left the room for a moment.

She returned and plunked a small bottle of whiskey between them. "Well, my friend, a drink to the end of the century." She refilled her cup and topped Arianna's off.

"Is it that time already?" Arianna lifted her mug to Beth's.

"Aye, as of this moment we toast in the nineteenth century."

The two friends drank and set down their mugs.

Arianna rested her arms on the table. "This is a monumental occasion."

Beth nodded. "Without a doubt."

"I should be a married woman right now."

"What's a few more minutes?" Beth grinned and shrugged.

The crowd in the parlor hollered with merriment. "I'm glad you're here," Arianna said.

"Where else would I be?"

Arianna turned somber. Beth was due to leave for college the next day.

"You remembered," Beth said. It was more of a statement then a question.

"Aye." Arianna sighed.

"I'd hoped you wouldn't. At least for tonight."

"You're my best friend. I was bound to remember."

Beth didn't like to get emotional. "Shall I go check out front and see if the men are on their way back in?"

Arianna nodded, took another drink of whiskey and sat back. This night is cursed.

"Uh, Arianna?"

Arianna glanced to where Beth stood in the doorway of the kitchen. She looked worried.

"You may want to come see this."

Arianna was out of her seat in an instant.

People suddenly overflowed the foyer and blocked the front door so she detoured down the hallway that ran beside the staircase and exited out the back door. *Oooh, these bloody skirts!* She yanked them up so they wouldn't drag through the snow.

When she rounded the corner, she stopped, horrified. A circle of men stood halfway down the front walkway from the house, their lanterns a fiery eye against the dark.

Fyne was violent. She bucked and kicked sharp hooves into the air. Everything about the horse bespoke of lust and need. Pure instinct drove the animal to near insanity.

"Fyne!" Arianna cried and raced forward. She sidled the perimeter of torches and tried to get closer.

"Subdue the animal," Richard said.

Other men spoke.

"Shoot it."

"Stab it."

"The beast is crazed."

They have guns and knives? *No!*

Then Richard Huntington raised his gun. With skilled precision, the man circled the wild animal. Fyne's mane shone auburn against the circle of candles, her coat a polished combination of oak and cherry.

"No, stop!" Arianna pushed forward but met the wall of Edward's arm.

"Let her through," Liam said.

Edward's arm released her and Arianna surged forward into the ring of torches.

"Easy, lassie, easy. 'Tis just a wee bit of excitement this eve, luv. 'Tis just you and me, girl. 'Tis always been and 'twill always be, my Fyne. These folk dinnae what they do. You cannae hold that against them. Aye?"

Fyne's wild eyes met hers. "Come now, they didnae mean to scare you. They widnae hurt you. We all know o' the feelings you have right now."

She put her nose to Fyne's muzzle. "Aye?"

The horse stomped one leg.

Arianna pulled back with a giggle. "Are you sure my friend?"

Fyne turned calm and lowered her head.

Arianna turned to Uncle Liam. "'Tis all good now."

"What has her in such a state?" Edward asked.

"*That* is a very good question," Liam said. "Arianna, we need to get her back into the stall."

Arianna nodded. "I agree." She scratched behind Fyne's ears. "It would be best if I do that."

"Aye." Marie stepped out the front door. "I'll come as well and check on the other horses."

Liam addressed the men. "Thank you gentlemen, please go back in and join your families in the festivities. We'll be back in little time."

"We'll stay with you," Richard said. "In case you run into another problem." A few others decided to come as well.

Liam nodded at Richard and Edward. The group of men escorted Arianna, Fyne and Marie to the big barn where they proceeded to light more lanterns hanging from intermittent posts on either side, running the length of the building.

"Edward, stay with the women. Richard, perhaps you'd go upstairs and look around?"

Richard nodded and Liam turned back to the other men. "We'll search outside to see if we can't discover who let Fyne out of this stall." He frowned at the latch on the stall door. It wasn't damaged therefore the horse hadn't broken free of its own device.

Everyone went in his or her consecutive directions. Marie went down one stall, checked on her own horse, then proceeded to check on Liam's horse three stalls down.

Arianna led Fyne into her stall and checked on water and food. The horse trotted to the back of the stall and cast a cautious eye at the barn door.

When she turned back Edward stood at the stall door. "Are you alright, my love?"

No. She looked down at her mother's wedding gown. Bits of dry hay stuck to its wet hem. "I could be better."

"I know. This has all been very...distracting." He walked over and pulled her into his arms. "Very soon, we'll go back into the house, take our vows and go home."

Arianna shivered. "Aye."

"Let's shut this—" He stopped mid-sentence and froze. "Get behind me, Arianna."

Before she could respond, Edward was yanked from her and tossed against the stall wall with a dagger tucked neatly against his jugular vein.

Was she dreaming?

Arianna fell back against the wooden wall of the stall. Iain? It couldn't be. She blinked to clear her eyes but he remained. Not dead, but very much alive.

As if she'd dreamt up until this point, everything sharpened. Horrible pain. Loss. How had she forgotten how much she loved him? Needed him? It was as if she'd been under a spell. Now he stood before her even more majestic than she remembered. Her Scottish warrior. Her husband. Come to life here in New Hampshire.

At least five inches taller than Edward, Iain's dark brows crashed together and his eyes narrowed. He pushed the blade tighter against Edward's neck. "I should kill you now for touching her, Sassenach."

"Iain?" That's all she could whisper. *Stop. Don't. He's innocent. I'm yours.*

"I can assure you—" Edward started to talk but stopped as the blade dug deeper, a trickle of blood rolled down his neck.

"Drop the knife." Richard stood at the stall entrance with a gun pointed at Iain's head.

Iain disregarded him. *He doesn't know what a gun is!* "Iain, listen to him. He can kill you from where he stands."

He didn't look convinced so Arianna continued. "That weapon will propel a small ball of lead at you that travels so fast that it will go through your head."

Iain appeared to consider his options and then spoke to Richard. "That gives me enough time to slice this man's throat."

Edward tried to move but Iain held him tight.

Richard held his gun steady. "Then you assume I care if he dies."

"Of that I havnae doubt. He shares your blood," Iain said.

"You don't know that."

"That's where you're wrong." Iain released Edward anyway. "However, I will not use this man as my shield and Arianna doesnae want him dead."

Edward stumbled to Arianna's side.

"Richard, lower the gun." Marie spoke from outside the stall.

Richard eyed the stranger. Arianna couldn't blame him for not responding. Iain was an imposing figure clad in black save for his plaid. His battle-axe adorned his back as well as a sword and multiple other blades scattered along his muscled body.

"Richard." Marie stood in front of him. "Lower the gun."

"He's to remove his weapons and I will." Richard kept his eyes trained on Iain and his gun raised.

"Not likely." Iain crossed his arms over his broad chest.

Marie cast an imploring eye over her shoulder at Arianna.

Arianna took a step forward. "Iain, do as he asks. Please." Edward took her arm and allowed her to go no further.

Iain met her eyes. *No.*

His voice in her head startled her. He was inside her again, his baritone depths as hot as his skin when it touched her body. She hooded her eyes from his direct gaze and pleaded with him.

"Please. I can't lose you again." As if he heard the words aloud, Edwards's hand tightened on her arm. Iain's eyes narrowed on Edward and the emerald turned to slits of black.

"Lad, remove your weapons." The wizard Adlin appeared beside Richard, his long robes aglow beside the hanging lanterns.

Iain scowled. "Nay."

Adlin stepped past Marie into the stall. "If you don't, you *will* lose her forever."

No one moved or spoke as Iain met and held Adlin's eyes. They're talking to each other through their minds. Arianna was sure of it.

At last, Iain began to remove his axe and whistled for his mount. Adlin flicked his wrist and Fyne stayed calm when Iain's black warhorse trotted into the barn and came up beside Marie and Richard. Both stepped back.

Iain strode from the stall and put his axe into a strap on the great horse. One by one, he removed his remaining knives and sword. When the last blade was sheathed on the animal, Richard lowered his gun.

Edward kept hold of Arianna's arm when they stepped from the stall. *I need to go to Iain.* She tried to pull her arm free to no avail.

"I did what you wanted," Iain said to Richard. "I would suggest you tell your son to release my wife. *Now.*"

"I don't know who you are stranger, but Arianna is my wife, not yours and I have no intentions of releasing her," Edward said.

The look Iain shot Edward was far sharper than a blade. "I can assure you that she is my wife, fully consummated."

Edward swallowed a cough as Iain redirected his dark gaze at Arianna. "Why does he claim you as he does, lass?"

She felt the worst kind of agony and struggled to push the words past her lips, past the pain she saw in his gaze. "Because we were...are to be married this night."

Marie was about to speak when Liam and the other men entered the barn. She smiled at her husband. "All is as well as it can be. Please put down your guns."

Liam looked from her to Iain, and then to Arianna and Richard. His gaze fell on Adlin last.

"What are...how are you here?" Liam asked.

Adlin shrugged. "I just couldnae stay away."

Marie kept her gaze on Liam. "You know him?"

"Aye, he was me brother Shamus's gambling partner when he first left us to travel from Dublin to London. I met him briefly when I first arrived in London back in 1767, after Shamus had such good fortune at the game tables. Then he vanished. My God, man." He looked Adlin up and down. "The years have been kind to you. In fact, you don't look as though you aged a day."

Everyone looked at Adlin, except Iain and Arianna. They kept an eye on each other.

Adlin preened and smoothed his white robes. "I thank you kind sir."

"Arianna, is everything oka—" Beth came around the corner. Her words died on her lips as she stared in rapture at Iain.

"Beth." Arianna tugged her arm free from Edward and stepped forward.

Iain went to block her path.

Richard raised his gun again.

Edward stepped forward to stop Arianna.

Fyne whinnied in distress. Iain's horse sniffed and raised its head.

Marie and Liam said, "no," in unison.

Adlin sighed.

"Enough."

~Fate's Monolith~

Chapter Twenty

A curious wind howled in off of the distant North Atlantic as white light poured through the barn door like mist. It slid along the wooden floors of the barn, crawled up the wall and formed a ceiling of clouds.

The doors slammed shut and the ceiling of murky alabaster fell like rain over them until nothing existed but Richard, Edward, Arianna, Liam, Marie, Iain, Adlin and Beth.

They stood in a circle of fathomless silence, scentless white and could see only one another. Arianna looked at the sea of faces around her. Marie appeared expectant, Liam confused. Edward, Beth and Richard appeared frightened.

Iain looked aggravated.

"I chose intervention this eve for I've other things I must attend to." Adlin's voice was different. Musical. Young. Dominant. His eyes again shone the color of blue ice and his hair had a life of its own.

He looked at Marie and smiled. "'Tis nice to finally meet you."

"And I you." Marie smiled back.

Arianna looked at her aunt, confused. "Aunt Marie, you know Adlin?"

Marie waved her hand dismissively and looked at Arianna with a blue-eyed twinkle, a tilt of her head and a grin that could only be described as deviously angelic.

Adlin sniffed and shook his head. "I just helped fate along a little."

"I figured as much." Marie turned her attention from Arianna to Adlin, only to end up at Liam.

Adlin's gaze fell to Liam. "Do you understand?"

"I think so." Liam gave a slow nod. "Had it not been for you, me brother would have never become known at the London game tables for his good fortune and met his wife, Lady Havensworth, a peer by birth. I would've never had the opportunity to thrive in England being the poor, Irish lad that I was. Of course, if I had never moved to London, I wouldn't have ever met me Marie. "

"Aye." Adlin chuckled. "You Irish never let me down." The wizard cast a rueful glance in Arianna's direction. "I had nothing to do with making sure Marie made it to London for she was connected to Arianna's pre-ordained fate."

Arianna looked at him, her heart in her eyes. "My parents?"

She'd intended to further interrogate her aunt but all thought was lost in light of Adlin's answer.

Adlin nodded. "Aye, lass. Your parents. Their fate was to pass on that day. I assure you that I had nothing to do with it. But they are happy. Do you remember seeing your mother, Arianna. In the place between the twelfth and the eighteenth century?"

Arianna gasped. "I didn't dream that?"

"No, child. She was there sitting on that bed telling you what a beautiful woman you've become and urging you to keep walking through the snow to safety. Your da stood just behind her but your spirit didnae see him. He loves you very much."

Arianna blinked back tears.

Adlin raised his forefinger to the corner of his eye. "No, no sweetling, don't cry. You will see them again."

A strange sense of peace overcame her. A slow warmth started just beneath her ribcage and eased the wild rhythm of her heart. She looked at Adlin. "Thank you."

Adlin nodded before his eyes drifted to Iain who'd never taken his gaze off of Arianna. "Lad, you need to still your heart while this gets sorted out."

Arianna's heart gave a heavy thud and then fluttered.

Iain scowled.

The wizard disregarded him and looked at Edward.

"You need to listen to your heart."

"Who are you? Where are we?" Edward asked.

"Good question, son." Richard clenched and unclenched his fist.

Adlin looked first at Edward, and then Richard. "We are still in the barn but you cannae see it. Can you accept that explanation?"

Richard's finger's stilled. His thin body became elongated as he stood taller and met Adlin's eyes. Though his gaze was shrewd, his voice was tentative. "I can if there's a good reason for it."

"Aye, 'tis a good reason indeed." Adlin turned his attention to Edward. "And you lad? Can you accept your current circumstances?"

Edward's lips thinned. "I don't see how I've any choice."

Iain laughed. "Mayhap he's not as ignorant as he looks."

Adlin shot him a dark look and Iain quieted.

The wizard turned his attention to Beth who appeared to accept her present situation. "And what do you think?"

Beth's eyes rounded. "I think that when one finds themselves in an unusual predicament that doesn't pose any immediate threat, it's best to stay quiet until they know more and then act upon that knowledge."

Adlin smirked and wagged his finger back and forth. "Ever the over-thinker."

Beth grimaced. "You say that as though it's a bad thing."

"It is in this case." Adlin redirected his attention to Edward. "Are you in love with Arianna?"

Arianna gasped.

Iain growled.

What an odd question.

Edward appeared taken aback. "Of course I am."

Adlin scratched his head in question. "Are you sure?"

"Quite," Edward said with indignation.

"Then why do you continue to carry that locket?"

Edward looked stunned and his hand floated to his right pant pocket. "What locket?"

Arianna watched Edward's hand and heard Iain grunt.

Adlin smiled and shook his head. "Just take it out. It's obvious to everyone that you hide something."

Edward frowned but removed the tiny gold piece from his pocket.

Adlin turned back to Beth. "Do you recognize that?"

Beth squinted.

Adlin walked over to Edward. "May I?"

Edward paused a moment as he looked at Arianna then he dropped the locket into Adlin's waiting palm. The wizard turned and brought it to Beth.

"Well, child, don't tell me you don't remember this."

Adlin dropped the small, gold heart into Beth's hand. She stared with trepidation at the piece for a moment and then pried it open. Beth looked at Edward, an indefinable emotion in her eyes. "You still have this?" She closed it and handed it back to Adlin.

Her gaze flickered to Arianna for a moment before they returned to Edward. "Why?"

Edward looked down. "I...it...I don't know."

"Aye, you do." Adlin handed the locket to Arianna.

Confused, she looked at Edward and Beth.

Stoic, Edward wouldn't meet her eyes. Beth's met hers without a flicker. It was obvious Beth was innocent. Her best friend had neither planned nor anticipated this moment.

"Go on lass, open it," Adlin urged.

Careful, Arianna placed her thumbnails between the two halves of the closed heart. Click. It opened. On either side were two miniscule drawings. One was of Edward who looked to be about fifteen, the other was Beth, who was about thirteen. She looked at Beth. "Did you draw these?"

Beth's lips pursed a moment in contemplation. "Yes. Many years ago."

Arianna looked back at the portraits and then turned her attention to Edward. "It seems to me that you did not answer Adlin truthfully."

Arianna should have felt hurt. Betrayed. But she didn't. Instead, she felt hope.

Edward stood straighter. "I do not lie."

Adlin took the locket from Arianna and gave it back to Edward. "Mayhap it has less to do with you lying to me and more to do with lying to yourself."

Edward looked down his nose at the wizard. "Then we're at a stalemate old man because I have no idea what you speak of."

Arianna bit her lip. *Careful Edward. Careful.*

"I take my previous statement back. You are as ignorant as I thought you were," Iain said and stepped closer to Arianna.

Edward sneered and took her arm. "Stay away from her stranger."

Iain tried to take another step forward but couldn't. "I'll see you dead. That's a promise."

Edward turned pale.

Arianna tasted a bit of blood in her mouth when she bit her lip this time.

Liam broke the tension. "Why would you carry that locket on your wedding day, lad?"

Edward looked at him, unable to answer.

"Answer the question, son," Richard said.

Edward glanced at his father and seemed to relax. "I suppose out of habit."

Richard looked stern. "You carry a locket of you and another woman on your wedding day out of habit?"

"I carry this locket every day for good luck." Edward's face turned red.

Richard's lips curled into a tight circle and his brows drew together. "You are a Huntington, son. Do you have any concept what that implies? Arianna is to be your wife. What the bloody hell is going on?"

Richard took a moment to gather his breath. "It appears this Scotsman is not one to be disregarded. It also appears Arianna knows him. Regards him with respect, if not some confusion..."

Iain's eyes darkened at Richard's vague words.

Richard was quick to clarify his meaning. "It appears she holds quite a bit of regard for him son, so if you ever had the opportunity to voice your feelings, now would be the time."

Edward offered his father a nervous laugh and then spoke. "As always father. I appreciate your input and welcome your insight."

Arianna pulled her arm away from Edward. "Does it not strike you odd you carry a picture of my best friend out of habit or for luck?"

Edward looked guilty. "I never really thought about it."

You never thought about it?

Arianna decided she wasn't getting anywhere with him so she looked at Beth. Dare she ask her? Oh yes. "Do you carry one as well?"

Beth's face remained impassive. "No."

Arianna knew she'd answered honestly. But Beth was a writer and writers knew their way around words.

Time to rephrase the question.

"Do you have a locket as well?" Arianna didn't miss the slight jut of her chin.

"Yes."

Arianna shook her head. "Can you tell me why you both have lockets with pictures of one another?"

A brief flicker of pain crossed Beth's face when she looked at Edward. "Because we promised...well...that we would always hold one another close to our hearts as friends...close friends."

Sweet Lord, was she free to be with Iain without guilt? She didn't dare hope. Arianna truly hadn't seen this coming. Though she probably should've. Her gaze traveled to Edward.

He didn't look at Beth, Richard, or Arianna. Instead he shoved his hands into his pocket and dropped his head.

Arianna sighed. She wasn't being told the whole truth. "Perhaps one of you would be willing to tell me what's going on."

"Nothing. It was an old promise. We were just children. Please believe me Arianna, there is nothing between us now," Beth assured.

Her voice had sounded strained. Arianna's heart thundered with wild anticipation. Could it be Beth loved Edward as well? "But there *was* and based on the fact that Edward still carries your picture, I'm fairly certain that something still does exist. At least for him."

Edward looked at Arianna though his gaze seemed far away. "I'm sorry."

A small sound came from Beth.

Adlin flicked his wrist and a simple wooden chair materialized behind Edward. The Englishman gave him a grateful look, sat down, placed his elbows on his knees and held his head.

Richard sighed but said nothing.

Arianna was about to speak to Edward when Beth raised a hand to silence her. "Why are you sorry Edward?" Though her voice sounded stony, passion burned in her eyes.

Beth *definitely* had feelings for him. If Arianna could grab Edward and Beth's hands, she'd dance in a circle. She kept silent and waited for Edward to speak.

When he raised his head and looked at Beth he appeared ten years older. "Because I do love you. I always have."

Richard gasped.

Arianna fought a smile. Glorious, wonderful Edward, he had excellent taste in women!

Beth strode forward, eyes full of fury. "What?"

Arianna clenched her fists. *No. It's all right. I don't love him.* She would've said as much if she could speak but nothing came out of her mouth.

With a mad scowl she glanced at Adlin. He wouldn't meet her gaze so she looked at Iain. He shrugged and frowned.

It appeared Adlin was in control.

Her attention returned to Edward who was clearly enthralled by Beth. He sat back and looked up at her as though she was a siren come for his soul.

"Why are you marrying Arianna then? Why would you do that to her?" Beth spit the words.

Yes, Beth, yes. Pull it out of him.

"I don't know." He shook his head in despair.

"You don't know? Bastard! How could you? Give me that locket."

Edward looked sullen as he handed her the jewelry. She threw it to the floor. "You're a fool."

Arianna watched the locket slide past her foot. This was very good.

Edward's face changed and he stood. Beth took a step back as he took a step forward.

"Edward," Richard said, concerned.

He held up a hand. "No, I've had enough." Edward seized Beth by her arms and peered down at her with narrowed eyes. "You're leaving. What point was there in telling you how I felt?'

Beth tried to shake him off but couldn't. Her words were ice. "So you were using Arianna."

Arianna looked at Adlin and implored within the mind; *let me speak. Let me help them.* He offered an infuriating smirk.

No such luck.

Arianna returned her attention to Beth and Edward.

Edward wasn't pleased with the accusation that he'd used Arianna. His eyebrows furrowed and he squared his shoulders. "I was not using Arianna. She is a beautiful, kind person that would make a good wife."

Iain growled again. "My wife."

Edward quirked a brow at him. "So you seem to think."

Adlin lanced Iain with a look of exasperation and shook his head. "I've the ability to silence you."

Iain crossed his arms in front of his chest and ground his jaw. Arianna attempted to reassure Iain with a smile. His eyes only narrowed a fraction at her.

The wizard looked at Beth. "He has a point, sweet girl, you were going to leave."

"That matters little. If he felt so strongly he should've said something and never—" She sneered at Edward. "Pursued, no, I'm sorry, wrong word. He should have never misled Arianna."

She's right about that. Arianna waited for Edward's response.

"I didn't mislead her. She accepted my offer to court her as well as my offer to marry her, which I would've gladly done," Edward said. "You are going away to school and I'm staying here with father and the business. Arianna and I will be very happy. She has no desire to travel. We will make a family together and be quite content right here in Salem."

Arianna had a lot to say about his explanation and looked at Adlin. He merely shook his head. Apparently, she wasn't going to be able to interrupt this interlude at all.

When Beth spoke again her voice had turned a bit shaky. "You try to convince yourself." It was obvious to everyone that the two had grown blind to the people around them.

"Just go, Beth." Edward released her. "It's obvious you find me repulsive."

She shoved her finger into his chest. "Don't turn things around. You're the one on trial. I did nothing wrong. I never have. I've been here all along. Not once did you ask me to stay. Not once did you tell me how you felt."

He grabbed the hand that accosted his chest. "I made a mistake. I meant no harm toward Arianna but had only faith in what we could be."

He wrapped his hand in hers. "As for you, I would never ask you to stay. You're a gifted writer. To do so would be to hold you back and I love you too much to do that. If I had told you how I felt, would you have gone?"

Arianna waited with bated breath. *Say no.*

~Fate's Monolith~

Beth sucked in her breath but didn't pull away. She appeared to contemplate his words. Her eyes rose to his. "Yes."

Arianna shook her head. *Wrong answer.*

Edward nodded. "So you see, I did what I thought was best."

Beth took her other hand and wrapped it around the hand that held hers. "No, you did what was safe. You took the easy route."

He tried to pull his hand away but she held fast. "Did it ever occur to you that we could have a life together even as I pursued my career?"

Edward's eyes softened. "Beth?"

"Yes."

"Are you telling me what I think you're telling me?" Edward moved closer.

Beth looked once at Arianna, and then at Iain before her eyes returned to Edward's. "What do you think I'm telling you?"

"Do you still feel the way you did when you said those words on the Spicket River so many years ago?"

She didn't hesitate. "Yes."

Edward smiled, pulled Beth close and kissed her deeply.

"This is so wonderful," Arianna said, her words soft and very much aloud.

Iain looked at Arianna and then Adlin. "Release me."

The wizard flicked his wrist and Iain strode to Arianna and took her into his arms. As he did, the barn returned.

The other townsmen still stood in the same spots with their lanterns. Albeit a bit shocked to see Beth and Edward embracing and the tall stranger with his arms around Arianna, they were magically oblivious.

"All is as it should be," Adlin said and looked at Liam.

Liam nodded and turned to the men. "What say you we all return inside?"

Marie ushered everyone back to the house save for Arianna and Iain. The wizard stopped at the door of the barn to address them. "Never doubt fate."

Adlin transformed into Father McGregory, turned and walked into the snowy night.

Chapter Twenty-One

Arianna was alone with Iain at last.

She leaned her head against his hard chest and closed her eyes. The wind blew through the barn and made the fire flicker in the lanterns. His hand snaked under the veil and stroked the back of her hair in slow, rhythmic fashion. *God, he smells so good, feels so good.*

She pulled back slightly. "How are you—"

He put a finger to her lips. Hungry, his eyes traveled her face. "Dinnae talk." He leaned close. Within mere inches of her lips, he stopped, grabbed a lock of her hair with his other hand and ran it through his fingers.

His eyes met hers while his finger trailed from her lips, over her chin and down the satin slope of her neck. She leaned her head back in welcome and closed her eyes.

Oh no! Her eyes flew open when he released her and she stumbled backwards. She landed in a pile of her own skirts.

Iain glowered down. "I'm not happy with you wife. You thought to marry another man? A bloody Sassenach no less!" His horse trotted back into the barn and looked down with the same distain.

"You can't be...what the bloody hell...you bastard of a..." She sputtered and attempted to stand. Fyne poked wide eyes over the stall door.

The black horse's tail flicked and brushed Arianna's head with contempt. She whacked away the tail. "Get away from me." The tail whacked her again.

Iain retrieved two small daggers from his horse, tucked them into his plaid and spoke to his animal. "Thank you my friend but I'll deal with her." The warhorse cast one last dismissive glance at Arianna, a look of promise to the chestnut mare in the stall and left.

She managed to get to her feet before Iain walked away. "What do you think you're doing with those daggers?"

He turned, expression grim. "I'm never without weaponry in a strange land, lass."

Arianna ran her hands down her dress, wiped back her veil and placed her hands on her hips. "In fact, how are you here...in this land, this time?"

"It doesnae matter how I got here, merely that I'm here." Iain shrugged and walked towards the house. He tossed casual words over her shoulder. "But I'll let you into my mind for a minute, lass. Let you know exactly what happened when you left me."

"Wait!" Arianna said. Before she could pursue him, a vision rose up and she froze. *I'm in his mind. Seeing his memories. Feeling what he felt!*

First she witnessed the clan war in an instant. Knew that they'd won but at great cost. So many had died, including his dear friend, David. He mourned but remained proud of all his fellowmen, dead and alive. Before she could focus she was...part of Iain. It was the day she'd vanished.

He could still feel the way the dry grass weaved around him as he knelt on the ground with his head hung low. The salty sting of moisture behind his closed eyes.

He'd never heard the arrow thump into the chest of the clansman enemy and didn't smell the blood warming the purple heather beneath his knees. He barely heard the pained words spoken to him. "She is not gone from you forever, Iain. This I promise."

He raised his head and looked up at the man standing over him. With a regal stance, eyes the color of pale blue sky and a face so similar to his own, Ferchar had the look of a great laird.

"You sound certain of that lad." Iain took the offered hand and rose to his feet.

"More certain than you could imagine." Slight fear and anxiety touched his words.

Iain glanced at the dead clansman. "Thank you Ferchar, you saved my life."

Ferchar wore a mask of contempt as he spared a glance at the dead man. "'Twas an honor."

"It appears you must've seen her disappear and carry further knowledge unbeknownst to me. Have out with it, lad."

Ferchar cleared his throat, uncomfortable. "'Tis old knowledge that I carry. Shown to me in a vision caught within the waves of the loch when I was a wee bairn. I went to the Shaman immediately and asked for guidance. 'Twas he who told me a vision was a selective thing, meant only for its receiver. To divulge what I had seen would forfeit the message and misguide fate. Please forgive me for never having told you."

Damn the old man and his endless riddles. "Go on."

Ferchar's gaze fell upon the trees and past them, as though he could see the ocean beyond. "It began here on the meadow this very day. I stood a ways behind you through the tree trunks as the wind blew off the sea and down through the mountains. As the mighty pines fell soldier to an ancient magic. Then I saw her, the beautiful angel with the golden hair. She held your heart to hers even in the midst of imminent death."

Iain's heart was a private place now, buried deep in his chest. Alone and confused. "Why didnae you warn me?"

"Warn you against what exactly? I wasnae absolutely positive when the vision might fructify. I wasnae willing to forfeit the chance of you falling in love with her because of my meddling with mere possibilities."

Ferchar took an unsteady breath. "The moment I saw her walk down the stairs of your castle, I knew it was she. I watched closely after that, stayed as near to both of you as I could. So many times I wanted to warn you but Adlin's words of past haunted me."

No doubt they did, intrusive blackguard of a wizard.

Iain shook his head as they walked back toward the horses. "Is there more? Foolish question, of course there's more."

Ferchar straightened his shoulders. "Aye, you have the right of it."

Iain swung onto his horse. "Continue."

"The fire of her sunlit hair as she vanished turned to the fire of a battle upon a mountainous plateau. The fire in the bellies of clansmen killing clansmen." Ferchar rode his horse alongside Iain's.

"'Tis the battle ahead you speak of, then," Iain said.

"I suppose it must be." Ferchar reined in his courage.

"In my vision, the fire of bloodlust turned to the fiery pits of hell. Through this hell you walked to her. Through this hell you forfeited everything you knew to be with her again."

Iain waited through Ferchar's silence. He knew his nephew's final words would change his life forever.

"And you left me behind in the battle of clansmen, amongst mortal men as their lifeblood drained away. You left me in a place of endings and new beginnings. Where the fire of battle turned to the fire of your castle's great hearth with me sitting before it. Laird of our clan until the day you returned home."

Iain shrugged.

"Eleven years later," Ferchar said.

Iain stopped his horse and stared at his nephew.

Ferchar became very serious. "As I saw it in my vision, if you go back to her, the next time we meet we shall be the same age."

Whoosh. Arianna zoomed out of the vision and once more stood in the barn. *Oh my Lord!* She still felt the pain he'd felt when he lost her. A pain that rivaled hers. And he'd given up eleven years for her? Walked away from his clan?

Iain had nearly reached the house.

"Iain, Iain, please wait!"

He stopped at the door and she caught up with him.

"We need to talk. Please," she pleaded, trying to catch her breath.

"Nay, I'm going inside. Is there not a warm fire in there?"

"You're upset with me because of Edward. Please let me explain."

He ignored the statement. "Is this your home, lass?"

"Aye, this is my home." Her lower lip trembled. "My life continued on without you Iain. I had to marry, start my own family."

Iain let a very long minute pass before he eased her suffering. "Aye, lass. You had no way of knowing that you would see me again." He cupped her check, the anguish in his expression apparent. "I also know you were cast under a veil of magic that cloaked your pain, your memories, and your heart. I'd have forgiven you even if you were not."

At that moment, the door flew open and Aunt Marie stood in the doorway. "Iain MacLomain, welcome to my home."

Pulling away from her, he nodded and met Marie's eyes. His eyes locked with hers for several seconds before he spoke. "You know magic."

"Aye." She eyed him up and down. "You are not welcome in if you mean any harm to my Arianna."

"Of course he doesn't!" Arianna said. "It's Iain, Aunt Marie. My husband."

"Aye," she replied cautiously. "I know well who he is. All full of powerful magic, this one."

"But Aunt..."

"Nay lass." She continued to eye him.

"I willnae enter your home if you dinnae wish it," Iain replied evenly, eyes locked with Marie's.

"Do you love her?"

Without hesitation he said, "I would not have come this far if I didnae."

He loves me! But she knew that. Had known it the minute he'd let her remember the day he'd lost her. Arianna wanted to wrap her arms around Iain and hold on tight but the moment didn't allow it.

Marie closed her eyes and released a long sigh. "Don't hurt her."

"Never."

"You may enter if you promise only peace within these walls."

He nodded.

"That means you can't kill Edward."

A hint of a smile played briefly at the corner of his lips. "You have my word, he's safe from me. But only because Arianna wishes it."

Marie eyed him for a few more moments, then nodded and opened the door.

~Fate's Monolith~

****

Beth and Edward were married that night. In actuality, it was the wee hours of the morning of the first day of the year 1800.

"Is that within God's eyes?" Arianna whispered to Marie when the guests began to filter out the door to go home.

Marie shrugged a shoulder and grinned. "I don't know."

"Aye," Adlin said behind them. "I was a priest but for a short time in the year 1142."

Arianna looked over her shoulder at Father McGregory. "It takes some getting used to you in his form. Where is Father McGregory?"

"Oh." Adlin shuffled his feet. "On a much needed sabbatical in Rome."

She frowned.

"No, no, really. He left just last night. All is well. I may be capable of many things, but harming an innocent human being is not one of them."

Marie stroked her forehead. "Will there be any repercussions?"

Adlin clucked his tongue. "Now lass, has there been anything but good repercussions since I became involved?"

Marie narrowed her eyes. "I'm still undecided on that point."

Adlin pulled his Bible to his chest and mocked her. "You've a bit too much pagan in your blood for my taste." With that he turned and walked away.

Marie laughed. "I like him."

"Me too."

Richard and Edna stepped forward to say goodbye to Arianna. They looked uncomfortable.

"We're so sorry. This is all so very awkward. Richard assures me that you're not heartbroken, but

I'm not so sure. Will you be all right dear?" Edna pulled her close.

Arianna smiled into her shoulder. "Aye, I will. This must be rather distressing for you but know that I hold no grudge against your son. He had no choice but to follow his heart. He loves Beth and she will make you a superb daughter-in-law."

Edna pulled back and studied Arianna's face. It seemed she liked what she saw there and smiled. Before she turned to leave, Edna leaned over and whispered in her ear. "It appears, perhaps, you will have a tall, very good looking, though incredibly old fashioned Scotsman available to heal your wounds."

Arianna giggled. "Aye, perhaps."

Richard stepped forward. "You're a good girl. I'm so sorry about all of this confusion. By the way, you won our costume contest. As requested by your aunt, the gift basket was given to charity."

Smiling, she gave him a brief hug and assured him all was well before he departed with his wife.

She faced the next couple. Here goes. "You two look very happy." How cliché.

Beth said the last thing that Arianna would have expected. "I will write a book about you."

Arianna was speechless.

Beth looked over her shoulder at Iain who sat in the parlor. "I have little doubt that yours is a story that needs to be told."

Arianna was doubtful. "My story is a long one."

"That's what I'd hoped you'd say." Beth pulled her close. "When I come home next summer, maybe you'll be here to tell me." She held Arianna at arm's length. "And if you're not, I'll bet I can whittle the details out of someone else." She winked at Marie.

"I love you," Arianna said. Tears welled in her eyes.

Beth cupped Arianna's face briefly in her hands. "Yeah, I love me too."

They laughed and hugged each other once more before she stepped back and Edward stepped forward.

"Can you ever forgive me?" He glanced at Iain uncomfortably.

Arianna followed his gaze. "It seems we should ask that of one another?"

Edward looked at her. "Perhaps we should leave things as they were. Friends?"

She smiled and hugged him. "Friends."

When Arianna pulled away Iain's large form leaned against the entryway to the foyer. She could've sworn she heard him growl.

"Take good care of her," she said to Edward.

"I will."

Beth turned back at the door and said, "I believe the title of my book shall have something to do with fate."

Arianna wiped away a farewell tear as Beth and Edward disappeared into the night.

Those who remained commenced to the living room.

"Please, sit down," Liam said to Iain. He nodded at the chair across from him. Marie and Arianna sat together on the settee.

Adlin stood with his back to the fire. Father McGregory was gone and he was again in his original form. His long white hair glowed in the firelight and power shone in his eyes. "Well, my friends, I'm afraid that my time here is short lived."

Marie stood and walked over to him. "I've been eager to know, Adlin, why was it so important to have Arianna married on New Year's Eve?"

Adlin snickered. "'Twas really just a selfish request."

Marie frowned and cocked her head.

"You see, 'twas my mission to ensure that Edward and Beth discovered their love for one another. 'Twas also my mission to ensure Iain and Arianna came back together in such a way that you, Edward and his parents would somehow understand the strange circumstances. I knew Iain would arrive here in Salem when he did which would be at a late hour, indeed. It was the perfect opportunity to accomplish everything at once, for everyone would be here and awake to toast in the New Year," Adlin said.

Marie bit the corner of her lip. "It seems you had your hands full." She appeared to consider something. "But how did you know that Edward would propose? For surely, if he hadn't, things would not have lined up so neatly for you."

Adlin rocked back on his heels and shrugged. "Now that, lass, was just a stroke of good luck."

Marie laughed. "I'm so thankful to you. I would not have Liam or my children if it weren't for you."

She looked down at her belly with pride and then to Adlin. "Will we meet again?"

His gaze flickered from her stomach then back to her eyes. "One never knows what fate intends."

She smiled and embraced him.

Liam walked over. "Is it appropriate to merely shake the hand of a man such as yourself?"

"I would be honored." Adlin shook Liam's hand. "You have done well Liam O'Donnell. I knew you would."

Arianna stood when Liam and Marie sat. Iain looked at her from beneath his brow.

"I don't know what to say. You have been a good friend to me. When I found myself in an impossible situation, you were the only one who believed me." She took his frail hand. "Was that because it was you who sent me back?"

"Nay lass." He studied her face. "As I said before, 'twas pre-ordained by God and magic."

Arianna nodded. "Aye."

She squeezed his hand. "I would have been just as thankful had it been you. It was a wonderful experience and..." Arianna broke off when she looked at Iain.

"Say no more." Adlin smirked. "Though he is difficult to deal with you were meant to meet one another."

Iain scowled at Adlin. "Be off with yourself old man. I will see you again soon enough."

Arianna smiled at the wizard. "So you will be back?"

Adlin cast Iain a weary glance. "Nothing is for sure, lass."

She looked from Adlin to Iain, confused. "But you just said—"

Then it hit her. Iain had said he would see Adlin again, which could only mean one thing. Her body turned numb.

"You're not staying, are you?" She asked Iain.

His emerald eyes turned dark and he sat back. "No."

Arianna's heart tightened. "I need to sit."

"Come, child." Marie sat her back on the settee and wrapped her arms around Arianna.

She shook her head and sat forward, stiff backed with her eyes straight ahead. How cruel fate was. "Why did you come here?"

"I had to see you again," Iain said. "Look at me, Arianna."

She didn't look at him. "Just go. Leave with Adlin." Arianna looked to the wizard but he was gone.

"Did you not travel with Adlin?" She glanced at Iain. So regal and handsome. So out of place in this house.

"I traveled alone." Iain opened his closed fist.

Her hair. Arianna stared at the small twist of golden hair in his large palm. "But...how?"

"Adlin, that's how. After you left he sought me out and told me your tale." Iain's eyes traveled to the hair. "The same one you tried to tell me time and time again."

Arianna walked to him. She closed his fist around her lock of hair. "Keep it if it will please you."

She turned her back to him and concentrated on the fire. "You've seen me again, now go. However you came, go and please don't ever return."

Then he was behind her. His hands wrapped around her waist and pulled her back against him, his mouth so close to her ear that when he spoke she could feel the warmth of his breath. "I have not traveled six hundred years to merely see you, lass."

She shivered with awareness. "You still haven't told me how you traveled here. I was sure it must have been with Adlin."

"Nay, I didnae even know he'd be here. As for myself, 'twas Adlin who gave me a bit of help. I knew that whatever it took, no matter the peril...I had to find you."

Arianna hung her head. "Go on."

"Adlin created what he called a vortex over the shore of Loch Holy. 'Twas incredible magic. Power unlike anything I'd ever seen. He told me to ride into it with your lock of hair and will myself to find you." He paused. "So, without a second thought, I spurred my horse and raced down the shoreline. 'Twas like riding into the heart of a hungry thundercloud. As I rode, I poured my heart and soul into locating you. I said the same words again and again. "I will find you."

She turned to face him. It couldn't be.

"Then there was wind. A powerful wind that led me to a stone deep in these woods. The next thing I was aware of was snow. 'Twas not hard to find you then," he said.

Arianna trembled with understanding. Terrible, sweet confirmation. The day at the monolith and the magic she witnessed. His words on the wind. "I will find you." 'Twas the monolith's premonition. Her one true love in the mirror in the basement on All Hallows' Eve. 'Twas her premonition.

Iain leaned close. "I had to find you." He kissed the corner of her lip.

Liam cleared his throat. "It appears you two need some time alone."

Arianna burned with embarrassment and pulled away.

"I agree," Marie said and stood.

"Lass?" She held her arms out to Arianna.

Arianna hugged her aunt. "Thank you for everything tonight. I'm sorry things didn't happen as planned."

Marie held her at arm's length. Wisdom filled her blue eyes. "No need to be sorry. I believe that everything did happen as planned."

Arianna blinked back tears. "Where would I be without you?"

Marie brushed back Arianna's hair. "You'll never be without me."

They hugged again and Marie tucked a small crimson velvet pouch into Arianna's hand and closed her fist around it. "Your Christmastide gift."

"Let me have a gander at her, wife," Liam said.

He pulled Arianna into his arms. "Life is never dull with you, lass. Handle your Scotsman and try to get a good night's rest."

Arianna smiled. "Goodnight."

Marie turned back at the door. "I love you."

"And I you," Arianna said.

Arianna stared at the door after Marie left.

"Well, luv, what is it?"

She looked at the pouch in her hand. With care, she pulled apart the tiny strings that cinched it together and poured the contents into her palm.

It was the golden ring Liam gave her so long ago in London. She'd forgotten to put it back on the eve of Samhain after she'd adorned her costume.

It had been altered.

Now, in the center of the heart held by two hands sat a blazing emerald. Arianna's birthstone. And the color of Iain's eyes. She'd swear it glowed. Thank you, Aunt Marie. A sense of rightness, family, infused her as she slipped the ring onto the finger that Edward's ring had been on so briefly.

At the very least, she'd come full circle. If Iain had to leave, she'd suffer. It wouldn't be easy. While the thought terrified her, she felt stronger, more sure.

What choice did she have?

Chapter Twenty-Two

"Come with me, Arianna."

Her heart leapt. "What?"

"To the barn." He flicked his wrist and the candles sunk into their wicks, then diminished into thin streams of smoke. "My horse cannae be trusted alone with yours for much longer."

Arianna sat. "Take your horse and go then."

"Damn, lass."

"What are you doing?" She yelped as he scooped her up into his arms and carried her out of the house.

"Put me down." She struggled against his strong arms. The wind drove a heavy snowfall across the drive.

"Be still." He strode forward, his dark hair already covered with a layer of white snow. The barn doors she closed earlier flew open and the lanterns flared to life. Once they were in the barn, he tossed her onto a pile of hay and brushed the snow from his hair. The barn doors slammed shut and warmth flooded the air.

"If you throw me to the floor one more time." Arianna sat up in the pile of wedding gown and hay. "I'll ensure you don't return to Scotland a whole man."

He pulled his wet tunic over his head and offered a wicked grin. "I'd like to see you try."

Sweet saints above. His broad muscled chest glistened against the lantern light. A light layer of black stubble covered his strong jaw. Arianna couldn't look away if she tried.

Iain held a hand down to her. She allowed him to pull her up. Arianna stepped out of his reach and walked over to Fyne's stall. Her horse stood, sound asleep at the back.

Arianna turned around. "There is one more thing I've yet to understand."

"Aye?"

"I saw you die."

Iain leaned against the opposite stall and crossed his arms over his wide chest. His tartan hugged his lean waist. "So you did."

Arianna leaned against Fyne's stall and pulled up her bodice. "How was it that I saw you die and yet you stand here before me? Are you a phantom?" If magic existed, then anything was possible.

His interested eyes fell to her hands as they fumbled to keep her cleavage intact. "Nay lass, I'm flesh and blood."

She removed her hands and hid her bodice beneath crossed arms. "Just tell me."

His eyes returned to hers. "Adlin is my grandfather."

Arianna stood straighter. "Oh."

She frowned. "But what does that have to do with you dying? Did he resurrect you?" There was little doubt in her mind Adlin was capable of most anything.

"He's a bloody wizard, lass. Wizards dinnae resurrect."

Then who does? She didn't want to know. "Then tell me, my laird, how are you here?"

Though her words were sarcastic Arianna had never been happier to see anyone in her life.

"'Twas not my horse I rode on that day. Adlin carried me into battle. He was determined to see that I live, one way or another." Iain's jaw twisted. "The old pagan ritual was to be a last resort. Regrettably, we were left with little choice."

She shook her head. "You must be mistaken. He was here when the battle took place, that I can assure you."

Iain lowered his head a fraction. "Only in spirit was he here, lass."

A chill ran through her. "I don't understand. What pagan ritual?"

"It was a ritual born of last attempts made many thousands of years ago by Viking wizards. They made a pact, a very powerful pact that harvested the energy of the middle ground between a soul's earthly body and its next destination. A place between Heaven and Hell. Where wind blows the lost souls in circles."

Iain nodded at the barn door and it blew open. His warhorse trotted in with a hurricane of snowflakes before the doors slammed shut.

"When they sealed the pact, they gave it to their bloodline. Not the ability to resurrect at all, but a simple *avoidance* of death. An escape."

Iain touched the space between the horse's black eyes.

"Is that Adlin?" Arianna whispered.

"No, just a horse." He ran his thumb in circles. "A wizard of this same ancient bloodline must be with another wizard of the same bloodline for the magic to work. Together, in the midst of death, they can pass from the plane of mortal existence and re-enter whole, unscathed and very much alive."

Iain's gaze appeared far away as he continued. "Adlin and I walked together through the wind of souls. We could see the green trees, blue water and humankind far above us as though they were the sky. Below us, like fish beneath the sea, were worms of fire. Twisting and beautiful, mesmerizing."

Arianna sank back further against the stall. "You make it sound as if you desired what lay beneath."

Iain removed his hand from the horse and it trotted to the far side of the barn. "I did. As did Adlin."

He took a step closer to her. "Every man has good and bad in his heart. Mankind would not be such without it. Evil is a tempting thing. That is its strength. That is how it's able to turn a man."

"But good is better," Arianna reminded.

"Aye, lass, but not half as easy. It takes a much stronger man to be good."

She squished back against the stall wall now. "And are you, were you, as strong as you look?"

A slow, devilish smile crept over his face as he moved closer. "Stronger."

He stood within six feet now. "The blood in my veins is a gift. Both Adlin and I returned to our bodies, wounds healed, when the time was appropriate."

"How do I know that?"

Iain closed the distance. "You dinnae."

Arianna slammed her hands; palm first, back against the wooden stall as Iain's hands met the stall on either side of her head.

She started to pray.

"Shush lass." He leaned so close she could see the varying shades of green in his piercing eyes. "Here, feel." He pried one of her hands from the wood and placed it over his heart.

Her fingers started to curl and he flattened her palm over his skin. "What do you feel?"

Thud. Thud. Thud. She closed her eyes. *It feels so good to touch him again. To know he's with me. How could I think for a second he'd turned evil?* Arianna opened her eyes.

"What do you feel?" He repeated softly.

"I feel you," she whispered. Her eyes stung. "I feel you."

Iain raised his hand to the crown of emeralds on her head. One by one, he removed the pins beneath it. "You look as lovely in jewels as you did in flowers."

He reached behind her and gathered the veil as he removed the crown. Carefully, he wrapped the veil into a small circle and placed the headpiece on the small, three legged stool beside them.

"So you are a…wizard," she whispered.

"Aye," he murmured. Visions rose up in her mind. Ones he put there. She closed her eyes and welcomed the impressions he burned into her mind. How he felt the first time he saw her walk down the stairs in his castle. Her dancing around a fire and her hair whipping in the wind as they stood on the shores of the Holy Loch. The pride he felt when he married her. The blatant fear he'd felt when she was nearly raped by the enemy clansmen. The passion he felt when he made love to her. The enjoyment and respect born of their many conversations.

The final image was the pain he felt when he'd lost her. The lasting regret that he'd not been able to tell her he'd fallen in love with her.

"Arianna." She opened her eyes. "I do love you. I'm so sorry I didnae tell you sooner."

At long last, he'd said it… and he meant it. She tried to swallow but couldn't. "Then don't go. Stay with—"

He broke her words with a long, deep kiss.

Arianna's thoughts and worries disappeared. He was all that was left. She buried her hands in his thick, dark hair. Lord, she loved him. There was so much to say, yet it all slipped away as he lifted her into his arms.

All the lanterns blew out save for the one hanging at the far side of the barn. A bed of hay with a green and blue tartan spread over it lay at the edge of the lantern's meager light.

She cocked an eyebrow at the miraculous bed. "You're good at what you do."

"Aye," he whispered in her ear as he lay down on his side next to her. He took her arm closest to him and pulled it over her head. Her entire left side cuddled against him when he leaned down and kissed just above the line of her bodice. His hot lips trailed up the side of her neck as he took her other arm and pulled it up above her head. "I can do many other things."

"I'm sure you can," she murmured in between kisses.

Iain propped his elbow beneath him and looked down at her. His eyes churned with lust. "You have no need of this."

He ran his hand down the front of her dress.

"No?" she said. Cool air slid over her bare skin.

His calloused fingers skimmed her vulnerable flesh. Arianna enjoyed the sight of their suddenly nude bodies next to one another. Iain's hooded gaze slid over her body with raw appreciation. "No."

Eager, she arched up and caught his mouth with hers. Their hungry kisses made the world vanish. His fingers explored her breasts as though he touched her for the first time.

"You've been in my mind," he murmured against her skin.

Breathing heavily, she nodded.

"Did you know?"

Arianna shook her head. What was he talking about? She couldn't focus on anything save the way he was making her feel.

He tilted her chin up so their eyes connected. "Adlin told me. I never knew. Your magic has allowed you to hear my thoughts often since we met."

Aye, so she hadn't been insane.

He spoke within her mind. *"I'm so sorry I pushed you away at the beginning. That I feared your magic equaling mine. And that I never believed you when you said you were from another time."*

Arianna shook her head, lost in his intense gaze. Softly she said, "And I'm sorry I turned coward and ran when the Broun clansman came. I never should–"

"Nay, lass. You did what you had to. I found you in the end, aye?"

"For all the good it will do us," she whispered. His finger wiped away the escaped tear. He licked it from his finger. She gazed at his mouth, the curves of his lips. "I don't want to be without you, Iain."

"I know, lass." His lips slowly lowered and brushed against hers. "I know."

Arianna wanted to whisper don't go yet again. But she wouldn't.

"Spread your legs, Arianna," he whispered.

Aye. Anything for you.

When she did, he rolled on top. She closed her eyes and relished the feeling of his heavy arousal against her belly. The feeling of his weight covering her body. Inch by cherished inch, Arianna ran her hands down the sides of his face, then lightly ran her fingertips down his neck until she curved them up over his shoulders.

If this was to be the end, she meant to build a slow, easy fire. His breathing increased and his member throbbed against her. Still, Iain didn't move. Instead his eyes watched her face intently.

Gingerly, so slow that she knew he felt every little sensation, she ran her fingertips down his muscled chest and scraped her nails lightly along the sides of his torso until she curved her palms over the tight globes of his backside and lifted her legs high and wide.

He licked his lips, breath choppy. His hips jerked forward a fraction. Arianna shook her head and denied him entrance, simply let him feel her soft, hot folds and the smooth friction of her legs wrapped around him.

"I think I taught you too well, lass," he choked, strain and need plastered on his intent face. Slowly, he leaned down and flicked the tip of his tongue lightly over the corner of her lip, obviously enjoying the game she played. She smiled and locked her lips on his. Their tongues twirled and lapped. Arianna rolled against his body, kneading his backside eagerly.

"But you underestimate," he said so softly she barely heard him.

"Hmm?"

One strong arm quickly snaked beneath her lower back and lifted. Before Arianna had a chance to shift away, he thrust and buried himself deeply. *Ahhh!* Breath blew from her lungs. Hands still on his backside, she felt the muscles constrict as he plunged.

Iain didn't kiss or touch her during their intimate contact. He merely stared, his eyes glowing such an intense shade of Emerald she thought them on fire. That fire burned below as he slowly moved in and out. She met his pace, enthralled by the domination in his eyes and the thrilling pleasure growing below.

An urgent pinching sensation started just beneath her bellybutton. Arianna dug her fingernails deep into his backside and thrust up, needed more. With a small, secretive smile he rolled his hips. The pinch fanned out, rippling the muscles in her lower stomach, down her inner thighs. *Ohhhh!* Before she could shift, he rolled his hips the other way. She screamed with pleasure. What felt like crippling lightning shot down her legs and up through her torso.

"Iain," she gasped against his chest, almost afraid.

One strong hand cupped her head and the other beneath her backside as he angled her where he wanted her. Then he began moving faster and faster and faster. Restrained ecstasy sizzled, burst and flared through every part of her body, desperate for a release only he could give, only he would allow. A vision shot into her mind of how he saw her beneath... startled, aroused, mouth parted, eyes half shut, chest heaving, nipples tight.

"Let go, Arianna," he whispered into her mind. *"Come with me. Let go."*

Iain rolled and thrust sharply. Every muscle and sinew in her body locked then started to vibrate and unravel. Delicious shudders wracked and tore at her body. She tried to hold onto him. Ripple upon ripple upon ripple ate away at her until she exploded. Arianna screamed. And screamed. And screamed.

She couldn't move as rapturous feeling enveloped. A sizzling glow, hot as the sun, filled her. Small flecks of light swam in her vision as though a thousand fireflies surrounded them. The air cooled and her breath turned to fog.

Iain's intense cry and endless throbs of release sounded far away at first, then closer and closer. She felt so hot. So alive.

Arianna sighed with relief, relishing the cool water trickling over their entwined fists. Bliss held her so tightly she couldn't say how much time passed. At last, she was able to open her eyes. Tall pines shot to the blue sky overhead. Bright sun blinded.

It couldn't be. Had she really returned to Scotland? Though the answer shone clearly in his intense eyes, she whispered to Iain, "You didn't leave me behind."

"'Twas never even a possibility, lass," he whispered back.

Iain rolled over and cuddled her on his lap at the edge of the stream, the very one they'd been married by. His warhorse and Fyne nuzzled one another across the way.

A white eagle soared far overhead and cried with triumph.

A rainbow arched down, wrapping them in memories and promise before he kissed her.

Scotland...wherever and whenever it may be...was theirs.

"Welcome home, my love."

SNEAK PEEK ...

Destiny's Denial (The MacLomain Series-Book 2)

Prologue

"Don't be afraid, I'm not."

He laughed and dove after his nephew. Cool mist sprayed his body as he descended within the waterfall. Cold, mountain born water sheathed his hot skin when he hit the river. The lad's legs retreated ahead in a sea of underwater foam.

"'Tis glorious," he bellowed as he surfaced. The tall and mighty pines basked their needles in the springtime sun.

He turned to his aunt, who sat on a wide rock. Her knees were bent. She leaned back on one elbow.

"You should join us," he urged.

She sat forward and wrapped her arms around her knees, "Nay..."

Blatant alarm shot from her green eyes.

"What is it?" Fear trickled down his spine.

She jumped from the rock and scanned the water. "Where is William?"

He spun.

The lad was nowhere to be found.

Impossible! *He was right in front of me.*

He scanned the river then dove. Surely the lad jested. He pushed his way back to the waterfall's base. White bubbles and river current pushed at him but he kept his eyes open and searched until black flecks threatened his vision.

When he finally surfaced for air, his aunt tugged anxiously at his arm. The octave of her voice chilled him to the bone. "Where is he? Tell me now, where is he!"

He again scanned the river then dove. *This isn't happening. There's no way.* But William was nowhere to be found. Panic rose.

He searched and searched, desperate.

Still nothing.

Out of breath and about to resurface, he spied something. With renewed strength he kicked his way down to the piece of fabric caught on the rock below and yanked it free. His aunt grabbed his arm the moment he surfaced.

They stared at the scrap of bloodstained, blue and green tartan in his grasp. *Please, this can't be real. This has to be a nightmare.* But he knew it wasn't.

Her face turned white.

"No. God no," she whispered.

He caught her just before she fainted. For the scrap of tartan belonged to her son.

Chapter One

North Salem, New Hampshire

Present Day

"No! He's not dead!" Caitlin sat up, rolled off the bed and fell flat on her face. The hardwood floor turned slick with tears as she pressed her cheek against its cool surface. *Breathe. I've got to keep breathing.* Would this horrid nightmare ever leave her alone?

She released a deep breath and rolled onto her back. Falling out of bed in the morning was a common occurrence. She sat up with a growl and worked to untie the knot of sweat soaked sheets from her legs. As usual, both her down comforter and pillows were scattered around the room.

"Damn dream." Caitlin sat on the bed and held her head in her hands. She didn't know what to make of it. For three years now she'd been having the same dream, well, more of a nightmare. The worse part of it? She was inside this stranger. That he was a man she had little doubt. Caitlin felt the horrible agony he experienced in losing his cousin. She spent every night locked inside of him, replaying the same excruciating moments over and over.

His pain tore through her and broke her heart every single time. She kicked the balled up sheet away, walked over to the window, whipped it open and stuck her head out into the fresh spring air. The ancient oak tree outside her window was full of new, green leaves. She reached out and fingered one of the soft stems.

"You're going to be late for work."

Caitlin disregarded Shane's words as they floated up. Her brother had just walked out the front door and was heading for his car. As usual, he was reading a book with one hand and drinking a cup of coffee with the other.

She shook her head and yelled down to his retreating form. "I've got plenty of time."

He ignored her, jumped into his silver Acura and peeled off down the drive.

Caitlin glanced at the clock. Half an hour to get to work. She grabbed a shower and threw on a pair of khaki colored pants and a navy blue polo shirt. God, she needed a cup of coffee. Grabbing her apron, she rushed downstairs.

The house was empty. Amanda must've left for work. Her best friend held a job as a social worker and she was never home anymore. Caitlin and Shane's mom and dad had died in a car accident when they were twelve and Gram had taken them in. When they turned eighteen, she agreed to let them live in the old colonial house on her property. They paid a small rent just to cover the taxes and paid for their own utilities. She knew Gram was a wealthy woman and didn't need the money. Charging them rent had more to do with instilling a sense of responsibility into her grandchildren.

A couple of years ago, Amanda moved in with them, desperate for a cheap place to live while she got her career going. Gram had always liked Amanda so there was no problem.

Her horse whinnied from the adjacent barn as Caitlin flew out the door. "Morning baby, I'm leaving for work. We'll go for a ride when I get home."

C.C. offered no response. She would've preferred spending time with her horse rather than going to work, but at some point she needed to continue her college education and the only way to do that was to make money.

"Ah, good morning to you as well sweetheart." This time she was talking to her Ford Explorer Sport. Though only a 2004, she looked pretty in red with silver trim. Caitlin jumped in and cranked the radio. Rolling down her window, she waved to her grandmother as she drove down the dirt lane that connected to the main road.

Lucky for her, Dunkin Donuts was quiet. She was out of the drive-thru in thirty seconds flat. Record time. Medium French Vanilla iced coffee in hand, Caitlin swung into the parking lot of the restaurant where she worked. She really did love working here. Weathervane Seafoods stood like a silent ship on Route 28 at this hour and she enjoyed getting here before it filled up with hungry customers.

"Hey girl, you made it," Rick said as she entered through the back door into the kitchen, slid her timecard and plunked her purse down on the ice cream cooler.

She glanced at the clock and winked. "I'm on time today, so relax."

Rick laughed and pushed a box of donuts her way. "Care for something sweet? Or maybe a donut?"

Caitlin rolled her eyes and entered the dining room through the swing doors. She switched on both coffee makers and stretched.

What was up with her dream? It was all she could think about lately. *The glimpse of a young boy diving off a cliff in front of her. The love of the man who dove after him. The woman on the rock and the pain that flooded her face.*

"There you are."

Caitlin jumped at the sound of Jessie's voice. She turned and smiled at her manager. "I'm right on time. Aren't you proud of me?"

"Of course." Jessie placed a hand on her shoulder and issued a wide smile.

Caitlin slumped. She knew that smile. "Oh no, really?"

"You know me too well." Jessie gave her the puppy dog eyes she couldn't refuse. "We're in a tight spot."

Jessie needed her for a double shift. It was Friday after all, not such a surprise. Time to bargain. "Can I lose my day shift tomorrow?"

Even though she needed the money, doing a double today would rob Caitlin of her Friday night with her grandmother. Her gram was her best friend and Fridays had always been theirs. She would spend Saturday with her instead.

Jessie's eyes softened. She knew. "I'll see what I can do. No promises."

Caitlin smiled. Whenever Jessie said that it meant: *Don't worry, I'll get it covered. You do me a favor, I do you a favor.*

Five hours later, Caitlin took her break. It was three o'clock and a perfect day to sit out at the picnic table situated behind the restaurant for employees. Regrettably, there were three other waitresses plus two cooks already on break. Not that she minded the company but there was nothing better than solitude after four hours of waiting on tables. Not going to happen today apparently.

"Caitlin, I've got a spot all warmed up for you," Rick said as she approached the table.

She slid in next to all six feet of him, well aware that he didn't move over much. She slid her tray of fried chicken tenders with honey mustard sauce down, wishing it were a plate full of whole bellied clams and sea scallops. What was the point of working so hard if you were going to waste it on a fourteen-dollar plate of food when you could instead order a seven-dollar plate of food?

She hated her reasoning as she gazed at the plate of fried oysters across from her. Hell. Her gram said it was the Scottish in her. Frugal to the bone. She shoved a piece of chicken into her mouth and pretended it was a delicious piece of Haddock. In short time, everyone began to filter back inside until it was just her and Rick.

"Good money today?" He'd managed to make five french fries last twenty minutes. She knew why.

"Not bad. It's been better," Caitlin said.

He pushed his plate away and folded his hands on the table. An unruly light brown lock fell forward over his forehead as he seemed undecided as to what to say next. "You make me nervous, Caitlin. I don't get nervous."

She stopped eating and focused on twirling the claddagh ring on her finger. He turned his head slightly and gave a slow grin. Sexy...definitely sexy. Was she normal? This guy should have her sweating all over.

"It's just me, Rick." They'd worked together for at least a year now.

He pushed back and swung one of his legs over the bench seat of the picnic table so he straddled it in her direction. His dark-blue eyes grew serious. "Yeah, I know."

His position was more intimate...erotic somehow. A picnic table behind a restaurant. She was just about to laugh at her thought process when his hand slid down her forearm and covered her hand on the table.

The air vibrated and her vision blurred. Then it cleared. Transfixed, she watched his hand change, become tan and lengthen. The palm widened, became stronger, more sure. A burning sensation started beneath her fingernails and slowly crept over her hand as though first fire and then scorpions clawed the delicate skin.

Caitlin tried to talk, tried to tear her gaze away from the hand covering hers, but couldn't. Something was wrong. Everything around her hand and his was wrong. The air compressed and it felt as though tiny bolts of lightning zapped every inch of skin on her body.

The restaurant vanished. The traffic pulling into the parking lot faded away. The trees were gone, the nearby post office, the dumpster. Everything. Not even the sky above remained. A rush of heat rushed over her and sucked the air from her lungs.

That's what made her panic. She couldn't breathe.

"He's not dead. He can't be." A deep voice saturated her eardrums.

Pain ripped through Caitlin. Fresh, pliant, raw pain. Physical, psychological, mind-blowing pain. Rick was gone. She was with *him*. The person she became late at night, under the cloak of sleep, year after year. But where was he? Her eyes couldn't find him. The hand tightened over hers. She felt so exposed. Possessed.

"Let me go." My voice doesn't sound right...it's far too distant. Panicked, she screamed. Nothing came out.

"Who are you?" His question held incredible rage. Blatant accusation.

Fresh fear bombarded her. Shards of ice streaked up her arm until her chest seized. Was she having a heart attack? I'm too young to die. A horrible, hot wind blew over her and she turned away. She tried to get away.

A strong arm seized her from the back before she could flee the bench. Bare and muscled, it squeezed tightly across her ribcage just below her breasts. Caitlin was pulled back against the phantom man until he straddled her backside on the seat. His anger poured over her.

"Who are you?" He breathed against her ear. His resolution dripped into Caitlin. Her body began to shake. He squeezed tighter still. His free hand came up to her throat. Though it didn't squeeze her neck, the power beneath his fingers was palpable. Ready to easily take her life.

"Rick?" The word was a week squeak of hope through clenched teeth. Though she knew it wasn't Rick, maybe he'd get spooked if he thought her "boyfriend" was nearby. Her sense of reasoning suddenly seemed ridiculous. Whoever this tyrant was she had the very distinct impression that he feared no man.

His breathing shifted, became abstract, as if her question incited him to switch tactics. His hand slid from her throat down through the top of her polo shirt to skim the top of her bra.

Caitlin meant to scream but purred instead. Literally purred. Electricity traveled from his hand straight down to her throbbing womb. Sweet pleasure scorched her, burning a tunnel of need straight through her that only he could satisfy. Caitlin's body quivered. Then, before she could comprehend what was happening, a sharp orgasm raked her body. *Ohhhh!* Though her lower half arched off the bench in pleasure, the arm locked beneath her breast held tight.

"Will you tell me now?" His soft words teased her, tickled and aroused places he couldn't possibly be touching.

For all the violent, hateful things she wanted to do, her body was putty. What was going on? Thankfully, when all else failed, one emotion always seemed to take over. Anger. Caitlin had just been used. In the worse way possible. That's all it took.

"Get away from me!" She did the only thing she could think of from this angle. Clawed. Never one to keep long nails, she used what she had and dug deep, then raked with all her might from his wrist to his elbow.

The minute she did it his other hand caught her chin and whipped her head sideways. "This isn't over. I'll find you."

Before she could jerk her head free he attacked her with what he knew would work. The dream. The horrible pain of loss. Death.

Caitlin bent over and threw up. She felt as though every person close to her had just ceased to exist. Bastard. What a tormented, horrible soul.

"Caitlin?" Someone was shaking her. "Caitlin, are you okay?"

"Rick?"

"Yeah, you okay, hon?"

Caitlin opened her eyes. Though cloudy, the day was painfully bright. The soft wind blowing up behind the restaurant hurt her skin. If she never ate again, it would be too soon. She raised a shaky hand and nodded. "I'm all right."

"Are you sure?" He kneeled down beside her. "One second, I was telling you that you made me nervous, the next second you're over here by the fence all curled up and shaking. I didn't mean to...well, I don't know. Did I scare you that much by telling you I was interested in you? I'm sorry if I did. God, you look horrible."

Caitlin brushed away his hand. She needed to be alone. "Thanks."

He sat beside her and brushed the hair away from her face. "Come on, you know what I mean. Just because you just threw up fifteen shades of green doesn't mean you're any less fine to look at."

Caitlin sat back against the fence, pulled her legs up and wrapped her arms around her bent knees. This guy still found her attractive after she'd just lost everything she ate for the past twelve hours? That should mean something. Right now, it meant less than nothing.

She lifted her head and offered him her best attempt at a smile. "You're a good guy, Rick. Thanks. Mind if I have a few minutes alone?"

He studied her face. "You sure? You want me to tell Jessie you're sick?"

"No." She shook her head. "Just head on in, I'll be right behind you."

Rick rose to his feet. "If you're not inside in two minutes, I'm coming back out."

Caitlin tried to smile at his retreating form. What was the matter with her? Taking deep, steady breaths, she leaned her head back against the fence, closed her eyes and tried to relax. Something strange was going on and she couldn't begin to comprehend what. Then an odd revelation hit her. In her dream, she understood the verbal exchange on some subconscious level though she never actually heard anyone speak.

Her mystery man had just spoken and with a thick Scottish brogue.

"Caitlin? You coming in?" Rick asked.

She got to her feet and retied her apron. "Yeah."

He stood at the backdoor and waited. As she passed he touched her elbow. "You sure you're okay."

Caitlin nodded and pulled her arm away. Wow, was she sexually charged right now. Men beware. She headed for the bathroom. It wasn't that she didn't like sex. What experiences she'd had were okay. The problem was they didn't even come close to what just happened to her outside. Caitlin rubbed her temples against a newborn headache and stared into the mirror.

As disturbing as the whole nutty experience had been, it agreed with her. Her cheeks were rosy and her eyes shone a lighter gold than usual. She looked like a sated woman. Leaning over, she splashed cold water on her face, reapplied some lip gloss and went back to work.

An hour into the dinner rush, Caitlin realized how grateful she was to still be here. Keeping busy kept her from thinking too much about how insane she felt.

~Fate's Monolith~

Was she cracking up? It wasn't as if she was under pressure. With a steady job, great friends and a growing savings account, Caitlin led a fairly stress-free life. About the only thing that bothered her on occasion, besides the reoccurring dream, was her uncanny ability to foresee things. It happened on rare occasions and was usually as simple as dreaming about what parking space would be available when she went to a crowded shopping center the next day. Gram told her it was just heightened intuition and it ran in the family.

As always when waiting on tables the evening passed quickly. There was nothing like stepping out the door after a busy shift with two hundred and fifty dollars wadded up in her apron. Caitlin looked forward to a hot shower and a good book.

"Hey, Caitlin, wait up." Sean the busboy ran to catch up with her halfway across the parking lot.

"Oh no, I didn't tip you? I could've sworn I did." Caitlin reached into her apron pocket.

"No, you tipped me and if you didn't I wouldn't chase after you for it. You always tip me too much." Sean smiled and blushed.

"What's up, then?" Caitlin fished around in her purse for her keys.

"Well I was wondering if maybe your grandmother was looking for some yard help again this year. Maybe some spring clean-up."

Caitlin opened her door, threw her stuff onto the back seat and jumped in. She started the vehicle and rolled down the window. "I'm sure she is. You did a really great job for her last year."

"Thanks." He rested his arms on the door. "Actually, it wouldn't be just me this year. I've got a new foster brother that wants to help too. He's only twelve but he's a big kid and really nice."

"Sure, I don't see why not. I'm hanging with Gram tomorrow. I'll let her know you're interested."

"Great." Sean ran his hand through his light blond hair. "We could take care of your yard too, if you want."

Caitlin let her hair down. Not such a bad idea. Between her and Amanda working so much and Shane pursuing his literary career they could use the extra help. "That sounds good. Let me talk to Shane and Amanda and I'll get back to you."

"Alright." Sean headed for his car. "Have a good night."

"You too," Caitlin said. She was about to pull the shift into reverse when someone knocked on the passenger side window. Startled, she jumped. It was only Rick. She pressed the button on the side console and the electric window rolled down.

"Hi, sorry, didn't mean to scare you." His face broke into a not-so-sorry grin.

He looked tired. It'd been a hard night in the kitchen and Rick was the guy that always kept his cool. He handled stressed managers, frenzied wait staff and emotional cooks like a pro. That's why the restaurant was going to hate losing him at the end of the summer.

"What's up?" Caitlin asked.

"My brother just called and can't pick me up. You think I could grab a ride?"

"Sure." Caitlin unlocked the door. "Hop in."

"Thanks." He jumped in, filling up the Ford's interior. They made small talk as she took a right hand turn onto Route 28, then onto route 97.

"You want to swing into Sam's for a drink?" He said.

"No. Not tonight, I'm too tired." They drove by Samantha's Restaurant.

"That's cool." He leaned over and turned up the music a little.

He lived a half-mile from the Salem library so they didn't have to go far. Rumor had it Rick's family was wealthy but he lived in a fairly small house. As Caitlin pulled into his driveway she felt the tension rise within the truck.

"Here we are." Caitlin shifted into park.

"You're the best." Rick had his hand on the door handle but hesitated and cleared his throat. "Caitlin, I never got a chance to talk to you earlier."

She held back a sigh. For a confident guy who was recently accepted into Harvard Law School he appeared pretty nervous. Maybe she should give him a chance. After all, he would be leaving in a few months and she could use a casual fling. Actually, she could really use some male companionship.

Caitlin decided to make it easy on him. "Yes, I'd love to go out with you sometime."

The breath he'd been holding blew out of his lungs and he turned to her. "Really?"

"Really." She smiled. "You have my number, give me a buzz."

He leaned over and brushed the top of his knuckle across her cheekbone. "You got it."

Caitlin watched him enter the house and then pulled out. She felt pretty good. Maybe, if he played his cards right, she would make it a summer to remember for him. She smiled ruefully to herself as she drove through the back roads of Salem into North Salem. Maybe, he might be able to make her feel like she did today at the picnic table with a Scotsman at her back.

****

Mildred awoke at 9:00 a.m. sharp, just like she did every morning. She let Remington, her Lhasa Apso, out the back door and sat down in her favorite reclining chair beside the huge, multi-paned window that overlooked her front yard. Sunlight streamed through the glass and lit up the colorful array of blown glass fixtures she had hung.

Birds flitted around a feeder that hung near a round temperature gauge attached to a nearby maple tree. It read fifty-five degrees. Not bad for an April morning. Mildred had just grabbed one of her hard candies when Caitlin pulled into the driveway. She set the sweet aside when she saw the coffees her granddaughter had in hand.

"Morning, Gram." Caitlin came through the door behind her and gave her a kiss on her cheek. "I brought your cinnamon donut and coffee just like you like it, small, cream and two sugars." She set her own ice coffee on a coaster and went to let Remington in before his incessant barking drove all the birds from the forest.

"How are you feeling?" Caitlin asked as she plunked down in the chair beside her and took a long sip from her drink.

"Horrible," she said and smiled.

Her granddaughter ignored the response because it was the same one Mildred gave everyone. Not that she was a pessimistic person, she wasn't. Just sick of being in a body that didn't get around quite like it used to. She eyed Caitlin and sipped her coffee. Beautiful to the bone, that's what Mildred always thought. Her long, wavy chestnut hair was her crown of glory. All full with streaks of flaxen and gold.

They chatted a bit. Mildred figured she did well to talk casually as long as she did before finally asking Caitlin what was wrong. The girl was a ball of tension and fidgety to the point of distraction.

Her granddaughter was silent for a time, appearing to contemplate her next words. When she did speak, it was with a light sheen of tears in her eyes. "I promised myself I wouldn't say anything but the truth of it is, Gram, you're my confidant. I just can't not talk about it anymore."

Mildred placed her hand over the curved top of her cane and leaned forward. She couldn't remember the last time she had seen Caitlin cry. "What's going on dear?"

"I've been having the same dream for three years now and if that isn't enough, yesterday at work my dream started to infiltrate my reality. I think I'm losing it, Gram." Caitlin sat back and wiped away a tear.

"Tell me about your dream." Mildred handed her a box of tissues. She didn't like the sound of this.

Caitlin let out a puff of air and then told her about the dream. Detail by painful detail. It was obvious her emotions were all wrapped up in it.

When she finished, Mildred sat back. Her mouth felt dry. Her heart beat a bit faster. "So, you don't know where you were?"

Caitlin stared down at the inch of coffee left in her cup. "No. I suppose after what happened yesterday I could speculate."

That bad feeling Mildred had was getting worse. "Go on."

Caitlin told her about the man in her dream accosting her at the restaurant. Theirs had always been an honest relationship so when her granddaughter told her about the sexual interplay Mildred was neither shocked nor embarrassed. She knew well that the blush flooding Caitlin's face had more to do with remembering the event than telling her grandmother about it.

"I take it he must have had an accent and that's how you know where the dream might have taken place." Mildred met Caitlin's eyes and knew for a fact she wasn't going to like what Caitlin said.

Caitlin shrugged. "He had a very thick Scottish accent, so perhaps it was Scotland."

Coffee forgotten, she reached over, unwrapped a caramel candy and popped it in her mouth. That is exactly what she was afraid Caitlin was going to say.

About the Author

Award-winning New Hampshire native, Sky Purington writes a cross genre of paranormal/fantasy romance heavily influenced by history. From Irish Druids to Scottish Highlanders many of her novels possess strong Celtic elements. More recently, her vampire stories take the reader to medieval England and ancient Italy. Enjoy strictly paranormal romance? Sky's latest novels follow three haunted houses and the sexy ghost hunters determined to make sense of them. Make no mistake, in each and every tale told you'll travel back to another time and revisit the romanticism history holds at its heart. Sky loves to hear from her readers and can be contacted at **Sky@SkyPurington.com.**

Find out Sky's latest news at SkyPurington.com

Twitter @ SkyPurington

Facebook Sky Purington

Made in the USA
Lexington, KY
10 February 2012